THE SKY PEOPLE
CAST IRON FARM BOOK 4

ALI SPOONER

THE SKY PEOPLE
CAST IRON FARM BOOK 4

ALI SPOONER

Affinity
Rainbow Publications

2023

The Sky People
© 2023 by Ali Spooner

Affinity E-Book Press NZ LTD
Canterbury, New Zealand

1st Edition

ISBN: 978-1-99-104035-0 (paperback)

All rights reserved.

Editor: A Koenig
Proof Editor: Lisa M
Cover Design: Irish Dragon Design
Production Design: Affinity Publication Services

ACKNOWLEDGMENTS

I thank my fans for following my stories and providing great feedback and encouragement. Writing wouldn't be so much fun without you. Thanks to Affinity, Irish Dragon, for the cover art and the team of editors, readers, and publishers who continue to help me grow as a writer.

DEDICATION

I dedicate this story to my Bubba, whose family has been a model for this fictional family in this series. Never forget, I love you MOST.

TABLE OF CONTENTS

CHAPTER ONE

Whit Brewer sat in front of her computer monitor, staring at the words on the screen. She unconsciously twirled the ring Eli had given her when Eli proposed to her on Christmas. Whit was behind schedule on the textbook she was developing, so she promised Eli she would spend several nights in her treetop lab working on the project.

Winter at Cast Iron Farms was progressing well, but Whit was restless without a farm project needing her attention. Mark and Mitch were settling into their new home, and Carol and Julia's relationship blossomed. Carol had been her best friend since childhood, and Eli was grateful to have her nearby. Julia, a jeweler, had become enamored with Carol and agreed to move in with her. Eli stayed busy splitting wood or helping Mark in the forge during the day and enjoyed her carving around the fire at night.

Whit had never felt this level of contentment in her life. She had a wedding planned for the spring, new family and friends, and dreams of starting a family with Eli. She and Eli had traveled to Asheville to meet with a physician regarding artificial insemination and received a file of prospective donor profiles. Eli wanted Whit to review the potentials, and when she had pared her selections down to the top four, they would review them together and make a selection.

Whit had reviewed over fifty profiles but found her attention returning to one man in particular. There was something that felt familiar about him. He was handsome, and his IQ score was impressive. He was a professional in the medical field, and Whit decided he would be her top choice. She minimized the document she had been staring at for an hour and pulled up his profile.

A brilliant smile filled the top right corner of the screen. Dark blond hair and blue eyes sparkled in the photo. The eyes were more profound than Eli's but not as bright as Mitch's or Mark's. He had her hair coloring and Eli's eyes. She wondered if Eli would have the same reaction. After reviewing her other choices, Whit's eyes returned to number 143.

Whit closed the file and stood, needing a stretch. She walked outside to the deck and looked around. She could see the glow of the forge inside the cave where Mark was working some steel. The cool air carried the sound of the power hammer as it tapped out a steady rhythm. The flash of headlights coming up the drive revealed Mitch was returning home from a date with Jessie. Eli had lit the fire pit down by the creek, and the shadows from the flames danced across the yard. Eli would sit in her chair, whittling on some piece or another with Cruz stretched out beside her. Life was good.

Whit returned inside the lab and smiled at Oscar sleeping on the bed beside her desk. She softly stroked the cat's coat. "I can't seem to focus tonight. Are you about ready to head home?" Whit sat at the computer to shut it down, and a glowing from her bookcase caught her attention. The crystals from the cave she had stored in a small bowl were emitting a soft blue light. She watched them pulse for several seconds before they stopped abruptly.

"That's odd," Whit said and called to Oscar. "Let's go home."

Oscar stood and stretched before jumping down to race Whit to the door. Whit locked the door behind them and started down the steps from the lab, then crept behind the wheel of the Gator. Whit reached the bridge and looked up the mountain contemplating a visit to Mark. She noticed a blue glow near the top of the mountain and turned right to investigate. As she neared the cut-off to Mark's, the light disappeared. Since she was close to Mark, she drove to the cave outside his home.

Mitch looked up when he heard Whit approach. Mark was quenching a blade and smiled when he saw her step out of the Gator. Whit saw several blades on a nearby workbench. "You've been busy."

"I've got orders on top of orders," Mark said with a grin. "People must think I have a talent for creating fine blades."

"Undoubtedly so if you're getting that many orders. You make some mighty fine pieces," Whit said as she examined one of the finished blades.

Mitch looked at her. "Were you up at the lab tonight?"

"Yes, I'm just coming down. I've lost my focus for the night."

"Did you see a falling star or something a few minutes ago?" he asked.

"I thought I saw a blue glow for a few seconds, but then it was gone. What did you see?"

"Just a quick flash of light blue. That's what made me think of a falling star."

"You weren't smoking any wacky weed, were you?" Mark asked.

"No. Besides, Whit saw it, too," Mitch replied.

"Were you smoking wacky weed?" Mark teased Whit.

"No, but maybe we need some," Whit said and rolled her eyes. "I'm going to leave you guys to your man cave stuff and see what Eli's doing. I'll see you tomorrow."

"Goodnight, Whit."

"You two don't stay up too late. I think Eli wants to go to the diner tomorrow."

"I'll finish this blade and shut it down," Mark replied.

"I'm out of here, too. I'm whipped and going to head to bed," Mitch said.

"The chick-flick wore you out, Son?"

"I could barely keep my eyes open." Mitch grinned. "Goodnight."

Mark walked to the Gator with Whit. "Come up for breakfast in the morning. I want to break in the Blackstone griddle I got for Christmas."

"That sounds great. Any particular time?"

"Whenever you get up and moving. I'll send Mitch down for eggs."

"We can bring them," Whit offered.

Mark shook his head. "That's how I motivate him to get out of bed on the weekends."

Whit nodded, climbed into the Gator, and drove home. After parking the vehicle in the barn, she walked around the end of the house and saw Eli sitting by the fire. Eli had a long stick across her lap as she carefully removed the bark with the knife in her right hand. Whit watched her lover as her hands worked to smooth the wood. The peaceful look on Eli's face made Whit smile.

Whit stepped into the fire circle. "Would you like some company?"

Eli looked up and smiled at her lover. "I'd love some."

Whit sat beside Eli. "Everyone is busy tonight except me. I can't seem to focus."

"Is there something on your mind we need to discuss?" Eli asked.

Whit shrugged. "I honestly don't know what it is. My life has never been more perfect." Whit stared at the crystal necklace Eli was wearing. It often glowed when they were together, but tonight it seemed brighter. "Has that been glowing tonight?"

"More than usual," Eli replied. "Generally, it's just when you're close."

"The crystals in my lab were glowing tonight, too," Whit replied. "Then Mitch and I saw a shooting star or something a few minutes ago."

"Are there any meteor showers on the horizon or anything that could be triggering some cosmic energy?" Eli asked. "That could be why you find it hard to focus."

Whit shook her head. "No, nothing for weeks yet. Odd, but nothing to worry about, I'm sure."

Eli continued to shave the bark. "Where did you see Mitch?"

"I dropped by the forge to see what Mark was up to, and Mitch had just come home from a date. Mark's business is taking off, isn't it?"

Eli looked up from the stick. "Yes, and he couldn't be happier. Mark is doing something he enjoys and makes decent money at it, too. Mitch has an off day from school Monday, so he and I are making a trip to the junkyard for more leaf springs. Mark told me those are easy to cut and work with."

"Using the cave for a forge was a great idea. Even when it's cold out, Mark can work in the warmth of the cave," Whit remarked.

"He'll be rolling it outside in a few months," Eli replied. "The power hammer was a good move. It saves him hours of work and pain by not having to flatten the metal with a hammer."

Whit reached down to pet Oscar. "I noticed he still rubs his wrist at times. If we had a bracelet made, would he wear one made out of crystals? It worked for you when you were having headaches."

"It's worth a try. Do you think Julia could make him something that looks manly but not so big it interferes with his work?"

"I'm sure she can. I'll go up to the cave tomorrow and see if I can find some smaller pieces. Do you still want to hit the diner for lunch?"

"Yes, I think we need a break from cooking. I'll hike up to the cave with you if you want some company," Eli offered.

"I would love the company. That reminds me, Mark is cooking breakfast for us in the morning. He wants to start breaking in his new Blackstone."

"Great, I love Mark's breakfasts. Hell, what am I thinking? I love all his cooking." Eli stopped carving. "I hope he'll make some breakfast burritos. Those things are off the chain. Damn, now I'm hungry," Eli said.

"Would you care to join me for a slice of pie before bed?" Whit asked.

"Apple with cheese? Count me in," Eli replied. "Let me clean up here, and I'll be right in."

"Coffee?" Whit asked.

"Sure," Eli replied and wiped the shavings from her lap. She used a little rake to gather them while Whit went inside to start the coffee and pie. Eli dropped the shavings in the fire pit and closed the lid to extinguish the flames.

†

Mark shut down the forge and sat on a stool to admire the latest blades he had forged. There was still a lot of work to finish the knife, but he had completed the most critical task. Mark picked up one of the blades and inspected it for cracks and a warp. Finding none, he smiled at the beautiful Damascus pattern in the steel that would come to life as he began honing the edge to finish the blade. Mark looked around the cave for blocks of wood he would use to create the handles. Time to cut more blocks. Mark reached up to turn off the light and left for home. His phone pinged with a text.

Your sister is hoping for breakfast burritos.

Then breakfast burritos she will have. Mark added a smiley face to the text. *See you in the morning.*

†

Whit stirred Eli's coffee, and when the microwave dinged, she pulled out a large slice of apple pie. She looked up when Eli walked in. "You have impeccable timing, my love." Whit pointed to a stool and placed the pie and coffee in front of Eli.

"Perfect," Eli said after taking a bite.

"Thanks. I'm glad you enjoy apple pie. It's my favorite to make."

"My favorite to eat, too," Eli replied as she cut another bite. "I could eat this every day."

Tomboy stretched on the back of the sofa, looked at them, and blinked his green eyes. He jumped down and ran up the stairs. Cruz followed behind him. "I think our animals are trying to tell us it's time to go to bed." Eli smiled.

"It is getting late," Whit said as she rinsed the dishes and wiped her hands. "Do you have big plans for tomorrow?"

"Breakfast. Crystal gathering with you. Lunch at the diner, but after that, I'm free. Is there something you want to do?"

"I think I'm ready for us to review the potential donors," Whit replied.

"Do you want to do that first?"

"No, it can wait. There's no rush," Whit replied.

Eli walked to Whit and wrapped her in a hug. "Are you having second thoughts?"

"About having a baby? Absolutely not. I can't wait to have a baby together."

"We have a month before the wedding. Do you want to wait until after we're legal to get the procedure?"

"Would you prefer that over a shotgun wedding?" Whit laughed.

"The timing doesn't matter to me. I love you with all my heart, with or without a child."

"I never get tired of hearing that from you."

"Do I say it enough?" Eli asked.

"Yes, and when I hear you say those words, it makes my heart dance."

"I hope to make you a happy woman for another fifty years," Eli vowed.

"Just fifty?"

"For starters." Eli laughed and took her hand. "We'd better head upstairs before the posse comes looking for us."

CHAPTER TWO

Eli crept from bed and pulled on a robe before going downstairs. Cruz danced at the door, eager to relieve her bladder. When Eli stepped outside, the chilled air of a late winter morning greeted her. "Hurry, Cruz. It's cold out here." The warmth of her breath turned into frost as she spoke. "We'd better dress warmly this morning. It's chillier than it has been." Eli reached down to pet Cruz. "Are you hungry?"

Cruz dashed for the door and pushed it open. Eli chuckled and followed her inside. Whit was coming down the stairs when Eli stepped into the cabin. "Brrr, it's cold out this morning."

"You want some coffee before we shower and start the day?" Whit asked.

Eli opened her arms to Whit and pulled her close. "Good morning, my love. Coffee would be great. I'll stoke the fire if you brew the coffee."

Whit looked at the weather report on her phone. "It's only thirty-six degrees outside. No wonder you think it's cold."

Eli removed the screen in front of the fireplace and added logs to the glowing embers. "What's the forecast for today?"

"A high of forty-nine," Whit reported. "Oh my, there's a cold front coming our way. We may get a dusting of snow in the next few days."

"It's kind of late for snow, isn't it?"

"Generally, yes, but it does happen from time to time," Whit answered.

"Mitch will be on cloud nine if it snows," Eli said. "I worry about him driving in snow and ice, though."

"Mitch has done well so far," Whit reminded her. She handed Eli a cup of coffee.

"Yes, he has. Going to school daily has given him more experience than the rest of us," Eli agreed.

"He seems to be doing well in school. Have you talked about it much with him?" Whit asked.

"Just a bit on what he's learning, but not in great detail. I think he's enjoying the classes so far. He doesn't seem convinced that's what he wants as a career yet." Eli smiled. "I can't believe he's already finished his assignments to be able to graduate this spring."

"Mitch knew that was a requirement for starting mechanic school. He's young and needs to experience several types of work before he chooses a career," Whit reminded her. "Mechanic skills will come in handy around here. He appears to enjoy working in the forge with Mark, also."

Eli took a sip of coffee. "I wish Mark had a bit more patience working with Mitch. He adores projects with Mark, but he can get short with him if Mitch doesn't read his mind or move as fast as he wants."

"Have you talked about that with Mark? He listens to you."

"I think I need to," Eli replied.

"Why don't I take Mitch to the cave to hunt for crystals while you chat with Mark?"

"I wanted to go hunt crystals," Eli replied with a playful pout. "I know it will give me some time to talk privately with Mark."

"We also need to finalize the plans with Mitch for his tiny home. Graduation will be here before we know it," Whit reminded her.

"Yes, it will. Speaking of ceremonies, do we have everything in place for ours?" Eli asked. "You, Carol, and

Julia have been secretive about our 'Big Day,'" Eli said, making air quotes with her fingers.

"We've got everything under control. The only other thing we need to nail down is the house we'll rent at the Outer Banks for our honeymoon," Whit replied.

Eli grinned. "Our honeymoon. That sounds great. I didn't ever think I'd be having a honeymoon."

Whit reached out to stroke Eli's cheek. "It will be a well-deserved break for both of us. Life hasn't slowed down for either of us since you arrived. It's been one project after another, but think of all we've accomplished."

"We have gotten a lot done. More than I'd ever dreamed we could in such a short time."

"We've got great friends and family that have helped. Mr. Henry has gotten certified as Justice of the Peace, so he can perform our ceremony."

"Seriously?" Eli said.

"He's wanted to do it for years to help with his church. We will be his first wedding," Whit said with a smile.

"That's fantastic news. I wasn't thrilled with the thought of someone who doesn't know us performing the ceremony," Eli said. "Mr. Henry will be perfect."

"I think he's almost as excited as we are," Whit said. She drained her coffee. "Let's hit the shower and get this day started."

"Sounds good to me. I'm hungry," Eli commented.

Whit reached for her hand. "Lots to do, people to see, food to eat. Let's roll."

✝

Mitch was exiting the chicken coop when Whit and Eli walked outside. "Look, we've got a fox in the henhouse raiding our eggs," Eli called out.

"Busted," Mitch hollered back, raising his hands in surrender.

"Careful not to spill those eggs," Whit called out.

"Good morning, ladies," Mitch said.

"Morning, Nephew," Eli said. "Did you walk down?"

"Yeah, it's such a nice crisp morning," Mitch answered.

"Have you checked the weather report?" Whit asked.

"Nope, I haven't been awake that long. Dad got me up to raid the henhouse."

Whit smiled. "We have a chance for some snow this week."

"Awesome," Mitch cried out. "I'd love more snow before the warm weather arrives."

"Hey, after breakfast, I need your help with something," Whit said. "Will you go with me to the cave?"

"You know I can't say no to a beautiful woman," Mitch teased. "What are we doing?"

Whit scoffed. "You're so smooth. I want to gather some smaller crystals. I want Julia to make your dad a bracelet to see if it will help with his wrist and hand pain."

"That's a great idea. I'd be more than glad to help." Eli looked at Mitch. "We also need to finalize the plan for your tiny home. Do you realize graduation is only two months off?"

"I know. I'm not stoked about walking at graduation, but Mom is desperate to see me complete the whole high school graduation thing."

"Well, there were some times when it took a lot to get you motivated. You are definitely on the right path now. I couldn't be prouder of all you've accomplished in the last year." Eli wrapped an arm around his shoulder.

"You two have played a big part in that. Before you came up here, I had zilch for motivation. Your excitement was contagious, and I caught the mountain bug. I knew I had rules to follow and things to complete before moving up here, and I'm so glad to be here sharing this with y'all."

"You've been a big part of our success, and I hope that will continue," Eli praised.

"I don't have plans to leave the mountain," Mitch replied. "I do need your help, though."

"With what?" Eli asked.

"Jessie asked me to go to the prom with her last night. I have no clue about tuxedos or flowers."

"Has Jessie picked out her dress yet? The tux you rent will depend on her color selection," Eli replied.

"As will the flowers," Whit added.

"See, I do need your help. All I know is that Jessie's dress is blue. I'll see if she can send me a picture."

"That would be helpful," Whit said.

"Will I have to wear a tux to the wedding?" Mitch asked.

"Not unless they make one using cargo shorts," Eli teased. "We've decided to keep things casual."

"That's comforting. I'd dress up for y'all in a heartbeat, but give me deck shoes and cargo shorts, any day over a tux."

"We want everyone to be comfortable. Especially since the ceremony will be out here," Whit said. "We also want you to house and animal sit for us while we're on our honeymoon."

"That's not a problem," Mitch said. "I'll do that anytime you two want to take a trip. Are you going back to Pensacola?"

Eli shook her head. "No, we're going to the Outer Banks. Neither one of us has gone in years."

"That sounds like it will be fun. Are y'all taking a Gator up or walking?"

Eli looked at Whit. "I think we'll walk up with you. It is a nice morning for a stroll."

"We need to stop off at the barn to feed everyone first," Whit reminded them.

"Nope, I did that already. Even the chickens," Mitch said. "Molly wanted out, but I didn't think you wanted her out this early."

"Good call. Especially with us not here to monitor. We'll let Molly out later when it warms up," Eli said. "Thanks for feeding the crew."

"No problem," Mitch said. "I know they are all altered, but I swear the cats are multiplying," he joked. "I opened the door, and black cats were everywhere."

"With that bunch, they could be out recruiting," Eli joked back. "I wouldn't put anything past Cajun."

"One of them spends time in the cave with Dad when he's working in the forge. I couldn't tell which one for sure."

"It's probably Goliath. He's the youngest of the bunch and took a shine to Mark right off the bat," Eli said.

"Dad's almost as crazy about black cats as you are," Mitch said. "When it warms up, he will see if Doc Loren has any to adopt."

"I'm sure she will," Eli answered. "We may have to rename this place Black Cat Haven." She chuckled.

"Hey, I may have to join the fun and name my tiny home that." Mitch grinned.

"There's an idea. I don't think there will be a lot of room for cats, but maybe one or two," Whit replied.

"Maybe I can build them a tiny cat house connected to mine," Mitch said. "With a tunnel up to my loft and a small kitty window for them to go outside."

"I can just see it now. You'll have a bed full of black cats once they figure out the tunnel." Eli smirked. "Will Danny be able to get up the steps?"

"Naw, she'll stay at Mom and Dad's with Riley. I'm sure I'll be seeing lots of her."

"We will get you some kittens to keep you entertained." Whit reached for Eli's hand. "I think everyone needs a couple of good cats. I know I lucked out with Oscar and now Walter."

"Walter is a trip." Mitch laughed. "I love watching him try to keep up with the kittens on the slide."

When the cabin came into view, they saw Mark out on the deck. The smell of bacon filled the air. He looked up when Cruz rushed ahead and climbed onto the balcony. "There you are. I was wondering if you got devoured by Henny Penny," Mark teased.

"Those are some damn mean hens," Mitch replied. "I've got your eggs."

"Good morning, ladies," Mark said with a smile. "I hope you're hungry."

"Always," Eli said. "What you cooking?"

"I heard someone had a craving for burritos, so that's what we're having on this fine, chilly morning."

"What can I help with?" Eli asked.

19

"I've got a bowl of diced onions and potatoes. You can bring those out with a pack of tortillas. I'd love a fresh cup of coffee, too."

"I'll get his coffee if you bring the vegetables out," Whit said, walking over for Mark's cup.

"Thanks, Sis," Mark said and kissed Whit's cheek. "I think it's too cool to eat out here, so if you want, y'all can set the table inside. Send Mitch out with a dozen whipped eggs and some cheese. There is sour cream and guacamole in the fridge you can put on the table."

"That makes my mouth water," Whit said. "I'll be right back."

Eli brought the bowl of vegetables out and handed them to Mark. "Those are going to taste so good. How many pounds of bacon did you cook?"

"Two, but there's more if needed. I hope to fill the tortillas with all kinds of goodies," Mark said as he spread oil on the grill and dumped the contents of the bowl. "I think I'm going to love this Blackstone."

"I bet it would be great for hibachi meats and some kicking fried rice and veggies."

"We will have to test that theory soon," Mark replied.

Whit walked out carrying two cups of coffee. "I'll get the table set, and Mitch will be out soon."

"Do you need some help?" Eli asked.

"I've got this. Enjoy your coffee and stay out of the bacon," Whit teased.

"I've got my eye and spatula ready for her," Mark said.

"You two are no fun," Eli griped. She watched Whit return inside. "How are things going with Laura and Brad?"

"Laura's getting a total dose of Brad. He's in that know-it-all, untouchable teenager phase right now. I think she's regretting how much we've babied him."

"Hopefully, he'll pass through that phase unscathed," Eli said.

"I don't know. Brad almost got suspended for making a loud-mouthed inappropriate comment to another student last week. He claims they were both playing around, but you know the second person is always the one to get caught. That behavior won't be acceptable anywhere, much less a Catholic school."

"Do you need to go home and get him on the right path?" Eli asked.

"I'll probably go down next week. Laura needs a good taste of how obstinate he can get. It's a learning time for her, too," Mark said. "We were hard on Mitch and have been the opposite on Brad. Now we have to pay the piper."

"Mitch wasn't an easy kid to raise, but he's turning into a fine young man," Eli said.

Mark nodded. "He's matured since he's been up here with you. I know he's probably going to make more mistakes, but I think, for once, he's gotten serious about his future."

Mitch walked out of the kitchen with the eggs and tortillas. "Man, it smells good out here. If I weren't already hungry, I would be. What else do you need, Dad?"

"I think I have things under control here, Son. Let me cook these vegetables more, and I'll start on the eggs. Do you want to add some peppers or olives to yours?"

"Oh, some Greek pepper rings might be tasty," Mitch replied.

"That does sound interesting," Eli agreed.

"We won't know until we try them. Go bring some out, Mitch." Mark looked at Eli. "There's one good thing about Mitch. He's not afraid to experiment and try different things. Brad can be such a picky eater at times."

"Two very unique young men, for sure," Eli said.

"That's an understatement," Mark said as he turned the veggies. "Will you open the pack of tortillas?"

Mitch returned with the peppers.

Mark took the container. "Will you also bring out a cookie sheet?"

"Yes, sir," Mitch replied.

"Hey, please drop this bowl in the sink, too." Mark looked at Eli. "Toss a couple of those on the flat top while I scramble these eggs. Go ahead and put two cheese slices on each one when I flip them, please."

"You got it," Eli said, separating the cheese slices. As soon as Mark flipped a tortilla, she placed the cheese on the hot side and watched the cheese start to melt.

Mark placed a layer of hot vegetables, then bacon, and added the scrambled eggs to the pile. "Would you wrap them and put them on the cookie sheet when it arrives."

"Sure thing." Mitch arrived with the cookie sheet. Eli looked up at him. "How many peppers do you want on each one?"

"Five or six will do." He grinned. "You going to try one with me?"

"Of course I am," Eli replied. "Your dad is, too," she said, winking at Mitch.

Together, they made ten breakfast burritos and placed them on the cookie sheet. "Get them inside before they start cooling down. I'll be inside in just a few." Mark picked up a squeeze bottle of water and cleaned the flat top. "You, too. I won't be out long."

Eli picked up the spatula and seasonings, carrying them into the kitchen.

"Apple juice for you, Eli?"

"Yes, please." Eli smiled at her lover.

"Better make it all around," Mitch said. "I have milk, too. Do either of you want some?"

"Nope, I'm good with juice. Thanks, Mitch," Whit replied.

Eli served the first burritos, and when Mark arrived, they added sour cream and guacamole. The flavors exploded in Eli's mouth when she took the first bite. "Those peppers bring the eggs to life," Eli said and licked a drop of sour cream from the corner of her mouth.

"They are excellent," Whit agreed.

"*Eggssalent.*" Mitch laughed. "You outdid yourself on these, Dad."

"I have to admit they are decent," Mark replied.

"More than decent," Eli said and took another bite. "If you don't like them, I'll eat your share."

"Nobody mentioned not liking them, but if you're still hungry, I'll make more," Mark said.

Mitch's phone rang. He looked at it. "Mom," he told Mark. "Can I rub it in?"

"Go for it." Mark smirked.

"Good morning, Mom. You aren't going to believe what Dad cooked for breakfast." He turned his phone around so Laura could see the massive burrito.

"That certainly looks better than my cold cereal," Brad said as he looked over Laura's shoulder.

"Dude, you will love these," Mitch replied. "Stuffed with all the goodies."

"Thanks, Bro, be sure to eat one for me," Brad groaned.

"I think I can handle that," Mitch said.

"You look all wrapped up. Is it cold there this morning?" Laura asked.

"A bit on the chilly side, and we have a chance of snow this week," Mitch reported.

"Oh, you suck," Brad said. "It's just cold and rainy here."

"Watch your language," Laura growled. "Maybe you should stay for confession after mass. I think a few thousand Hail Marys might help your attitude."

"Sorry, Mom," Brad said.

"If I believed that for a second, I'd accept that," Laura said.

Mark stood up from the table. "Hand me your phone, please, Mitch."

Mitch's eyebrows shot up, but he gave his dad the phone. "I'll be right back."

Eli looked at Mitch, then at Whit. "I think baby bro is about to get an earful from your dad."

"It's about time. Brad gets away with so much, and it's not funny." Mitch returned to his meal.

Mark returned to the table a few minutes later, and Eli could see the frown on his face. "Sorry about that, ladies. My youngest needed a reality check because Brad's obviously bounced."

"I'm sure he got your message loud and clear," Eli said.

"I hope so. Other than drilling a hole in Brad's hard head and packing in common sense, I don't know what else to do with him," Mark replied. "He and a friend passed inappropriate pictures with racial and sexual slurs during class. Of course, Brad was the one to get caught. He's lucky he didn't get expelled from school."

"You should know the second child is always the hardest," Eli claimed. "I mean, after me being such an angel and all, I'm sure it was hard for you to follow in my footsteps," she joked.

"Ha! Angel, my ass. You were just too clever to get caught in most of your shenanigans," Mark replied.

"Oh, I got caught in plenty," Eli replied. "Dad wore my ass out many times, yet here I am today."

"Mom always said these two would be her revenge on me. I know she was right now." Mark looked at Mitch. "You've seemed to turn a corner. What do you recommend I do with Brad?"

Mitch had just taken a bite of food and choked as he tried to swallow. His face turned red as he grabbed the glass of milk and drank. "You're asking me for advice on Brad?"

"Yeah, you're close to his age and know what hits him the hardest," Mark replied.

"His social life. Take away his cell phone, tablet, and X-box, which will get his attention." Mitch smirked. "There's not much else he cares about right now."

"That sounds about as good a plan as any," Eli said. "Can Laura enforce it?"

"Not so much a matter of can. It's more of, will she? Brad has always been her baby," Mark replied. "I'll admit, mine, too, so I have to buckle down with him."

"That will probably be the most challenging part, to be the enforcer and not give in to his whining and complaining," Eli said.

"Tell me about it." Mark shook his head. "I guess I'll deal with that later this week."

"You're going to Alabama this week?" Mitch asked.

"Yeah, I need to give your mom a break and see if I can get Brad back on track. Do you need me for something?"

"No. I didn't know you had plans to go," Mitch said.

"I didn't until this morning," Mark answered. "Do you want to go?"

"I've got school I can't afford to miss and stuff to do around here," Mitch said.

"Speaking of which, are you ready to head up the mountain?" Whit asked Mitch. She popped the last bite of her burrito in her mouth.

"Yes. If I eat any more, I'm going to explode. That was an excellent breakfast, Dad."

"I'm glad you enjoyed it. It did turn out pretty well," Mark agreed.

"You can make those again whenever you want," Eli added. "I'll help with the clean-up. I'll start on the kitchen if you need to finish the grill."

"The grill is clean. I just need to cover it once it's cooled down. That shouldn't take long in this weather. You rinse, and I'll load."

Whit kissed Eli and then nodded toward the door. "You ready?" she asked Mitch.

"Right behind you," Mitch answered. "Are you coming, Cruz?"

Cruz looked at Eli. "Go ahead and keep the bears away," Eli told her. Cruz stood and trotted over to Mitch, and they walked outside.

"I swear that dog understands every word you say," Mark said as he carried a stack of dishes into the kitchen.

"I just wish kids were that easy," Eli said.

"Amen to that. They can be a challenge at times."

"I wanted to talk to you about Mitch this morning. That's why Whit asked him to help her."

"Has he done something wrong?" Mark asked with a furrowed brow.

"On the contrary, Mitch is doing fantastic. It's you I'm worried about," Eli said, deciding to put the issue right out front.

"Me? Why are you worried about me?" Mark asked.

"I don't think you realize how much Mitch adores working with you. Sometimes, you are a bit short with him on patience, and I can see the hurt it gives him. I am not an expert on raising children, but I've seen him grow so much these last few months. He busted his ass to finish his requirements for graduating high school and has begun his mechanic courses." Eli sighed. "He hungers for your approval. He's often told me that he wants you to teach him how to forge knives, but he's afraid to ask much of you. I'm sure the issues with Brad will make things more difficult for you." Eli rinsed a plate. "I guess I'm trying to say to have a bit more patience when it comes to Mitch. He's going to make mistakes. We both know that, so don't blow up at him when he does." Eli took a deep breath and slowly released it. "There, I got it out."

Mark took the plate from her and placed it in the dishwasher. "I know I get short on patience at times. I've always expected so much from him. He's my firstborn, and I want the world for him, but he's also been difficult to raise. Less behavioral than Brad and his sassiness, but more motivational with Mitch."

"All I can say is that I've seen a lot of effort on his part to do what he needs to, and his maturity is growing. He's still a teenager and is going to make kid mistakes. Allow him to grow into the big man shoes you expect him to wear." She smirked at Mark. "Besides, you were still a goofy teen when you were his age. Don't expect him to be any different than the cloth he was cut from."

"I hear what you're saying. I'll try to do more to be positive with Mitch. I can see a lot of growth in him, and I know I can do better in helping him increase his self-confidence and skills."

"That's all I'm asking. Have fun with Mitch while he still wants to spend time with you and learn." Eli handed

Mark the last plate. "My job is done here. What are you going to do with Brad?"

"That's a whole other dilemma in itself. I think I'll start by taking Brad for a crew cut. Cut off those pretty little locks of his. If nothing else, it will reduce the time he spends preening in front of the mirror."

"That's cruel," Eli said.

"He's got to learn that there are consequences to his behavior, too. I like Mitch's suggestion about cutting out his social media addiction. I think that will affect him the most. He lives for Snapchat with his friends."

"You've got to come up with ways he can earn those privileges back, too," Eli reminded him. "If he just has to wait out his prison sentence to get his privileges back, he'll just be an angry slug."

"Oh, I've already got a list of things he can do to lessen his time. They won't be easy chores either. I plan to recruit Father Michael on this mission. I believe the parking spaces need new lines, and the church needs a good power washing, along with the sidewalks."

"Man, I'm glad I'm not your child." Eli grinned. "What else?"

"He can clean the gutters at our house and our neighbors, an elderly couple. It may be early, but he can also mow both yards."

"If Brad doesn't get the message after all that, there's no hope for him surviving his teen years," Eli said. "Doesn't he have Spring Break coming up, too?"

"He did have. Now, he has Hell Week. I'll go down and get him, and he will be so busy up here he will wish he was at the beach with his friends."

"I think it's time to start planning your garden plot. I know mine could use some tilling. My barn could use some fresh paint, too," Eli said.

"If he finishes all those assignments, I'll give him the option of what privilege he wants back after each one. By the time he finishes here, he should learn to put a filter on that mouth."

"Let's grab a cup of coffee and look for a garden spot," Eli said.

†

"I can't remember ever making Dad that mad at me," Mitch said. "I wonder what he said that got him in so much hot water?"

"I bet his ears were blistering after he got off the phone. Brad needs to learn to filter his comments, and it sounds like he has a hard time learning that lesson," Whit replied.

"I didn't think it was possible, but Brad's more hard-headed than me."

"That's pretty hard," Whit said, bumping her shoulder into Mitch as they reached the cave.

Mitch turned on his light and shined it inside.

"I'm glad you remembered a flashlight."

"My head may be hard, but I can still think occasionally. I hope there's nothing inside that wants to eat us."

"Good point. You go first," Whit teased.

Cruz ran past them and disappeared inside the cave, returning a few seconds later. She sat down and looked at them as if to say, "Y'all coming or what?"

"I think she's calling us out," Mitch teased. "Let's go."

As they made their way into the rear cave, Whit could feel the crystals begin to pulse before she saw them. *Something feels different, more energy than I've noticed before.*

"These things are glowing," Mitch said as they entered the large opening. He turned off the flashlight. "We don't need this in here. What size are you looking for anyhow?"

"The smallest we can find," Whit answered. "If we can't find any that will fit into a bracelet, he may just have to wear an amulet like Eli."

"Or both," Mitch replied. "A little extra couldn't hurt." He bent to pick up a crystal. "What about this?" He held the crystal out to Whit.

The crystal flared a bright blue when she touched it, then faded back. "That one likes you." Mitch laughed.

"A bit smaller, if we can find some," Whit replied. Whit felt goosebumps rise on her arms and the hairs standing up. It was cooler inside but not cold by any means. Certainly not enough to give her a chill. Cruz must have felt something, too. She was glued to Whit's side as her eyes scanned the cave. Whit thought they were not alone, but she wasn't fearful.

"Here we go," Mitch said and bent down to pick up four crystals that were the size of marbles. "I bet these would work, and you can use the first for an amulet." He handed Whit the crystals, and she quickly stuffed them into her pocket.

"Does it feel different in here to you?" Whit asked.

"It's not as cool as I thought it would be. It feels warmer than outside, which is weird. It's brighter than I can remember, too," Mitch added. "Do you think this has anything to do with the falling star last night?"

"Who knows?" Whit shrugged. She had to admit she had the same thought when they first arrived, but she didn't mention it to Mitch. "I've got what we need. Let's head back and see what Eli and your dad are doing."

As they turned to exit the room, a crystal dropped and hit Mitch on the head. "Hey, what the hell?" he cried out. He bent to retrieve the fallen crystal.

"I guess that one chooses you," Whit said. She looked at the crystal. "That would be a good size for an amulet for you. Would you wear one?"

"Heck yeah," Mitch replied.

"Let me have it, and I'll see what Julia can do for us." Whit took the crystal and tucked it away.

†

The sun broke through and burned off the mist as they headed back down the mountain. They saw Mark and Eli outside walking around when they reached Mark's cabin.

"Did y'all lose something?" Mitch asked.

"Nope, we are just scoping out a garden plot for your brother to till during his Spring Break," Mark announced.

"Damn, no beach for him. He's gonna die," Mitch said.

"He will wish he had kept his mouth shut when I get done with him. I've got lots of things he will be doing over the next few weeks. All without his cherished electronics," Mark said.

Mitch just shook his head. "I almost feel sorry for Brad."

"Don't. Brad's behavior caused all this. He has to learn there are consequences for making crude remarks."

"I think this will be a good spot. Not too many rocks to have to pry up, but enough to work him hard," Eli said.

"Mitch can help me measure it out and mark it later. What time were you thinking about hitting the diner?"

"Why don't we leave here at about noon? My burrito will be long gone by then," Eli replied.

"Sounds good. We'll come to pick you up. Mitch and I will mark the garden plot and heat some steel in the forge."

"Alright," Mitch said.

"I can walk you through the forge while I work on honing some edges," Mark told his son. "You ready for that?"

"Yes, sir. You bet I am," Mitch nearly crowed with excitement.

"We'll see you two later then. Thanks for a great breakfast," Eli told Mark.

"Anytime, Sis. We'll see you at noon."

"Don't work too hard," Eli said, then wrapped her arm around Whit's shoulder as they started for home.

"It looks like we have a relatively free morning. What do you want to do?" Eli asked Whit.

"If you don't mind, I'd like to visit Carol and Julia to discuss making some jewelry. We found some excellent crystals for a bracelet and an amulet for Mark. When we were leaving, one fell and hit Mitch in the head, so I wanted to make him an amulet, too. It appears the crystal was choosing him."

"That sounds good. A bit odd, but that place has strange energy," Eli said.

"It felt different today."

"How so?" Eli asked.

"I don't know how to describe it. Like maybe we weren't alone, but not in a scary way. Very comfortable and almost warm in the crystal cave."

"That place is full of mystery," Eli said as she slid her hand inside Whit's as they crossed the bridge.

"Yeah, it is," Whit agreed. She didn't mention her and Mitch's thoughts about the strange sensations related to the falling star they thought they had witnessed. "Let's go see a jeweler." She grinned at Eli.

†

After returning from lunch, Mark and Mitch decided to do some more work in the forge. "He did well this morning," Mark praised.

"It's a lot of fun working with you, Dad," Mitch said.

Eli's heart swelled when she heard how well they had worked together. "Maybe once Mitch gets the forge work down, you can focus on the finishing work," Eli suggested.

"Eventually, but he needs to learn the whole process, too. We've even discussed branching out some. This knucklehead wants to try his hand at a small Viking-ax," Mark told them.

"I think they would be a good seller," Mitch said. "More woodwork, but less iron."

"Are we still going to get leaf springs tomorrow?" Eli asked.

"I told Mitch he and I would go since he has the day off from school," Mark said.

"That's fine with me," Eli said. "What kind of wood do you need for an ax handle?"

"Birch or hickory would be traditional," Mitch replied. "There is a hickory tree a couple of hundred yards behind the camp shelter going east that Brad and I found on our trip. I might hike to see if it had some branches that broke during the winter."

"We could hike up there when we get home," Mark suggested.

"That would be cool with me. It's not all that far, and we can walk off some of that pie we just devoured." Mitch grinned.

"Good point. What do y'all have planned for dinner?" Mark asked.

"I can't even think about food right now. I'm full from that lunch," Eli groaned.

"How about a run at the fried rice and hibachi chicken you mentioned this morning?" Mark asked.

"That wouldn't be heavy. Sounds good, but not until later in the day," Eli replied.

"Should we shoot for about seven, then? That will give us a bit to work in the forge, and you can nap if you want," Mark teased.

"Hey, that's not a bad idea," Whit agreed.

"I guess we'll see you later tonight. Do we need to bring anything?" Eli asked.

"Nope. We've got it covered. See you later."

Eli laced her fingers with Whit's as they walked into the cabin. "Are you ready to look at those profiles?"

"Yeah, let's go ahead with that. Then a nap does sound good." Whit smiled.

"I'm going to grab some water. Do you want anything?"

Whit walked to the computer. "No, thanks. I'm good."

Eli pulled a chair up next to Whit. "What are we looking for?"

"Someone who looks nice, has a strong IQ, and good qualities. I know the agency vets out the donors, but it's nice to learn more about them from their profiles. These are my top four selections." Whit moved her mouse to the first profile and allowed time for Eli to read through the contents.

"Okay, who is next?" Eli asked.

Whit pulled up profile 143 next and held her breath until Eli spoke.

"He's nice looking, has a good IQ, and is a medical professional. He must be new. He has not been a donor yet. The first profile had twenty selections."

"Is that important to you?" Whit asked.

"No, not really. The man looks familiar," Eli said.

Whit smiled. "I thought the same thing. His hair coloring is close to mine, and his blue eyes are a close shade to you."

"Huh, that is true. Who's next?"

Whit moved the mouse to bring up the following profile.

"Wow, he's been busy," Eli joked. "Thirty-five males and twenty females. Do you have any preference?"

"Not at all. I think any healthy child will be a blessing to us," Whit answered.

"I agree," Eli replied. "Who is the last one?" She waited for Whit to move the mouse and shook her head when the photo appeared. "He's got strange eyes," Eli said.

"What's weird about them?" Whit asked.

"I don't know. The eyes just look off to me," Eli answered.

"Did you like either of them? Or do you want to look at more?"

"Let's look at two and three again," Eli said.

"I need to empty my bladder, so you study them while I'm gone," Whit said. "I'll be right back."

Eli shifted over to the office chair and clicked the mouse. She studied each face and read over the profile information carefully. Eli was reading over 143 for the third time when Whit returned. "Do you have a favorite?"

Whit sat next to Eli. "Yes, but I want to make sure we agree. Do you have a preference?"

"This is a big decision," Eli replied. "Let me think about it for a bit."

Whit was slightly disappointed they hadn't made a selection, but Eli was right. It was an important decision, and they needed to be sure they agreed on the donor.

"I'm going to do a bit of carving while I think. Do you want to take a nap?"

"Not if you aren't beside me. I think I'll make a dessert to take to Mark's."

"Okay, I'll be at the firepit if you need anything," Eli replied.

Whit watched Eli gather her supplies and walk to the firepit. Then she walked to the pantry and opened the doors in search of a dessert idea.

†

Eli stretched out in her favorite chair and opened the blade of her knife. The piece she was working was coming along nicely, revealing beautiful wood grains beneath a thick bark. Her hands moved mechanically as her thoughts returned to the four faces that had stared back from the computer screen. Whoever they picked would potentially be the father of their child. However, by the contract terms, they had no legal claim to a child they had supplied the seed to create for her and Whit. The agency assured them they would maintain their and the donor's privacy. Eli had to make sure of that. She knew she would go nuts if something happened to allow the donor to claim the child. Eli's concentration wavered, and her knife slipped off the wood, slicing open the palm of her hand.

"Dammit," she cried out and rushed to the kitchen.

Whit saw the blood flowing down her wrist as Eli entered the kitchen. She reached over to turn on the flow of water in the sink. "What happened?"

"My knife slipped, and I sliced my palm," Eli said.

"Bad enough for stitches?" Whit asked.

"I don't know. Blood covered my hand so fast I couldn't tell."

"Rinse it carefully under the water while I get the first aid kit," Whit instructed and rushed from the kitchen.

Eli placed her hand under the water and winced as the cold water rushed into the cut. Whit returned with the kit and pulled out a large pack of sterile gauze.

"How does it look?"

"I don't know. I'm afraid to look," Eli replied.

Whit looked at Eli's hand and saw a two-inch slice open across her palm. She pressed the gauze against the cut and applied pressure to stop the bleeding. "It's not horrible, but I'd prefer you get checked for a stitch or two. Have you had a tetanus shot recently?"

"Not that I can remember," Eli said.

"Let me grab a towel to wrap your hand in, and we'll head to town."

"Do we have to go?" Eli asked.

"Yes, we do. I want you checked by a professional, and get a booster and stitches if needed." Whit looked at Eli. "Do this for me, please."

Eli nodded and allowed Whit to wrap her hand in a small towel.

"Do you want some Tylenol before we go? Does it hurt?"

"No, I'm good. It's more embarrassing than painful," Eli said.

"Accidents happen. Nothing to be embarrassed about," Whit told her. "Were you distracted by our conversation about selecting a donor?"

"Yeah, I was lost in thought and not paying attention," Eli admitted.

Whit nodded. "I should have known better than to allow you to work with a sharp blade when you were contemplating something important."

"That's probably not a bad idea moving forward," Eli said. "I'm sorry."

"For what? Being human? You can't always be a superhero, baby." Whit kissed Eli softly. "Try to keep your hand elevated. I'll grab the truck keys. Let's go."

†

Whit helped Eli into the truck and they headed into town. She pulled into the parking lot at the emergency room. "Are you okay to walk?"

"Yes, dear," Eli said. "It doesn't feel like it's bleeding any longer."

"Let's go then," Whit said, shutting down the truck.

Eli was relieved to see the emergency room had very few patients, and she was checked in and placed in an exam room rather quickly. Whit sat beside her, and they both turned when they heard a knock on the door.

The doctor who had treated her head injury stepped into the room and smiled. "I thought I recognized that name. Didn't I tell you not to come back?" he joked.

"You did, but it's been almost a year. I missed you," Eli joked back.

"What happened today?" he asked when he sat beside her.

"I was carving on a walking stick, and my knife decided it wanted a taste of me," Eli said as she unwrapped her hand.

He smiled at Whit. "Do I need to lecture you on monitoring her around sharp instruments?" he teased.

"I guess I need to get her a chainmail glove that meat cutters use," Whit replied.

The doctor examined the cut across Eli's palm. "That probably wouldn't be a bad idea. Let's get this cleaned up so I can get a better look. Come with me," he said and reached for Eli's hand. He took her to a sink, opened a drawer to pull out a Betadine scrub, and handed it to her. "You get the honors."

"Me? I have to clean it?" Eli asked.

"Yes, you. You can tell how painful it is where I can't," the doctor replied.

He monitored Eli as she cleaned the cut. "That doesn't look too deep, but I'd like to close it with a stitch or two."

"I need a tetanus booster, too, according to the other doc in the room." Eli nodded at Whit. He stepped over to the computer system and tapped a few keys. "No, you're good. We got you when you tried to fly. That should last you for ten years."

"Good," Whit said. "Neither of us remembered a shot."

"I'll still need to give you a shot to deaden the area for stitches," he replied. "Unless you want to go Rambo on me."

Eli shook her head. "No, I'll take the shot."

He smiled. "I'll be right back then."

When he returned, he deadened the area, made two quick stitches, and then wrapped her palm. He looked at Whit. "You know the routine. Keep it dry and protected, then bring her back in ten days to remove the stitches." He grinned at Whit. "Or you can take them out. Just make sure there is no drainage or redness. And please, by all means, get her some protection if she's going to play with sharp objects."

"I will, Doc," Whit replied.

He handed Whit a bag of supplies. "Pay the lady on your way out, and do try to stay safe. If you want to visit, just stop in any time." He chuckled, shot Eli a wink, and left the room.

Whit paid the bill and helped Eli back into the truck. She looked at the clock. "Now, do you want a short nap?"

"Will you snuggle with me?" Eli asked.

"I'd love to," Whit said and drove them home.

†

Cruz rushed over to Eli, smelled her bandaged hand, and sneezed at the antiseptic smell. "I'm okay, Cruz," Eli told her and stroked the top of her head.

Whit followed Eli upstairs and pulled her boots off. "Be careful of that hand," Whit warned as Eli stretched out.

"I will," Eli replied, patting the bed with her right hand. "Come snuggle."

Whit kicked off her shoes and stretched out next to Eli. She tucked a small pillow under Eli's left hand to elevate it and hopefully add protection while Eli encircled Whit with her right arm. Whit laid her head on Eli's shoulder. "Are you feeling okay?"

"Fine as wine," Eli replied. "I'm sorry if I scared you. I reckon I should come with a warning label that reads 'Clumsy at times.'" Eli grinned.

"It doesn't matter what warning labels are attached. I still love you." Whit's hand rested on Eli's stomach. "I'm glad it wasn't more severe than it turned out."

"Me, too," Eli said. Her hand stroked down Whit's arm. "My mind was playing too many what ifs. I was worried about if the donor could have a claim as a parent that would force us to share custody."

Whit turned to look at Eli. "From what I've heard and read, the donor would have no claim or even be aware of who chooses him as a donor. That is not something we need to worry about, sweetie."

"It would kill us to lose a child," Eli said.

Whit could see the tears in Eli's eyes. "That could not happen. Are you having second thoughts?"

"No, not of having a baby. Not even for a second. I just worry that a stranger could show up and ruin our happy family," Eli said.

"We can check with the agency to confirm everything is in order and a donor has no legal claim to any child." Whit smiled at Eli. "Would that make you feel better?"

"Yeah, it would. I like the second profile we looked at, even though he doesn't have a prior history of births."

Whit raised her head to rest on her elbow. "He was my choice, too. For some odd reason, he feels like the one."

"I know. I kept coming back to the profile," Eli said. "Like I was being pulled back to him. Does that sound strange?"

"No, I felt the same thing. Like to a magnet. I felt attracted to the man's eyes. Something warm and intelligent in them."

"I'm glad we agree on that part," Eli said. "Now we need to decide upon when."

"What about after we return from our honeymoon?" Whit suggested. "That way, we can focus on having fun together and nothing else."

"I think that's perfect," Eli said.

"So, promise me one thing. You'll be extra careful with sharp objects from here on out," Whit teased.

"I like the idea of a protective glove when I'm carving. It certainly can't hurt," Eli said, kissing Whit's head.

"I'll order one when we get home tonight. If not before," Whit said with a chuckle.

†

After a short power nap, Whit woke Eli to go to dinner at Mark's. "Are you ready for the teasing Mark and Mitch are going to give you?"

"I'm used to their harassment," Eli replied. "I probably deserve it this time."

47

"Let's go then, and get it over and done. I can't believe it, but I'm hungry," Whit said.

†

"What on earth? Can we not leave you unsupervised for a day without you hurting yourself?" Mark asked.

Eli told them she got distracted by her thoughts and decided to test the sharpness of her blade.

"I could have found so much more for you to test with," Mitch said. "How many stitches?"

"Just two, so I'm making progress." Eli laughed.

Mark just shook his head. "Come on out to the deck. Mitch is going to cook dinner."

"Do I need to worry about my health with him cooking?" Eli asked.

"Nope, he's got this. We've talked it through several times, and I'll be with him. I'll protect you from sharp knives and cut the meat into small bites for you."

"Oh, good one, Dad," Mitch said, and they shared a high-five.

"Tag teaming me now, huh?" Eli said. "I'll remember that."

Mark winked at Mitch. "I'm not worried. Are you?"

"Naw, I think we're safe. I can still outrun Eli," Mitch said.

"Thanks, Son, that puts me right in her crosshairs. I never could outrun her," Mark said.

"That's the idea, Dad. Survival of the fittest." Mitch smirked.

"Okay, let's get to cooking if you want to eat before dark," Mark said. "Get the bird going." Mark watched Mitch spread the chicken breasts on the grill. "I think we're going to have an adult beverage. Would you ladies like to join us?"

"I'm not driving or handling any sharp objects, so yeah. I'll take one."

"Me, too," Whit said.

"Be right back. Don't let Mitch burn anything while I'm gone," Mark said and walked inside.

"I got this, Dad," Mitch said.

"I know you do, Son, or I wouldn't be leaving," Mark teased.

Mitch smiled at Eli. "You're doing great. Did you find the hickory wood you were looking for?"

"Yeah, we carried three great branches back. Dad will show me how to plane them after we put them through the mill. I should be able to get a bunch of handles out of them." Mitch grinned at Eli. "I was planning to ask you if you'd carve some of the handles, but given the circumstances, I think I'll pass."

"Whit is going to buy me a chainmail glove for protection," Eli told him. "I should be good as gold in two weeks. You get them ready, and we can check out some designs."

"That's a deal. If we can find something simple, I'll try my hand at it," Mitch replied.

Mark returned and passed out beers. "You can get your vegetables and rice going on low while the chicken cooks. Slap a couple of these on, too," he said, handing Mitch a plate of filet mignon.

"Now we're talking," Mitch said. "I know, low and slow," he told Mark.

"That's correct, Son. I do believe you listen sometimes." Mark turned to Eli. "Is it safe for you to ride to the junkyard with us tomorrow?"

"I think so. What time do you plan on going?" Eli asked.

"Probably around nine. I thought I'd let Mitch sleep in a bit."

"Yeah, like that's going to happen." Mitch smirked. "Whenever I can sleep in, I'm up with the chickens."

"That happens when your body gets programmed to wake up at a certain time. I feel like I've overslept if I make it until seven," Eli said.

"We can start working on an ax handle if you get up early," Mark told him.

"That will get me going. I can't wait to work on one of those."

"Do you have all your dimensions written down?" Mark asked.

"I've got them all right here." Mitch tapped his temple.

Mark shook his head. "We need to draw them out. Blade, handle opening, and handle. You need to see it in front of you, not just in your head."

"I'll draw them out tonight. I'll also look for some handle carvings and send them to you, Aunt Eli. We can look at them on the ride tomorrow and see what you think we can do."

"That will work for me. Maybe I can create a template to trace the design until we get used to carving," Eli replied.

"I need to make a run into town tomorrow. What if I pick up some carving tools for y'all?" Whit said.

"That would be awesome, Whit. Just tell me how much, and I'll pay you back."

"Nope, consider it my investment into your new venture. Maybe you can make me a small ax when you've gotten into a groove."

"I would love to," Mitch said as he turned the chicken breasts.

"That's starting to smell good," Eli said, nodding toward the grill.

"Don't forget to add some butter to the rice and steaks. Tell me when you're ready for eggs, and I'll whip some up," Mark said.

Mitch turned the rice. "I think you could go ahead and scramble them."

"I'll be right back then," Mark replied.

"Do we need to set the table?" Whit asked.

"You can help me while Eli supervises Mitch. I don't want her around anything sharp," Mark scoffed.

"Are you excited about working in the forge?" Eli asked Mitch.

"Heck yeah. I'm excited to learn some new skills from Dad."

Eli was excited by the smile on Mitch's face. "He can teach you so much if you pay attention and work hard without dragging your feet."

"I'm going to try my best," Mitch said. "I'm stoked he will help me make a mini Viking-ax. They could be great sellers if we can make a decent template."

"I think it's cool that the two of you will be working side by side. It almost makes me want to learn how to work with steel." Eli held her hand up. "May not be the best occupation for me, though."

"Whenever you deal with blades of any type, you risk getting cut. I'm glad Whit is going to get you some cut-proof protection."

Eli nodded. "I may ask her to get some extras for you and Mark."

"That's probably not a bad idea. Even better if they would protect from burns, too." He turned the chicken. "Man, this is starting to smell good."

"Don't forget to add more butter," Eli reminded him.

Whit stepped out of the house carrying a bowl of whipped eggs and handed them to Mitch. "Here you go. We're ready inside. Do you want me to bring some bowls and a platter for the meat?"

"Yes, that would be great," Mitch answered as he scrambled the eggs. He added soy sauce to the pile of rice and then began slicing the chicken and steaks. Mitch mixed the chopped scrambled eggs into the rice, cut the remaining vegetables, and dowsed them in soy sauce.

Eli held a large bowl for Mitch to fill with fried rice and then another with grilled veggies. She handed them to Whit, who waited for her at the door with a platter for the meats. "I could make a meal out of these," Whit said.

"Wait until you see the meat," Eli teased.

Eli carried the platter to the grill, and Mitch carefully moved the steak slices and a mound of grilled chicken onto the platter. "Take those in while I shut down the grill, please."

Mark had returned. "I'll do the cleaning since you did the cooking."

"I'll watch then and see how you do it," Mitch said.

"Don't stay out too long. The way this looks, there might not be much left," Eli warned.

"I don't think we have much to worry about," Mark said. "I'm saving room for those brownies Whit made."

"Oh, yeah. Brownies and milk will be great." Mitch shut down the gas and watched Mark pour water on the grill.

"Ta ta, boys," Eli said and carried the platter inside.

"You did good, Son"." She heard Mark say to Mitch as she walked inside.

†

Eli pushed her plate away. "That was an excellent meal and great dessert."

"You did a great job, Mitch," Whit told him.

Mitch's face beamed with pride.

"Not bad for a rookie, but I think you need more practice," Mark said. "Maybe again this week?"

"Whenever you're ready, Dad," Mitch said.

"Do you need help cleaning up?" Eli asked.

"Nope. We've got this." Mitch smiled at Whit. "You're leaving the rest of the brownies, right?"

"Ha! We have a full pan at home," Whit teased.

"We'll pick you up in the morning when we get the trailer," Mark said as he walked them to the door.

"That's perfect," Eli said. "You made Mitch's night tonight," she whispered.

"You are right. Mitch's growing into a fine young man," Mark said. "Thank you for helping me to see that."

"My pleasure. Now we have to work on the younger model," Eli said.

"Don't remind me. Mitch is beginning to look like an angel." Mark chuckled. "Damn, did I say that?"

"Yeah, you did, Bro." Eli laughed and hugged him. "See you in the morning."

"Love you."

"Most," Eli answered.

"Goodnight, ladies."

Eli climbed into the Gator and groaned. "I am so stuffed."

"That was a great meal. Mitch did a good job."

"Yeah, he did." Eli smiled.

✝

Whit parked the Gator in the barn, and they fed the animals. Cajun rode the slide down and wove his body between Eli's legs as she filled the feeders.

"I think someone wants your attention," Whit said.

Eli sat on a bucket and placed Cajun in her lap. "Have you been a good boy?" she cooed to the cat. Cajun began purring as soon as Eli started scratching him. "Do you want to let Molly out for a little bit?"

"Sure," Whit replied, and Molly pranced out of her pen and rushed out to find Cruz. Whit chuckled. "And they're off," she said as Molly and Cruz raced out of the barn.

"I love watching them play," Eli said. "Molly has been so good for Cruz."

"Yes, she has. She's the only one I know that can wear Cruz down," Whit replied.

Walter and Oscar trotted into the barn when they heard voices. "Hey, boys," Eli said. "I think everyone is ready for dinner."

"You'd think these two never get fed, the way they act." Whit shook her head.

"I'll let Cruz and Molly play for a bit if you want to feed those poor starving cats. Tomboy is probably stretched out on the couch and ready to eat."

"Okay, but don't forget we have more brownies," Whit reminded her.

"I haven't. I plan to have more with a glass of cold milk before we go to bed," Eli answered.

"I'll see you in a bit," Whit said. "Love you."

"Most," Eli answered with a smile. She watched Whit exit the barn, then returned to the herd of cats vying for attention. "It does look like we have expanded our numbers. Have you been recruiting?" she asked Cajun. Her only answer came from a loud purr. "What the heck. The more, the merrier."

Whit put food down for the cats inside the cabin and picked up her phone. She searched for cut-proof gloves and ordered a pair for each of them. Whit checked her email and then stretched out on the couch to check the weather channel.

She smiled when she saw the snowflake image on the forecast for Tuesday and Wednesday. "It looks like we will have snow after all."

CHAPTER THREE

Mark and Mitch didn't take long to work up a sweat, even with the low temperatures, as they removed a dozen leaf springs from various vehicles and loaded them onto the trailer.

"This should keep us busy for a while," Mark said, fastening the tie-down across the metal.

"Yeah, it will," Mitch said. "We should be able to make some great blades out of this. All of it is carbon steel, right?"

"Every glorious inch of it." Mark grinned. "I don't know about y'all, but I've worked up an appetite. How about some fried chicken?"

"Make mine chicken livers," Eli said.

"That does sound good. Let's grab some livers to take home," Mark suggested. "Does Whit like livers?"

"She does, but she prefers wings," Eli said.

"That works for me, too," Mitch said. "I'll even buy."

"No, Son, I've got this," Mark said. "You can call in an order, though. Wings and livers."

"I'm on it," Mitch replied and picked up his phone.

"Do you have any plans for the rest of the day?" Mark asked Eli.

"Not that I'm aware of unless Whit needs something. Why, what's up?"

"I thought Mitch and I could start processing some of this metal if you want to hang out with us. We'll cut it into workable sections and sand down any rust spots."

"I could do that one-handed," Eli said.

"We could secure it in the vise and hand you the sander," Mark said.

"That sounds reasonably safe. Safety glasses, and I'm good to go," Eli replied.

"Do I need to carry some firewood inside for you for tonight?" Mitch asked.

"That would be great if Whit hasn't already done it."

"Should I call her and tell her to hold off? I could ask her if she needs anything from town while I'm at it," Mitch said.

"That's not a bad idea," Mark said as he pointed out the clouds forming ahead of them. "I think we may get that snow earlier than expected." Mark looked into the rearview mirror at Mitch. "I can drop you two at the grocery store while I pick up the chicken."

"I know we could use some milk," Mitch said. "I finished it off this morning with the last of the brownies."

"Give Whit a call and see what we need. I hit the milk pretty hard last night, too."

"Do you have a pen and notepad, Dad?" Mitch asked.

"Look in the glove box, please, Eli. There should be a pad and pen in there."

Eli fished out the supplies and handed them back to Mitch. "The temp has started dropping."

"Yes, it has," Mark said. "It's already down to thirty."

"Will you spread some extra straw in Molly's pen and the hayloft for the cats?" Eli asked Mitch.

"Yes, ma'am. I'll feed them well, too," Mitch answered. He called Whit and started making a list. "Alright," he said when he ended the call. "Whit will make more brownies and a chocolate cake for dinner. She said to tell y'all we have chicken and dumplings tonight."

"That will be perfect for a chilly night," Mark said. "I'll get you to the front door and return as quickly as possible."

"No problem. We'll try not to buy out the store," Eli said as she climbed out of the truck.

"Good luck with that, especially if Mitch is hungry. You got a card, Son?"

"Yes, sir," Mitch replied.

Mark looked at Eli. "Pick up a twelve-pack for me, please."

"You got it," Eli said.

†

Whit finished deboning the chicken when Eli and the guys returned and carried groceries and lunch inside. "You've got things smelling good in here," Eli said as she placed a bag of groceries on the counter and kissed Whit.

"I thought I'd go ahead and get the chicken cooked. What time do we want to eat tonight?" Whit asked.

"I'm going to help the guys in the forge unless you need me for anything," Eli said.

"No, I'm fine. I'll plan on dinner at six if that's good."

"That sounds great," Eli said as she pulled the ranch dressing from the refrigerator. "What are we drinking?"

"Tea if you have it," Mitch said.

"Sounds good," Mark added.

Eli looked at Whit, who nodded. "That's easy. Mitch, will you pull out some fine china?"

"All over it, Aunt Eli," Mitch answered, taking paper plates from the pantry.

Eli poured glasses of tea and stored the groceries they had carried inside. Mitch helped bring the tea to the table.

"Let's eat," he said when his butt landed in the chair.

"Did you work up an appetite?" Whit asked.

"I did." He smiled. "Some of those bolts were monsters to get off."

"Were you able to get what you needed?" Whit asked.

"We've got enough steel to keep us busy for months," Mark replied, placing livers and wings on his plate.

"That's a good thing." Whit looked at Mitch. "Will you have school if it snows tomorrow?"

"I haven't heard anything about canceling," he said. "I wouldn't mind another day off."

"Are your classes going well?" Eli asked.

"Yes, ma'am. I've learned quite a bit already," he said.

"That's good to hear. Do you enjoy the work?" Whit asked as she passed the ranch dressing.

"It's been challenging, but I'm not sold on it as a career yet," Mitch answered.

"There's no rush to settle in on a career," Mark said. "You need to try several different things to see what you enjoy. In the meantime, you're learning skills that will be helpful around here."

"That's true. I'm getting a great education on John Deere equipment."

"You can always work for Jessie's dad," Eli said.

"Yes, I can. Jessie's dad has already offered me a position whenever I'm ready," Mitch told them.

"Have you heard from Evan recently?" Eli asked.

"I talked to him last weekend. He wants to come out over Spring Break. Hopefully, it will be warm enough to fish." Mitch grinned.

"It will be good to see him even if you can't fish. I got used to seeing him often," Eli lamented.

Mitch chuckled. "He asks about you and Whit every time we talk."

"Well, I'll be damned," Mark said, pointing out the window. "You talked it up, Whit."

All heads turned to see what Mark was referring to and found snow falling.

"I guess we'd better finish lunch and get that trailer unloaded," Mitch replied.

"No rush. We've got the rest of the day to start preparing the steel," Mark told him. "Eat a good lunch because I have plans to work you hard."

"Yes, sir," Mitch replied with a grin.

"You, too," Mark warned Eli. "You can still run a sander with one hand."

"Aye, aye, captain," Eli teased.

"Make sure she wears gloves and protects those stitches." Whit hid her smile.

Eli looked at Whit. "We'll be ready for those chicken and dumplings tonight."

"They'll be ready with a big pan of biscuits. I have a chocolate cake and brownies to bake for dessert."

"Sign me up," Mitch said.

Mark nodded. "I love your desserts."

✝

Whit watched Eli and the boys leave, then picked up from lunch. Thanks to Mitch, there weren't many leftovers. She stored the few remaining livers. *Eli can snack on those before dinner if she's hungry.* Whit opened the pantry and smiled to see a large jar of cooked apples. She would cook a pie for Eli this week. She removed the cake and brownie mix and started to close the door, then decided on a second brownie mix. She glanced out the window and smiled when she saw the snow was sticking.

Whit wasn't sure who was the most excited about the snow. Mark and Mitch were like kids when it came to snow, and Eli wasn't far behind them. Seeing how much Eli enjoyed spending time with her brother and nephew made Whit smile. The joy on her face made it evident how much she loved them. Whit placed her goodies in the oven to bake and walked over to the computer. *I might as well try to get some work done, too.*

✝

Mark pulled the trailer close to the cave entrance, and he and Mitch worked quickly to place the springs inside. Eli found a small chair and put it in front of the vise. Mark gave each of them a pair of safety glasses. She listened to Mark instruct Mitch on dismantling the springs and cutting the metal to workable lengths for the blades. Then, once a spring was cut, Mark brought a section for Eli to work on.

Mark secured the length of steel in the vise and picked up a small sander. "If this doesn't work well, we can move you to the grinder. It doesn't have to be perfectly smooth. I just need you to remove any buildup on the outside of the steel." Mark demonstrated how he wanted Eli to sand, then handed her the equipment. "Careful. I don't want to get on Whit's bad side."

"I think I've got this," Eli replied.

Mark watched her briefly and then started the fire in the forge. If his calculations were correct, he would create several blades from each section of spring and have enough steel to cut and stack to teach Mitch how to make the ax heads he wanted. As Mitch brought them inside, he cleared off a workbench section to stack the steel. They would be within easy reach of Eli and still allow her room to stack the clean steel.

†

Mitch carried over the first load. "What do you want me to do with the small sections from the ends?"

"I'd like you to cut them into four-inch pieces that you can stack and weld together for your ax heads."

"That's cool. No Problem at all." Mitch turned and began measuring sections for the ax heads.

†

Eli couldn't hear the exchange over the noise of the sander, but she could see the excitement on Mitch's face and knew that Mark had told him something that gave him great pleasure. She turned off the sander under the ruse of repositioning the steel.

"Aunt Eli," Mitch called out. "I'm going to cut sections for ax heads."

"That's fantastic news," Eli answered.

"We will use every inch of this steel," Mark replied.

"Sounds like a plan." Eli turned the length of steel in the vise and resumed cleaning. She looked up moments later to observe Mitch measure the steel lengths he needed. Eli was proud of Mark for making the extra effort with Mitch, and it appeared to be working well between them. She could see the look of pride on Mark's face as he watched Mitch.

†

Mitch's phone pinged with a message. He read it and then pumped his fist. "Yes. No school tomorrow, so can you show me how to weld the sections and start on an ax head?"

"I think so. If you keep working, you will have ample steel for us to work with." Mark scratched his head. "Eli, will you focus on cleaning his small sections?"

"Sure. That's not a problem. How many do you need?"

"Five or six ought to give us a good start."

Eli nodded and picked up the stack of shorter pieces. Mark placed a piece of steel into the fire to continue working a blade he had started.

"Do you need a break, Son?"

"No, Dad, I'm good. On second thought, why don't I run to the house for some water?"

"I like that idea." Mark smiled. "You're doing great, Son."

"Thanks, Dad. I'll be right back."

Eli waited for Mitch to get out of hearing range. "He's working really hard."

Mark smiled and nodded. "I'm very impressed with his work. It's good to see him so excited about a project."

"Would you mind if I start a handle for him? I think I've got a simple pattern I can use. We've already cut some two-foot sections. I'd like to sand one down and maybe do some carving tonight after dinner."

"That would be great. It will take most of the day tomorrow to create the head."

Mitch returned and handed them water. "The snow is starting to stick well."

Mark took a long drink. "It will make everything beautiful, but we'll need to keep an eye on downed limbs and trees."

Eli looked up when she heard a Gator approaching. Whit and Cruz pulled up next to the truck. "Hey, baby girl," Eli said, patting Cruz on her head. "Everything okay?"

"She wouldn't stop pacing, so I told her I'd bring her up to visit."

"You can leave her if you want. She can ride back with us when we stop for the day."

"I know she'd love that. She whined for five minutes when you left her behind."

"I'm sorry, Cruz. You can stay with us." Eli stroked the dog's head.

"Why don't we get a bed to leave here for her?" Mark suggested. "If you plan to continue to work with us."

"Of course I do," Eli answered.

"I'll go back to the house and grab her bed. We can pick up a new one the next time we go to town. She doesn't use the one downstairs often."

"That will work," Eli said. "Thank you."

"You're welcome. Do y'all need anything?"

"Thanks, Whit. I think we're good," Eli answered.

Mitch looked at Whit. "Do you have any brownies left?"

"I think I do. I'll bring some back. Anything else?"

"No, ma'am, that should do. Thanks."

Whit looked at Eli.

Eli shook her head. "I'm stuffed from lunch, but he's been working hard."

"Mark?" Whit asked.

"Well, since you're coming back, I'll take one if you have extras."

"I think I have enough for both of you. I'll be back soon."

Mark watched Whit leave and looked at Eli. "I love your woman."

"I do, too," Eli said. "I never realized how good life can be until we met."

"Hang on tight to this one."

"I plan to." Eli smiled and resumed working.

†

Whit returned with the dog bed, a plate of brownies, and a thermos of milk.

Mitch poured two cups of milk, handing one to his father. He looked at Eli. "Are you sure you won't join us?"

"Maybe just a little one," Eli answered after placing Cruz's bed beside her workstation.

"I'll see you all in a couple of hours." Whit bent down to kiss Eli. "Be careful."

"I'm being good," Eli promised.

Whit looked at Mark, who nodded his head. "She's been doing well."

"Good. I'll see you soon. Do I need to come back up for you?"

"Naw, I'll have Mitch bring her home and drop the trailer while I shower," Mark answered.

†

Once Whit left, they finished the brownies and returned to work. Eli finished cleaning the smaller sections for Mitch, then picked up a length of wood to begin sanding for a handle. The piece had a nicely curved area at the bottom, making the perfect hand grip. Eli worked carefully to preserve the beautiful grain in the wood while ensuring a smooth surface. Eli thought of the design she would use on the handle as she worked. She wanted to surprise Mitch with something she had created. Working the grip was much more tedious and delicate than sanding the steel, so Eli worked slowly and carefully.

†

Mark removed a piece of steel from the forge and walked over to the power hammer, passing Eli. He saw the intense concentration she was giving the project and smiled. Eli seemed to be enjoying the work. Mitch was steadily dismantling and cutting the spring sections and was nearly halfway through their haul. They had accomplished a good day's work, and he was proud of how well they worked together. Mitch worked hard and had the most strenuous task but never complained. Mark was excited to teach Mitch to forge weld and create the ax head. Mitch had decided on a simple design, and with luck, they would have the head forged, honed, and etched by the end of the day. When Mark had the blade hammered into shape, he looked at Eli. "I think it's time we call it a day."

"This has been a lot of fun," Mitch said. "I can't wait until tomorrow. Will you work with us again, Aunt Eli?"

"I probably won't be at it as early as you two, but I expect I'll be here shortly after breakfast."

"Mitch will probably have me up early to start," Mark teased.

"I can't waste a day off from school." Mitch grinned. "Do you want me to feed up for you tonight?"

"That would be great," Eli responded. "Will you let Molly out so she and Cruz can burn off some energy while you feed the crew?"

"No problem. Are you ready to head home now?"

"I could use a shower, too." Eli stood and stretched. "I'll see you in a bit," she told Mark. "Let's go, Cruz."

Cruz raced ahead of her to the truck. Mitch let Eli off at the house and then drove to the barn to drop the trailer. He went inside for Molly, and she and Cruz flew passed him to race across the yard. The snow was still falling, and a couple of inches had accumulated. Mitch laughed at the snow flying up into the air as they chased one another. He unhitched the trailer and returned to the barn. Mitch was swarmed by the cats. "I swear you guys act like you've never been fed," he teased as Cajun came down the slide. Mitch filled food and water bowls for them and Molly before spreading some fresh straw to keep all the animals warm. When he finished, he stepped outside to call Cruz. She and Molly ran toward the barn, and after securing Molly in her stall, Mitch closed the barn door and walked Cruz to the house.

"Here's your daughter," he announced when he opened the front door. "Everyone is fed for the night. I'll be back later."

"Thanks, Mitch. Will you bring the mail when you and your dad come for dinner? I forgot to ask you to stop just now."

"Not a problem. Do you need me to carry any wood inside before I go?"

Eli looked at Whit. "I would appreciate you bringing a couple armfuls onto the front porch. I restocked in here, but that would save me some steps."

"No problem. Love y'all," Mitch said and left.

†

"Come here, and I'll wrap that hand for you," Whit said as she held up plastic wrap and tape.

"Do you think it's too soon to unwrap it to shower?"

"Yes, I'd give it another day. I'll clean your hand and wrap it after you get done."

Eli looked at the counter where the cake and brownies were cooling. "Those look and smell great."

"I thought I'd make two. I'm sure we'll destroy one tonight, and the boys can have another half to take home for later. I'm going to send eggs back with them, too."

"I know Mitch will appreciate that."

Whit finished wrapping Eli's injured hand. "Do you need help in the shower?"

"You could wash my hair. You could do it much easier than me."

"Go on upstairs, and I'll be there in a minute. All I have left to do is bake the biscuits."

†

"That was delicious as usual," Mark said as he finished eating the cake. He also had a brownie.

"I've got another pan of brownies, and we'll split the cake so you can have another slice later," Whit told him.

"Mine may have to wait until in the morning. I'm ready to hit the sack."

73

"You'd better hope there will be some left," Mitch teased.

"If not, I'll eat breakfast burritos alone in the morning."

"Oh, that's cruel," Mitch said, patting his chest. "Makes my heart hurt."

"You ladies going to join us?" Mark asked.

"What time?"

"Seven too early? Mitch will be up earlier, but he can stay busy dismantling the last of the springs and cleaning the sections you didn't get to finish today. No cutting unless one of us is present."

"Gotcha." Mitch nodded.

"I think we could handle seven," Whit said.

"Do you want my help to clean the kitchen?"

"Thanks, Mitch, but it won't take me long." Whit portioned out half of the remaining cake. "Is there anything we need to bring to breakfast?"

"These eggs will be plenty," Mark said. "Thanks again for a fantastic dinner. That really hit the spot."

"Hey, have you planned to return to Alabama this week?" Eli asked.

"I thought I'd leave Thursday if this weather has passed. Why?"

"Well, I assumed we'd have another mouth to feed while you're gone, and I wanted to make sure we have enough groceries to keep him fed," Eli answered.

"Good idea. Mitch can eat you out of house and home if you let him. I don't know how we ever survived the cost of feeding two boys."

"Once your garden starts producing, it will make things easier here," Whit replied.

"That's true. I can't wait to break ground this spring. I'd like one at least your size, maybe a bit bigger."

"We will have vegetables running out our ears then." Eli smiled. "We can get your fencing and irrigation set up before spring."

"That would be awesome," Mark replied.

Mitch took the cake and brownies from Whit. "We'll see you in the morning."

†

Eli was rinsing dishes to hand to Whit. "Would you mind if I worked on a handle for Mitch for a little while?"

"No, not at all. I can work on the manuscript. Do you have a design in mind?"

"Yes, but it's secret." Eli laughed. "It's too cold on the porch, so I'll go to the workshop. You can holler at me if you need anything."

"Just bundle up so you don't get a chill, and wear gloves."

"Yes, dear." Eli laughed as she dried her hand. "You coming, Cruz?"

Cruz jumped to her feet and rushed to the door. "Like you even had to ask."

"I'll see you soon." Eli kissed Whit and wrapped her coat around her body. "Love you."

"Most," Whit said and closed the door behind them. "Turn up the heater."

†

Eli had imagined the design in her head all afternoon. She wanted something simple yet attractive for his first ax. She wrapped the wood in a soft cloth and placed it in the vise to hold it steady. It was chilly, so Eli turned on the small heater before sitting at her workstation. She turned on an LED above the workbench to give her more light. With the pencil, Eli traced the outline of the first symbol and then turned the handle over for the second. She measured ten inches from the bottom to mark the leather hand wrap she intended to use and then traced a spiral pattern down to the handgrip. Eli was undecided about carving out the spiral channel or using her wood burner. She decided on the wood burner since it would be a shallow design and began burning the design into the handle. It was tedious work, but Eli was pleased with her choice when finishing the first strand. The first symbol was relatively easy to carve and burn to give it a blackened color, but the second was more detailed and took longer than she expected.

She was bent over the project for nearly two hours before she finished. Eli stretched and walked over to a shelf of stains to select the perfect color. The stain would take all night to dry in the cold weather, so Eli would make that her final project. After coating the piece thoroughly, she placed it in a position to dry. She would check it first thing and, if necessary, add a second coat in the morning. Eli was pleased with the appearance so far. She opened a drawer and removed a spool of thick leather cord. If a second coat wasn't necessary, Eli would measure and cut the cord the length she needed for the handle design and hand wrap before adding a layer of clear coat to the wood. After all the surfaces were dried and hardened, Eli would request Whit's help to wrap the handle.

Eli checked her watch to see that it was nearly midnight. She had no idea it had grown so late. Eli sealed the can of stain and cleaned her tools before putting them away. "Let's go to bed, Cruz," she called as she turned off the heater. Cruz walked beside her back to the house, their footprints crunching in the snow. "It is beautiful when it snows." Eli laughed softly when the warmth of her breath turned into frost in front of her. "Let's go check on your other mama." When Eli opened the door, she saw Whit typing at the computer. "Are you about at a stopping point?"

"I will be in just a minute. Why don't you set the coffee pot for the morning, and I'll be ready."

Eli entered the kitchen and was working on the coffee when she felt Whit's arms circle her body. "I think I'm done for the night. My eyes were starting to cross. How is your project coming?"

"Better than I imagined. I will need your help to finish the work sometime in the morning. I need two good hands to do the final part; as you can see, I only have one." She lifted her left hand as evidence.

"I will be more than happy to help out. I know how excited Mitch is to make his first ax."

Eli turned in Whit's arms. "I bet he will be up before the sun rises tomorrow. I can't say the same for myself. I'm tired."

"It sounds like you all accomplished a lot today."

"I think we did. We've got enough steel to keep Mark and Mitch busy."

"Will you help Mark out on days when Mitch is in school?"

"If you don't need me for anything, I can help Mark some. Not much else I can do until spring arrives."

"Once that hand is healed, we can start work on the perimeter fence for his garden if it's not bitterly cold. I think the temperatures will become more moderate in the coming weeks. Has he said how long he'll be gone?"

"I'm not sure he's decided yet. I wouldn't think more than a week."

"Do you want to see if Mitch wants to stay here while Mark is gone?"

"I think it will be a good test for Mitch, but he knows he can join us anytime. He will definitely be here for dinner. He can handle breakfast on his own and will have lunch in town somewhere."

"I'd like to spend an evening with him looking at plans for his tiny home. Now would be a great time to get them started building it. We will also need a sewer system installed. Water and power won't be an issue."

"Maybe we could take him to the shelter on Saturday to look for kittens. He's been hinting that he and his dad wanted some."

"I'll let you two do that," Whit said. "I'd be too tempted to bring more home."

"I don't have a problem with that." Eli laughed softly and reached for Whit's hand. "Mitch talked about a small cat house for his kittens with a tunnel to get inside the tiny home and a small door to allow them outside."

"I can so see that happening," Whit replied as they walked up the stairs.

Whit climbed into the bed and snuggled into Eli after pulling the covers over them. She laid her head on Eli's shoulder and listened to her soft breathing. "I love you," she whispered.

"Most," Eli answered with a sleepy tone in her voice. She pulled Whit closer and, within minutes, was snoring lightly.

CHAPTER FOUR

Eli woke earlier than expected and crept from the bed and dressed. Enough light filtered through the window so that she could see that Whit slept peacefully with Tomboy curled up next to her. Eli planned to return to the workshop to take her measurements and add a layer of clear coat if the stain was dry and the desired color. Cruz followed her downstairs and walked out to the workshop. Her breath puffed out in front of her as they walked.

"It sure hasn't warmed up much," she told Cruz as they entered the building. Eli went straight to the heater and turned it on high. "Brrr."

Next, she checked the handle to find it dry and the perfect color. Eli decided against a second coat. The grain was well-defined, and she didn't want to hide the beauty by adding more color. Eli measured the length of the leather cord needed for the final step in the design and then added the clear coat. Once she had it staged to dry, Eli left the workshop and fed the animals before returning to the house to start the coffee pot. After eating breakfast with Mark and Mitch, she would bring Whit home, and if the handle was dry, they would finish the wrapping. If not, she would recheck it when they stopped for lunch.

Eli poured mugs of coffee and climbed the stairs to the bedroom. She placed the coffee on the table and sat beside Whit on the bed. She stroked her cheek. "It's coffee time, sweetheart."

Whit's eyes fluttered open, and she smiled at Eli. "That coffee smells delicious. I knew you would be up early today," she teased.

Eli shrugged. "I was excited to check on the handle. I put the clear coat on and measured the cord I'll need. I thought I'd bring you home after breakfast, and if it has dried, you could help me with wrapping."

"I'd love to," Whit said. "What time is it?"

Eli looked at the clock. "Six thirty."

Whit sat up in bed and took a sip of coffee. "That gives me barely enough time to drink this coffee and get dressed before we're due at Mark's."

"I'll go get a Gator and pour some travel mugs while you get ready," Eli told her. "Bundle up. It's still plenty cold outside."

"Is there still snow on the ground?"

"Oh yeah, and I think ice underneath. I slid about a foot after leaving the barn." Eli laughed.

"Be careful when you go out for the Gator, then. It's too soon for another emergency room visit."

"Don't jinx me now," Eli replied.

†

Whit could see the excitement shining in Eli's eyes. She was so excited about her project, and Whit could hardly wait to see the final product. She reached up to stroke Eli's face. "Did you sleep well?"

"Like a rock," Eli said. "I hadn't realized how tired I was."

"You all did a lot of work yesterday, and the cold tends to sap your strength, too."

"I guess so. Are you going to work on the manuscript this morning?"

"Yes, I thought I would. In a few more days, the rough draft will be done. There are enough leftovers for lunch. I can make some fresh biscuits if that's good for everyone. Maybe more brownies, too. How does that sound?"

"Totally delicious," Eli answered. "I'll clean more steel today while the boys start on the ax head. I imagine the first will take most of today to forge and they'll put the finishing touches tomorrow."

"Will you and Mitch still have work to do while Mark is away?"

"I'm sure we can find plenty for a few hours after he gets home from school and on the weekends. I'll work on more handles and walking sticks during the day."

"You enjoy that, don't you?"

Eli grinned. "It's relaxing, but I must remember to focus while carving."

"The safety gloves are supposed to be delivered today if the weather hasn't delayed them."

"No worries, I have plenty of other projects to keep me busy."

"Anything else you need my help with?"

"Not that I can think of right away, but that could change. I'll try to stay out of your hair so you can finish the textbook."

"You are never in my hair, but I'll admit, you are a pleasant distraction. I'd rather be working with you any day."

"If you need a break in the next few days, you could help me measure for Mark's garden and create a list of items we need to order. You are much better than me at doing that."

"I'll gladly help with that. Right now, we better get moving if we are going to get breakfast."

"I'll pour the travel mugs and leave them on the counter. Will you bring them out while I get a Gator?"

Whit left the bed to start dressing. "I'll be down in a few minutes."

"I'll have your carriage waiting out front," Eli teased. "Love you."

"I love you, too," Whit answered as she dressed. She entered the bathroom to brush her hair and teeth and nearly broke out laughing at the disarray of her hair. "She'd have to love me to put up with this bedhead," she told herself in the mirror.

†

Eli was disappointed when they returned from breakfast to find the clear coat was not completely dry. "I'll check it when we come for lunch. It's close, but I'd rather not rush the process. At worst, we can finish it tonight after dinner. Mitch won't be ready for it until Thursday at the earliest."

"It will be worth the wait." Whit stretched to kiss Eli. "I'll see you at noon for lunch, right?"

"Yes, ma'am. Mark is cooking bacon cheeseburgers for dinner tonight."

"Tell him I'll make some baked beans and potato salad to go with the burgers. I bet he was only planning to serve chips." Whit smiled. "Which would be fine, but beans and potato salad will be more filling."

†

Eli joined Mark and Mitch in the cave. She resumed cleaning the steel sections while Mark showed Mitch how to use the grinder to ensure his steel plates were flat. Once Mitch had the sections ground, Mark demonstrated how to stack them and place them in the vise to hold them firmly together.

"Now comes the fun part. Eli, I only have eye protection for two, so I'm asking that you and Cruz leave the forge for a bit."

"No problem, we'll go home and check on Whit. How long will you be?"

"No more than an hour," Mark answered.

"You want to break for lunch when you're done, and we'll pick up after lunch?"

"That sounds like a good plan. I'll let you know if it will be more than an hour."

"Let's go, Cruz."

Eli and Cruz drove to the workshop. She walked in to check the handle and was pleased that the handle was drying well. Eli had already decided to finish it after dinner so they wouldn't feel rushed. She drove to the house and parked out front.

"I didn't expect to see you back so soon." Whit was stirring a pot of boiling potatoes on the stove.

"Cruz and I got booted from the forge."

"Oh my, what for?" Whit's face was filled with concern.

"Mark was ready to teach Mitch how to TIG weld his steel plates, and he only has two sets of protective eyewear. They will come for lunch when they are done in about an hour."

"I guess I'd better get started on some biscuits soon."

"Is there anything I can do to help?"

"You can cut the biscuits once I have them rolled. Take the bowls from the dishwasher, and set the table. Then you can spray a baking pan for me for our biscuits."

"I can do that," Eli replied, setting the table. "I checked the handle, and it's not fully dry, so I'll wait until after dinner to finish the grip."

"That's probably a wise decision. There's no need to rush." Whit dumped the potatoes into a strainer, then set them in a bowl.

"Have you been able to work on the textbook this morning?"

"I've almost completed another chapter. I needed a break, so I peeled and boiled the potatoes for the salad. I've got the dumplings warming on low in the crockpot. I'll turn it higher when I put the biscuits into bake."

†

"That's it. Take it nice and slow. No need to rush this critical process," Mark told Mitch as he welded two layers of steel together.

Mark could see the bead of sweat running down his son's cheek. He knew it wasn't from heat or exertion but Mitch's anxiety about getting it right. He was proud of Mitch's growth and ability to take direction, and he appeared to have a talent for welding. The layers were sealed perfectly, and Mark remembered his own first lame attempt. He had to use the grinder to flatten his seams. He would demonstrate the technique for Mitch, but it would only take minutes if his quality continued. Mark felt his excitement growing about helping Mitch to forge his first steel. The ax would be a first for him, so it would be a learning process for them both. Since Mitch had mentioned the project, Mark had researched how to create an opening for a handle. He felt he understood the process and hoped his investigation time would help.

†

Eli took a break to watch them begin tapping out a hole for the handle using a punch and hammer. Mark picked up a tool and showed it to Mitch. "This is called a drift, and we'll use it to maintain the integrity of the hole during forging and shaping. We can't allow the opening to change once we've removed the steel."

Mark and Mitch worked on the piece for hours until they had created an edge and the proper dimensions of the ax head. After removing it from the forge, they gave the project a final look, and Mark nodded to Mitch. "I think we are ready to quench. Place the edge tip first and slowly lower the rest of the head. That will allow the edge to be strong."

Mark and Eli watched Mitch as he lowered the steel into the oil, and a hiss of flames filled the cave. Mitch was patient and slowly lowered the steel inch by inch and then lifted it from the oil.

"Place it on the cloth to dry, and then we'll do a different tempering process than I use for the knife blades." Mark grinned at Mitch. "I'm glad your mom isn't here. We will bake it in her oven for an hour and then leave it overnight."

"Where did you learn that?" Mitch asked.

"I've done some research on the internet, and that was one of the techniques they recommended. You've seen me etch a blade, so we'll do that tomorrow, and you can begin cleaning up your head and honing the edge. The etching will make the Damascus pattern stand out in the steel."

"I thought you were going to Alabama tomorrow?" Mitch asked.

"I am, but I want you to get up early so we can do this together before you go to school. I want you to wait until I return to place it on the handle."

"That's not a problem. We've got other stuff to work on." He turned to look at Eli. "We do have a handle, right?"

"I'll finish it this afternoon and bring it for inspection when we come for burgers," Eli promised. "I'm going to head home. We'll come up around seven."

"That's perfect. We will get this head tempered, cleaned up, and ready to cook," Mark replied. He looked at Mitch. "Just don't tell your mom."

"I won't. Do we have room for a small oven in the forge if I bought one?"

Eli looked around the space and then at Mark and Mitch. "I think it would be better in the workshop. More space there."

"Cool," Mitch said. "I'll start looking."

"Alright, guys. See you later."

†

Cruz and Eli returned to find Whit exiting the barn. "Welcome back. I thought I'd get everyone fed a bit early today."

"Thanks. Could I get your help for a little while?"

"Sure, I've got everything ready for dinner at Mark's. We just need a shower, and we are good to go."

"Hop in," Eli said, and they drove to the workshop. "The snow sure melted off quickly."

Whit nodded. "It started disappearing when the sun came out after lunch. Not much left."

"That's probably the last for this year, don't ya think?"

"I would be surprised if we got any more." Whit walked through the door Eli held open. "I assume we are working on the handle?" She grinned. "The boys can't wait to see it?"

"That is correct. The ax heads are baked in the oven to temper. Mitch wants a small oven, and I told him it would be better here. What do you think?"

"It would be better than crowding the cave; there's plenty of room here."

"That's what I thought, too." Eli pulled two stools close. "I will talk you through the process, but I need the strength of two hands to keep the leather tight."

"No problem. Just tell me what to do."

Forty-five minutes later, Whit tied the knot to the hand loop to finish the project. "I can't believe how perfect this length came out. I love the design you created. I can't wait for Mitch to see it."

Eli chuckled, and Whit cocked her head. "What's funny?"

"Look at the bottom of the handle."

Whit saw Mitch's initials engraved and realized why Eli was laughing. "MF. Does Mitch have a middle name?"

"Yes, but I think it's too classic to change. If anything, I'll change the future ones to CIF for Cast Iron Forge. Or do both."

"I think both would be good, but leave this one as is," Whit recommended. "It's perfect."

"Are you ready to shower?" Eli asked.

Whit nodded. "Are you ready to go without a bandage?"

"Maybe just a loose Band-Aid would do," Eli suggested.

"Bring the handle, and let's roll."

†

When he inspected the handle Eli had made, Mitch had tears in his eyes. "This is perfect. I love how you wove the Eye and the Raven into the design. They are symbols of Odin, and the leather is a nice touch. Thank you, Aunt Eli."

"You're welcome. Whit helped, too."

"All I did was manual labor because she needed two hands for the leather."

"Thank you both." Mitch pulled them into a hug while Mark inspected the craftsmanship.

"Wow, Sis, this came out great." Mark looked at the end of the handle and chuckled. "I love this." He showed the initials to Mitch and broke out laughing.

"We thought we could add CIF to future handles," Eli added.

"I love it," Mitch said, wiping tears. "MF is perfect, though."

"I like it," Mark said. "You did good work. I've been thinking about some branding for the forge. Maybe you could help?"

"What did you have in mind?"

"A howling wolf under a curved set of CIF letters. Something small that will work for all sizes of knives at the top of the handle."

"I think we could get a custom-designed piece to use with my wood-burning tool that would work nicely. I'll see what I can find while you're gone."

"Thanks. Grab a cold one and join me. I already have the bacon on the grill and am ready to add the burgers. Grab the plate of burgers and the cheese, please, Mitch." Mark looked at Mitch. "If you come back and slice an onion, I'll grill some for the burgers."

"Oh heck yeah," Mitch replied and headed for the kitchen.

Whit looked at Eli. "I'm going to get these beans heated. I'll be out in a minute."

Mitch handed each of them a beer and carried the plate of burgers to the deck. "Man, I'm starving."

"We've worked hard today and earned a couple of burgers." Mark took the plate and placed the seasoned burgers on the grill. "Rinse this and bring it back when you come, please."

"Sure thing." Mitch returned inside.

"You've been great with Mitch this week," Eli told Mark.

"I never dreamed he had a passion for forging, but he does, and he's got some talent. I want to keep that burning as long as I can."

"Mitch is happy when he works with you. Thanks for being patient."

"I hope it was good practice for dealing with Brad. I could strangle the kid every time I think of his antics."

"I think working his ass off and missing some of his luxury items will send him a message. Are you still planning on a crew cut?"

Mark laughed. "Not a flat top like Dad's, but it will be high and tight."

Eli smiled. "Other than cleaning the rest of the sections, what do you need us to do while you're gone?"

"I've already told Mitch no cutting unless you are present. Not that you're the best role model with sharp instruments, but he needs to learn to stay safe." Mark grinned after his teasing remark.

"Hilarious, smart ass," Eli said. "I think we can get the rest of the steel ready while you're gone."

"That would be fantastic, but I don't want him to fall behind on his studies."

"I assure you that any schoolwork will come first. Even if we don't finish the load, you'll have enough to keep you busy for weeks, maybe longer."

"That sounds good. Don't neglect your work to get it done; try to relax. Spring will be here soon."

"I won't. Whit and I will develop a plan for his tiny home this weekend. I guess I'd better ask your permission to look at kittens, too. Whit thought it might be good to check the shelter for black cats."

"No more than three since they do not have a barn to live in like your crew. Maybe we can build a small barn this year."

"I think Mitch will take one or more with him when he moves into his place," Eli answered.

"Pick me out some good ones. Definitely a little tom if they have one. I'd steal Tomboy, but I know he'd just return home to you."

"That's my boy," Eli answered.

†

"We are going to leave the beans and potato salad for you to snack on," Whit told Mitch. "I'll expect you for dinner every night, too."

"I'd like to grill us some steaks one night," Mitch said.

"That's fine. We can work on a menu tomorrow night."

Eli looked at Mark. "Let me know when you arrive in Montgomery, please."

"I will. I'll call you over the weekend to let you know when I'll return."

"Be safe, Mark."

"Always," Mark answered as they walked out to the Gator. "Thanks for joining us for a great dinner."

"Our pleasure," Whit replied. "Call if you need bail money."

"Oh snap. That was a good one, Whit," Mitch said, high-fiving his friend.

"That was a good one," Eli said as they pulled away. "What should we do for the rest of the evening?"

"I have a few ideas," Whit answered with a smile.

†

Eli took her time undressing Whit. They had all evening to enjoy one another, and Eli planned to make each minute count. She planted tender kisses down Whit's shoulders as she slipped the bra from her body. Eli smiled when she saw the pulse beating in Whit's neck. Her heart was racing with anticipation. "Have I told you lately how beautiful you are?"

"Every morning, but each time makes my heart skip. Especially when your voice sounds as sexy as it does right now."

"How so?"

"Your voice purrs against my skin with a warmth that spreads through my body."

Eli let out a soft laugh. "I love purring for you. Let's see what else I can do for you." Eli's mouth kissed a trail down Whit's body. Her tongue flicked out to tease Whit's nipples. Eli smiled as they grew hard, and she opened her mouth to take a breast into her mouth. Her tongue swirled around the nipple as her hand filled with the soft flesh. Whit released a soft moan. Eli pressed Whit backward onto the bed, her body stretched out beside Whit's. She caressed her cheek with the soft flesh while her hand lightly stroked Whit's stomach. Eli covered a breast with her mouth as her fingertips traced circles on Whit's silky panties. She could feel the dampness of her excitement soaking through the fabric as her hips lifted toward her touch.

"That feels nice," Whit said with a slight tremble.

Eli lifted her mouth and playfully nibbled Whit's nipple. "I want you to feel how much I love you." She cupped Whit's mound and gave it a gentle squeeze.

"I'm feeling it," Whit purred.

Eli eased her hand inside Whit's panties. "You are so hot and wet."

Whit trembled under her touch. "Feel free to take those panties if you want."

"Oh, I definitely want," Eli answered.

Whit lifted her hips off the bed, and Eli slipped the panties down Whit's legs. Whit kicked them off the bed and spread her legs to invite Eli to further explore.

Eli traced Whit's opening with her fingertips, teasing her while coating them with her wetness. Eli lifted her hand to her mouth, and her fingertips disappeared. "You taste so good," Eli said as her tongue licked up her middle finger.

"Be my guest," Whit replied.

Eli smiled at Whit. Her hand moved between Whit's legs, and her fingertips eased into Whit's opening, stroking the outer lips as a finger penetrated the wetness. "Damn, you feel so soft," Eli whispered. Her finger sunk into Whit and then curled as a second finger entered. Her thumb pressed Whit's clit as her fingers swirled inside.

†

Eli's touch burned a trail of desire down Whit's body, and when her thumb came in contact with her clit, Whit's stomach clenched. She clamped her teeth together, holding back the flood of pleasure threatening to erupt from her body. She could tell Eli enjoyed teasing her with her touches, and Whit would hold off as long as possible. Eli moved between Whit's legs, and when her warm mouth closed around the sensitive mound, Whit let out a loud groan. "Damn, that feels great." Whit buried her hand in Eli's hair, holding her in place as her pleasure peaked and her body trembled with her release. Whit closed her eyes and rode the wave of pleasure throughout her body. She felt Eli slowly withdraw her fingers and lay beside her on the bed.

"Is that what you had in mind?" Eli teased.

"That felt beyond fantastic," Whit purred.

Eli rolled onto her back. "I love the way your body responds."

"It's hard to describe how wonderful you make me feel. The looks you give me make my body melt. The passion in your eyes is so powerful, but your touch is gentle and teasing. I love every minute of our lovemaking."

Whit rolled on top of Eli. "My turn now." She grinned.

Eli's body was soaked and ready to be touched. Whit wasted no time in bringing Eli a powerful climax.

They snuggled and talked until the growling of Eli's stomach could no longer be ignored. "I think you need to feed that other hunger," Whit teased. "What would you like?"

Eli smiled. "Do we still have apple pie?"

Whit sat up in bed. "With cheese?"

"You know me so well," Eli replied.

"Relax, and I'll be right back," Whit told her.

Whit entered the kitchen, placed two pieces of pie on a plate, covered them with cheese slices, then removed a bottle of soda while the microwave heated the pie. Whit put a fork on the plate and returned to the bedroom.

Eli had propped up against the headboard, and she smiled when Whit returned. Whit placed the drink on the table and sat next to Eli.

Eli frowned when she only saw one fork.

Whit smiled and placed a bite in her lover's mouth.

"Oh, I could get used to this," Eli said after swallowing.

"I enjoy it when you allow me to spoil you," Whit answered. She took a bite of pie and served another bite to Eli.

Whit saw Eli scratch her palm. "Is your hand okay?"

Eli nodded. "It must be healing. It's itching like crazy."

"Take the bandage off, so I can take a look at it, please," Whit said, placing the empty plate on the table.

Eli removed the bandage and showed her hand to Whit. "What do you think, Doc?"

"It's pink around the edges but doesn't look infected. Do you think you can leave it open tonight? I'd like to put some ointment on it, but leave it open."

"I believe I'll survive." Eli smiled.

Whit walked to the bathroom and returned with ointment. She tenderly spread the cream over Eli's injury. "A few more days, and we should be able to remove the stitches." Whit kissed Eli's palm. "All better now."

Whit picked up the empty plate. "Do you need anything else?"

"Just your warm body snuggled next to me," Eli answered.

Whit smiled and leaned down to kiss Eli. "I'll be back. It won't take long to warm up beside you."

CHAPTER FIVE

Mark stopped by on his way to Alabama. "I should be home right after lunch, but I'll let you know I've made it."

"I hope things go well for Brad," Whit said.

Eli nodded. "Do you want some coffee for the road?"

"That would be great. As long as Brad admits he's been an asshole, things will go okay. If not, I may call for bail money."

Eli handed him a large travel mug. "We'll keep our phones handy. Be safe, and tell Laura and Brad hello for us."

"I will. Love y'all."

"Love you, too," Eli and Whit said together.

"Let us know when you're coming back, and I'll have a nice dinner ready," Whit said.

Mark grinned and nodded at Whit. "I'm so glad this one agreed to marry you."

"Hey, I was going to offer you Spam sandwiches," Eli joked.

"Like I said, I'm thankful for Whit."

"I am, too, Brother."

†

"What are we doing today?" Whit asked after they finished coffee.

"Do you need to work on your manuscript today?"

"Need to, yes. Want to? No. I'd rather spend the morning helping you."

"I'd like to measure and mark the dimensions for Mark's garden. Would you help me with that, and then you could develop a materials list and order while I clean some steel?"

"That's perfect. I'll get back to the manuscript after lunch. This will be the last I contract for at least a while."

"I think that's a good idea. You don't seem to have the ambition for the work like before."

"There's so much I'd rather be doing."

"Let's get started then. I'll bring a Gator around after feeding the crew, and we can grab tools from the workshop before heading out."

"I can go to the workshop and get the tools and supplies together. Just pick me up there."

"Deal." Eli pulled Whit into a hug and kissed her. "I love having you by my side."

†

It didn't take them long to plot out a garden space for Mark. Whit sat at Mark's workbench and developed the materials list they would need for fencing and an irrigation system while Eli cleaned several steel sections.

"I'm going back home to call in this order. I'll bring some water or coffee back when I come."

"Water would be great. Thanks, Whit."

"I'll see you in a bit. I may make a grocery list, too, before coming back."

"Take your time." Eli pointed to the stack of steel on her workstation. "I have plenty to keep me busy."

Cruz was curled up beside Eli. "I'll bring an extra water bowl up for Cruz. I can see she'll be spending time here with you." Whit leaned in for a kiss.

Eli continued cleaning the long sections of steel. It wasn't difficult to work, but she enjoyed seeing the immediate results of her effort. Eli's goal was to have everything cut and cleaned when Mark returned. She eyed the pile of steel that needed to be sectioned. A few hours after school one day should allow Mitch to finish the stack. Eli was deep in thought and didn't see Whit had returned.

†

Whit watched Eli work for several minutes undetected. Contentment was spread across Eli's face. Eli was happy doing the work and excited to help Mark and Mitch with their projects. It was heartwarming to see her love so happy. Whit realized how extremely happy she'd become as well. She no longer felt a need to drown herself in her work. Whit found she preferred working with Eli and the boys much more than sitting behind a computer. She would buckle down to finish the last manuscript but didn't feel she wanted that part of her life anymore. When Eli shut off the sander to examine her work, Whit entered the cave and handed her water. "You look thirsty."

"Thanks. I'd like to have everything clean for Mark's return. I'm confident I can accomplish that if Mitch cuts the remaining springs."

"I bet this is his first stop as soon as he gets out of school. This is an early day for him, isn't it?"

Eli nodded. "He should be home around two. It won't take but a few hours to finish the cuts. I can continue to clean while he's in school."

"I have an idea I want to run by you," Whit said. "The materials will be delivered tomorrow. Would you mind if I bring the tractor and start digging the holes for the fence posts?"

"I can attach the auger for you when we break for lunch."

"I'd like to go ahead and set up the irrigation system so we can use that for the concrete we need to set the posts. I can do all that while you clean steel, and Mitch can help when he finishes the cutting."

"Do you think we can build the garden fence before Mark gets back?"

"That's the plan," Whit answered. She smiled. "Do you think Mark would mind?"

"Heavens no. It would be a significant step toward getting the garden ready for spring. He intends to use Brad on spring break to start cultivating the soil and remove any rocks."

"I almost feel sorry for Brad," Whit stated.

"He has to learn the consequences of his behavior. Better from his parents than from other authorities. I can guarantee Mark will not go easy on him. I've never seen him so irritated, even with Mitch, who could press every button his mother has."

Whit placed the lid back on her water. "What do you want for lunch and dinner today?"

"Why don't we have some sandwiches for lunch. I can text Mitch to pick up a couple of pizzas on his way home, and we can keep them warm in the oven until we get ready to eat."

"It's been a while since we've had pizza. That sounds good to me." She smiled at Eli. "I'm going to walk down to the creek and decide on the spot for the irrigation system. We can go home for lunch after that if you're at a stopping point."

"I'll be ready," Eli replied.

†

Whit was surprised when Cruz joined her for a walk to the creek. The weather was beautiful. Still chilly but not downright cold. The sun had melted all the snow. The only spots left were the ones hidden in shadow, and those were receding from the warmer temperature. Whit picked out the location for the pump and decided she would need to build a small platform for it to sit on to keep it level. There were plenty of scraps around the workshop she could use. Whit decided that would be her first project in the morning while waiting for the material delivery. She used the heel of her boot to mark the site and began walking back to Eli. A hawk swooped down in front of her with a scream. Seconds later, the bird returned to the air clutching a small rodent in its talons.

"Lunch is served," she told Cruz, who watched the bird depart. "Let's get mama and get some lunch of our own."

Eli had just finished a section when Whit and Cruz returned. "That's great timing. Let me grab my water bottle for a refill, and I'll be ready."

†

Eli texted Mitch while Whit made sandwiches. "He's excited about pizza." Eli chuckled after reading Mitch's response.

"Chips and tea?" Whit asked.

"Yes, please." Eli carried the plates with their sandwiches to the table. "I'll attach the large auger to the tractor and take the small one in the Gator. I figured you'd want to start with your corner and gate posts first."

"When I finish those, I'll get your help changing the bits. I should be able to get them all dug this afternoon."

"I'd like us to help Mark build a small barn when time permits. He will need storage for garden equipment and tools."

"That should not be a problem. What size are you thinking? I can start a design if that will help."

"I'd guess a sixteen by sixteen, but I'll confirm with Mark when he returns."

"I would think that would provide ample space. I'll work on a design later," Whit said and popped a chip in her mouth.

†

When Mitch arrived home, Whit had only one section of holes to be dug. Mitch carried the pizzas into the house, placed them to warm in the oven, and then changed from his school clothes. He walked over to Whit.

"Do you need my help?"

"No, I've got this. Almost done. Eli wants you to work on cutting the remaining springs."

"I'm on it," he said and handed Whit water.

Mitch entered the cave and was impressed by the amount of steel Eli had cleaned. He waited for her to turn off the sander to hand her a drink. "You've been productive today." He grinned.

Eli nodded. "Not a bad day's work. How was Whit doing when you came home?"

"She's only got a small section to finish. Maybe six holes. She said you wanted me to work on cutting the springs."

"Please. I'd like to have everything cut and cleaned before your dad returns. He messaged an hour ago that he made it safely."

"Now the fun begins." Mitch shook his head. "I should be able to finish cutting these this afternoon. What else are we doing?"

"Whit ordered the materials for the garden fence, and they will be delivered tomorrow. Whit will build the irrigation system so we can use the water to mix the concrete for the post holes. I figured you, and I could work on setting the posts."

"Sounds like a plan. I'd better get to it."

"I'm going to stretch my legs and check on Whit while you get set up. I'll be right back, so wait for my return before cutting."

"You got it, boss," Mitch teased.

Eli walked out to the garden spot. "You've made good progress," she told Whit.

Whit nodded. "A few more holes, and I'll be done for the day."

"Mitch is about to start cutting, but I wanted to check on you. Love you."

"Love you, too. I'll come over shortly."

†

By the time darkness fell, Mitch had finished cutting the springs. "This was a great day," Eli announced. "I'm ready for some pizza."

"Me, too," Mitch agreed and put his tools away. "If we finish the fence, will you supervise me welding some stacks for ax heads?"

"Sure. I think we can have most of the posts planted tomorrow. Once they are delivered, I'll place the small ones in the holes, but I need help with the gate and corner posts."

"I only have one class tomorrow. My instructor for my afternoon class is sick, so I'll be home by lunchtime."

"Good. I'll give you money, and you can bring some livers and wings home."

"Thanks, but I'm good for the money. Dad left me some, too."

"Will you help me take the tractor and augers back to the barn while Whit gets pizza ready for us?"

"I'd love to," Mitch said. "I get to drive the tractor?"

"Absolutely, but I need you to place the large auger bit in the back of the Gator."

"Done," Mitch said, jogged over to the bit, and carried it to the Gator.

"We'll be back in a few if you want to set the table and get drinks ready for us," Eli told Whit. "We'll take the equipment back and feed up before coming back."

†

"Are you going to be okay up here alone?" Eli asked Mitch.

"I'm a big boy. I promise I won't let the bogeyman get me."

"Alright then. You are more than welcome to come to stay with us."

"Thanks. I need to practice being on my own for my tiny home."

"Good point. Why don't we go to the diner tomorrow night, and we can look at floor plans when we get back."

"Perfect," Mitch replied. "Can we go to the shelter Saturday morning?"

"I don't see why not. We'll have to get some litter box supplies and food."

Whit nodded. "I'll add them to my list. Unless you need me, I may sneak off to do some shopping while you two set the posts."

"I'm just looking for one for me right now. We must get the barn built before Dad picks out his lot."

"That shouldn't be a problem. I'm positive we can find a kitten for you." Eli smiled. "Boy or girl?"

"It really doesn't matter as long as we connect," Mitch said.

"That's very mature of you," Eli praised.

"I want one as lovable as Tomboy."

"He is a good boy," Eli agreed. "Call us if you need anything. If not, we'll see you at lunch tomorrow."

"Love y'all," Mitch said as he walked them to the Gator.

"Love you, too. Have a good night."

When the materials arrived, Whit and Eli went to work. Whit had built the platform for the pump earlier that morning. Eli shouldered the first of the posts and dropped it in the hole.

"Be careful. There's no need to rush," Whit reminded her with a smile.

"I know, but I'm excited."

"Me, too," Whit replied.

†

They broke for lunch when Mitch came home. "I'll put the large posts in the ground if you grab the wheelbarrow, hoe, and level," Mitch told Eli. "Are we good to go on the water?" Mitch asked.

"Yes, we've already got a hose and nozzle set up for y'all to use," Whit replied. "Is there anything you need from the store?"

"I could use some milk," Mitch replied. "I'm good with everything else. You're picking up some steaks for me to cook tomorrow, right?"

"Yes, sir, I am. Baked potatoes, salad, and some corn, too," Whit answered.

"What time does the shelter open?"

"Opens at seven," Eli replied.

Whit looked at Mitch. "I'll make some biscuits and gravy if you want to come for breakfast. Then we can go to the shelter."

"You have a deal. Let's get moving," Mitch called out as he left the deck.

†

"Can we start the fencing tomorrow, Aunt Eli?" Mitch asked as he poured concrete around a post.

"If these posts are set, I don't see why we couldn't start tomorrow afternoon."

"I'd really like to have it done before Dad gets home. He called last night and said he'd be back on Wednesday."

"How did he sound?"

"He was in good spirits, unlike Brad and Mom."

"She's got to realize she's part of the problem," Eli said. "That's just between us."

Mitch laughed. "That's exactly what he told her. I'd love to be a fly on the wall for that conversation."

"Be nice," Eli told him as she battled to hold in a laugh.

CHAPTER SIX

Whit returned from town, carried the supplies inside the house, and put the dinner groceries away while Eli and Mitch worked. She was impressed to see that they had only four posts to finish. "Looks good," she told them. "Y'all have been working hard."

"Dreaming about that coconut cream pie I'll devour at the diner tonight."

"Damn, that does sound good," Eli agreed with Mitch. "We shouldn't be too much longer here."

"I took the kitten supplies and put tomorrow's groceries away. Unless you need me, I'm going home to unload our groceries and hit the shower."

"Go ahead, sweetie. I don't think I'll be far behind you," Eli said. "Thanks for doing the shopping."

"No problem. I'll see you in a bit."

"Let's get these last ones knocked out," Eli told Mitch. "I'm getting hungry."

"We got a lot done today," Mitch said. He wiped the sweat from his forehead.

"I think your dad will be proud."

"Heck, he may decide to leave more often," Mitch teased.

"I doubt it. Mark would love to be in the middle of this project. It would take us twice as long to finish, though."

"I don't know. Have you noticed that Dad is moving better lately?"

"That's not what slows him down. It's overthinking things. Me? I just follow Whit's design with confidence." Eli nodded. "He does move better, though, and seems happy."

"He's like a pig in shit up here. I don't think he's ever been so happy."

"I can understand that. I think we work harder when it's on projects we enjoy."

Mitch finished tamping down the concrete. "I love it here, too."

"It's great having you all here. I can't wait for your mom and Brad to join us."

"If he survives school this year," Mitch said.

114

"He will. It may not be pleasant or easy, but he'll make it through."

"Man, that came out perfect," Mitch declared when they filled the last hole with the concrete mix. "Cleanup shouldn't even be difficult."

"Let's get it done so we can get cleaned up. Are you driving tonight?"

"I can, but you need to remind me to gas up. I'm running on fumes."

"Do you have enough to make it to town?"

"I do. The warning light just came on." Mitch grinned.

Eli shook her head as she rinsed off the equipment. "You are so your dad's son. I don't know how often I had to rescue him from the side of a road."

"Do you want me to store these under the shelter?"

"Sure, we may need them tomorrow."

✝

When Whit heard Mitch pull up, she looked at the clock and then at Eli. "Someone's a bit excited today."

"Yeah, he's eager to pick out a kitten. Come in," Eli yelled when Mitch knocked.

"I guess I'd better finish the gravy." Whit chuckled and returned to the kitchen.

"Good morning," Mitch said.

"Good morning to you. Did last night go well?" Eli asked.

"I took a long shower before bed and slept the night through."

"That's good. With a new kitten, that may be the last whole night's sleep you get for a while," Eli teased.

Mitch shook his head. "Nope, I'm picking the perfect cat today."

Eli smiled at his excitement. "Grab some plates, and I'll get drinks. Do you want milk, juice, or both?"

"Both, please." Mitch placed the plates on the table and returned for silverware. "You've got it smelling good, Whit."

"Thanks, Mitch. I hope you enjoy."

"I love your biscuits and gravy. What's not to enjoy? Are you going with us this morning?"

"Nope, I will stay and work on my manuscript while y'all are in town. If I go, I may be tempted to bring more home," Whit answered as she stirred the gravy.

Eli laughed. "Do you think I won't?"

"No, honey, I expect you to come home with a few if they are ready."

"That's entirely possible. Mitch gets the first choice."

Mitch was done eating, but Eli finished drinking her coffee. "We need to give Doc Loren and the staff time to get open and critters fed," she explained to Mitch. "I'm almost done. Why don't you feed the animals for me, and we'll go when you return?"

"No problem," Mitch said and left the house.

Whit smiled at Eli. "I was going to do that."

"He needs to burn some energy, and we need to give the shelter time to open. I don't think everyone will get adopted before we get there."

"Do you really think he'll stick to one?"

"I think so. For now, at least. It may be different once Mitch gets the tiny home we ordered last night."

"I can't wait to see it in real life," Whit said. "I think it will be the perfect home for him."

"You will in six weeks. Maybe sooner." Eli chuckled. "I loved that we added a small cat house to the outside with doors to the inside and outside. It will be perfect for the litter box and to give a cat indoor and outside access."

†

Erin welcomed them at the shelter. "Hey, guys. What's shaking?"

"We came to look at cats," Mitch explained. "I need a new companion."

"We've got a bunch to choose from. Does gender matter?" Erin asked.

"Nope, I'm looking for someone I connect with."

Erin started down the hall. "Let's see if we can find your match."

Doc Loren came out of her office. "I thought I heard Mitch. How are y'all?"

Eli smiled. "Doing well, Doc, and you?"

"Better, now that it looks like it will be warming up. What are you looking for today?"

"Mitch wants a companion. He'll have his own home once he graduates."

Erin and Mitch walked ahead and entered the cat room. Mitch took a seat on the floor and looked around at the cats. Several approached him curiously, but an older kitten rushed toward him and climbed into his lap. Loud purrs filled the air as he stroked the cat's back.

"Well, hello there," Mitch spoke sweetly. "Aren't you a sweetheart?"

"That's Tink. She's about six months old and has been here a few weeks."

"Altered already?" Mitch asked.

Erin smiled and nodded. "She's all ready to go."

Loren looked at Eli. "Are you interested in some kittens?"

"That's always a possibility," Eli said. "What are you suggesting?"

"These three," Loren said, pointing into a smaller room. "Brothers. Erin named them Bippity, Boppity, and

Boop. They are quite the characters. I'd really like to keep them together."

"Why are they sequestered?" Whit asked.

"They just finished their quarantine period today. All the tests have come back clear, and they are incredibly healthy, considering they came in during this cold weather."

Eli opened the door and stepped inside. She was covered in kittens within seconds and knew they had just acquired three more fur babies. The laughter coming from Eli further convinced her. "Can we shorten the names to Bip, Bop, and Boop?"

Loren placed her hand on Eli's shoulder. "You can call them anything you want. I know they will have a great home."

"Are they old enough to be altered yet?"

"Not yet. The boys need another week."

"Should we take them or wait?" Eli asked.

"I'd say wait. I'll have the brothers ready next weekend. It might be hard to separate them once they join the crew." Loren smiled. "I'd like to get a few more pounds on them, too. They were in rough shape when someone dropped them off in a cardboard box they had taped shut."

"I assume they cut air holes at least," Eli said.

"Whoever dropped them knew we'd open soon. The kittens had started chewing threw the holes, so they weren't left long before we opened. I just don't understand why they dropped them like that. We don't judge anyone for surrendering an animal."

The door opened, and Erin and Mitch emerged. An older kitten was snuggled in Mitch's arms. "Meet Tink," Mitch said.

"She's a sweetie," Loren said. "She will make a good companion for you."

Mitch turned at the sound of Eli's laughter. "I take it we are getting three more?"

"Aww, she's going to take the brothers?" Erin said.

"Yes, but we will shorten the names," Eli chuckled. "Bip, Bop, and Boop."

Erin grinned. "I can live with that."

Loren looked at Erin. "Why don't you start on Mitch's paperwork while I talk to Eli about getting the boys ready next weekend?"

"Good luck with that," Mitch said. "Let's go. I hate it when a grown woman cries."

"Follow me," Erin said. "Go get the carrier for Tink," Erin said.

Loren slipped inside the room and knelt down to Eli.

†

Whit had decided to stop on her way home from the store to see how the visit was going.

Eli nodded and looked at Whit. She motioned her to come inside the room.

"Are you okay with these three joining us?"

"Thanks for asking, but I couldn't say no to the joy on your face. I hear we are shortening the names, though. Bip, Bop, and Boop."

"I could never tell them apart anyhow," Eli said. "They look identical to me. Doc said they will be ready next weekend."

"Welcome to the family," Whit said as a kitten rubbed against her.

"I'll let you know when Mitch is set to go," Loren said. "He made a great choice."

"I think he did, too. I love the smile on his face." Whit scratched the kitten's chin.

†

Mitch sat in the back seat and held Tink all the way home. "Would you mind dropping me off at the house? I'd like Tink to get used to home before she meets the rest of the crew."

"That's a great idea." Eli had been watching him in the rearview mirror. "I can drive the truck back to you later."

"I'll come and get it. I'm not planning to go anywhere today. I have steaks to cook."

"We have an extra steak. Why don't you invite Jessie to join us? She can meet Tink, and we can finalize your prom attire."

"Crap. I had forgotten all about that," Mitch said. "I'll text to see if she's free."

"Whit's got the salad cooling already. I can bring it and put the potatoes in the oven at around three. That should give them plenty of time to cook."

"I can do that. I've already got the steaks marinating. What are y'all going to do the rest of today?"

Eli looked at Whit. "I'd like to work on the garden fence if the posts have set."

"That sounds like an excellent plan to me. It looks like it will be a sunny day. I'd rather be outside with you."

"I can help, too," Mitch said.

Eli shook her head. "You need to spend time with Tink. Maybe you can help after lunch if she seems content."

"Just don't forget to show her where the litter box is," Whit reminded him.

"I've already set it up in the laundry room and will take her there first. I have her food and water bowls already filled."

"Good. Let Tink explore this morning and get comfortable in her new home. Don't feel like you need to hold her the entire time." Whit grinned at him.

"I won't," Mitch replied. "I guess I'll see y'all in a bit."

"We'll head home, change clothes, and be back. "I'll drive your truck, and Whit can bring a Gator with some tools."

"You know where I am if you need me," Mitch said. He exited the truck with the cat carrier and entered the house.

"That's a happy boy," Eli said as she turned the truck.

"Yes, he is. What kind of tools do we need?"

"Hammers and the come-along to stretch the wire. Everything else is already on site. Are you sure you're up to this?"

Whit nodded. "I want to see it done as much as you. How much more steel do you have left to clean?"

"Not a terrible lot. Mark won't be back until Wednesday, so I can finish it while Mitch is in school. He's already cut the rest of the lengths." She looked at Whit. "Tomorrow, we should have a relaxed day. I thought we could ride the Gator to the top and find some downed limbs for ax handles."

"Admit it. You're having just as much fun as the boys in this forging venture."

"Oh, I definitely am." Eli looked at Whit. "I enjoy working with them. Especially when the weather is too ugly to work on another outdoor project. If the weather continues to warm, we can start breaking ground in our garden plots, can't we?"

"It won't be much longer. For sure, by the time we get back from our honeymoon." Whit smiled. "That's only a few weeks away."

"I know. It's creeping up on us fast."

"Any regrets?"

"Not one," Eli said as she parked the truck. "I am so happy you came into my life. I can't imagine spending the rest of it with anyone but you."

†

They worked on the fence and were halfway done when Mitch stepped onto the porch. "Y'all come in for some lunch. I've made grilled cheese and don't want them to get cold."

"On our way," Eli called to him. She hung her hammer on the fence. "Let's go."

Mitch had a stack of sandwiches, chips, and glasses of tea on the table.

"How is Tink settling in?" Whit asked.

Mitch smirked. "Like she owns the place already. Would it be okay if I took her outside and we watched you for a bit?"

"She's going to have to get used to being an indoor and outdoor cat," Eli answered.

Tink had curled up in one of the recliners, and she raised her head and blinked at them.

"I think she agrees," Mitch said. "She sat at the front window for nearly an hour watching what y'all were doing."

"You need to introduce her to Cruz. Cruz has become accustomed to the other cats, but we don't know how Tink will react to a dog." Eli glanced at Cruz, sitting patiently at the front door.

124

"Inside or outside?" Mitch asked.

"Probably inside. Tink seems comfortable here and knows where to go if she's scared. Outside, she may run into the woods."

Whit placed the paper plates in the recycle bin. "That was a great lunch, Mitch."

"Thanks, it really hit the spot," Eli said. "Are you ready for me to let Cruz in? She can sit beside me while you bring Tink over."

"No better time than now."

Eli walked to the door and called Cruz inside. She returned to her seat, and Cruz sat next to her. "Be nice when you meet your new sister," Eli told Cruz, stroking her head. Eli kept a hand on Cruz's collar as Mitch carried Tink over and sat on the floor with her in his lap.

Tink stared at Cruz and let out a hiss. Cruz looked at Eli with a sad look in her eyes. Mitch stroked her head. "It's okay. This is your big sister." He reached over to stroke Cruz, who wiggled with excitement. Tink climbed out of his lap and approached Cruz cautiously.

"Be calm," Eli told Cruz. She was amazed that Cruz and Tink were nose to nose, checking one another out. Tink turned her head and rubbed along Cruz's muzzle. "Good girls," Eli said, petting both animals. Eli could barely contain her laughter when Cruz licked the top of Tink's head.

"Aww," Whit said with a smile. "Good girls," she repeated. "Let's turn back to the table to drink and see what happens."

Cruz laid down at Eli's feet when no one paid attention to them, and Tink curled up next to her. "That's amazing," Mitch said.

"Bring a lawn chair and sit out by the garden and let's see how she does outside," Eli suggested.

†

Whit and Eli were securing the last section of the fence when Jessie arrived. "Good, we need another set of hands to hang this gate," Eli teased.

"Who is this?" Jessie asked when she saw Tink.

"My cat, Tink," Mitch replied with pride. "If you'll sit here and keep an eye on her, I'll help hang the gate."

"Deal," Jessie said, petting Cruz while Tink rubbed against her legs. "She's affectionate. Did you get her from the shelter?"

"Of course," Mitch replied, holding up the gate while Eli and Whit securely fastened it.

"There. All done," Eli said as she pushed the gate, which latched smoothly.

"I think your dad will be amazed," Whit said.

"Where is your dad?"

"He went home to Alabama to get Brad back on the straight and narrow."

"That doesn't sound like any fun," Jessie said.

"I'd hate to be Brad, but his behavior has brought it on. I imagine he's sitting in the barber's chair right about now. Dad's making him cut his hair short and is taking away all his fun stuff. He will have to earn his electronics back by doing extra work."

"That's one way to teach him there are consequences for his actions."

"I think he's learning that lesson the hard way." Mitch picked up Tink.

"Whit and I will take the tools home and get cleaned up. What time are you going to start the steaks?"

"In an hour or so. Do you want some sausage for an appetizer?"

"That does sound good. You can turn the oven off but leave the potatoes inside to stay warm. Is there anything else you need us to bring?"

Mitch frowned. "I didn't think about dessert."

"Lucky for you, I've got your back. There's a cold buttermilk pie just waiting to be cut," Whit teased.

"Thanks, Whit."

Whit looked at Jessie. "Do you have a picture of your dress? Mitch has asked for help picking out a tux."

"I most certainly do," Jessie answered. "We can take a look while Mitch cooks."

†

After a delicious meal, Whit and Eli decided to head home. "Thanks for a great meal," Eli told him.

Mitch smiled. "Thanks for helping me with a tux, Whit. What's the plan for tomorrow?"

"A relaxing day. Whit and I thought we would search for downed branches for handles."

"Would you mind some company?" Mitch said.

"We'd love to have you come along," Whit answered. "Do you want to join us for breakfast?"

"That could be arranged. What time?"

"Eight?" Whit answered.

"I'll come down and feed the animals and collect eggs for you."

"That sounds perfect. It was good to see you again, Jessie," Eli told her.

"I've missed seeing you all. Hopefully, with the weather warming, I can come out more."

"You're welcome anytime," Whit replied. "Be careful on the way home tonight."

"I will," Jessie promised.

"Don't stay up too late. Dinner was terrific. We'll see you in the morning," Eli said as she patted Mitch on the shoulder.

"Yes, ma'am. Love y'all."

"Love you, too. Good night," Eli answered. "Let's go, Cruz. I hope tonight goes well with Tink."

"She's already curled up on my bed." Mitch laughed.

"That's a good sign," Whit said.

Eli drove them home. "I think it's French toast time," Whit said as she pulled bacon from the freezer to thaw.

"That works for me. Come stretch out on the couch when you finish in the kitchen."

CHAPTER SEVEN

Sunday morning was beautiful. "You would never have known snow was on the ground just a few days ago. I'd still recommend a hoodie," Mitch said between bites. "It's still cool in the shadows."

"Will you bring a Gator around and load the small chainsaw?" Eli asked Mitch. "Check the fluids to make sure they are full."

"Yes, Dad," Mitch teased Eli. "He's drilled that in my head. Do we need any other tools?"

"I don't think so," Eli replied as she began rinsing dishes.

Eli watched Mitch and Cruz walk to the barn and disappear. "I think he's lonely. I hope you don't mind him tagging along."

"Absolutely not. I love having Mitch around," Whit answered as she took a plate from Eli.

"Just checking." Eli grinned. "Why don't you invite Carol and Julia for dinner? That pizza was so good the other night that I could do it again. Mitch and I can go to town to pick it up."

"Fine with me. I'll give Carol a call while you finish. Six, okay?"

"That should be fine." Eli finished loading the dishwasher and clipped her pistol onto her belt while Whit made the call. She slipped into a hoodie and handed one to Whit. Mitch pulled up to the cabin as they stepped onto the porch.

Mitch made a move to leave the driver's seat.

"Stay. You can chauffeur us today. How does pizza sound tonight?"

"I can always eat pizza."

"I thought you and I could go to town and pick some up. Carol and Julia will join us," Eli told him.

"I haven't seen them in weeks." Mitch grinned.

†

The recent storm had brought down limbs from the hickory and beech trees. Mitch cut the limbs into sections,

and it took two trips to haul the wood to the Gator. With the
bed of the vehicle filled, Eli looked at Mitch. "That should
keep us busy for a while."

"We can cut handles for axes and some for knives for
Dad."

"I need to see if I can order our brand, too," Eli said.

"Are we going to drop these at the cave or
workshop?" Mitch asked.

"We have the tools we need at the workshop, so let's
take them there," Eli replied.

"Can I talk one of you into supervising me while I cut
the branches into quarters for the handles? I need to go check
on Tink first, though."

Eli looked at Whit. "I can take my walking stick to
work on if you want to kick back and relax."

"I'll see if I can knock out the last chapter of the
textbook. I'll also look up the brand and text you what
options I can find." Whit smiled at Eli.

"That would be awesome. We can work a few hours
and then go to town for the pizza. Will that work for you,
Mitch? We'll make it an early night since you have school
tomorrow."

"Sounds good," Mitch said. "I'll drop y'all at the
house, unload the wood and check on Tink. I won't be long."

†

"I'm sorry if I've ruined our relaxing day," Eli told Whit when they entered the house.

"Darling, working on walking sticks is relaxing for you, and I want to finish this book, so I can concentrate on other projects." Whit leaned in to kiss Eli. "Mitch wants to impress Mark when he returns, so do anything you can to help."

"I think Mark will be pleased with all we accomplished," Eli stated. "The steel will be cleaned. Mitch has welded a few stacks for ax heads, the garden fence and irrigation system are in place, and we have wood gathered and cut for handles."

"Don't forget about Tink. She was a great find, too."

"Absolutely. Mitch got a diamond in her. Mark may want to steal her."

"The tiny home was ordered, too."

"Wow, we did accomplish a lot, didn't we?" Eli grinned. "I so love working with you."

"Enjoy your carving and use that glove," Whit teased.

"Got it," Eli answered, carrying her supplies to the workshop.

They fired up a small bandsaw when Mitch arrived, and she supervised him cutting the first log. "Go slow, and don't get careless. We have all day."

"Yes, ma'am," Mitch answered. Eli took her seat to begin carving but kept a close eye on Mitch.

Whit opened the door and entered, carrying a tray of hot chocolate and water. "I think it's time for a break. Wow, you've gotten a lot done, Mitch."

"He's getting great with the bandsaw and is wearing his gloves, too," Eli said. "Time permitting, we can run the pieces through the planer to ensure they are flat and smooth."

"Is that something I can help with?" Whit asked.

"Gloves and safety glasses are on the wall. I'll grab a stack and bring them to show you how to use the equipment. Hot chocolate first, though."

Mitch dumped the sawdust into the compost bin and tossed the wood trimmings in a bucket. "You can use these in the firepit, right?" he asked.

"Yes, they are a perfect size. I'll take that bucket and empty them in a few."

"I got this, Aunt Eli," Mitch said, rushing out the door.

"He is so excited. Thanks for your offer of help."

"I'll admit, I was missing y'all, and the last chapter was short," Whit replied.

By four, they had all the wood prepped for handles. "I've got my work cut out for me," Eli said. "I'll start sanding and shaping after cleaning the last steel sections."

"Can I do more welding while you're there to supervise?"

"I don't see why not. Why don't we get cleaned up, and you can drive the Gator down to ride into town for the pizza? I don't know about y'all, but I'm hungry," Eli said.

"We worked right through lunch," Whit reminded her.

†

After dinner, Julia opened up her bag and pulled out several items. "I'm not sure if these will work, but it was the best I could come up with. You can't drill or cut those crystals." She pulled out two pendants and then a bracelet. "The best I could do was to build a stainless crate and solder them inside. If they are too gawky, I understand. Those are the darnedest things. I tried every method I could, but they are impenetrable."

Eli fastened one of the pendants around Mitch's neck. "We'll try the other one and the bracelet on Mark when he returns. It looks sturdy, so hopefully, it will work."

"If he doesn't wear it, I will," Mitch said. "That looks cool."

"Bring me more of the smaller crystals, and I'll make one for you," Julia told him with a smile.

"Awesome," Mitch said. "I need to head out, feed Tink, and get ready for school tomorrow."

"Take the rest of the pizza in case you get hungry or for lunch tomorrow," Eli told him. "We'll see you when you get home from school. Love you."

"Love y'all, too. It's good to see y'all again, and thanks for the pendant. Do y'all need any firewood split or anything?"

"Now that you mention it, some split logs would be great," Carol replied.

"I'll take care of that tomorrow. Good night, ladies."

"Good night, Mitch," they called out to him.

"He's grown into a fine young man," Carol said. "I hope Mark gets Brad back on track."

"I have confidence he will," Eli stated.

"I think we'll head out, too," Carol said.

"What do I owe you for the jewelry?" Eli asked.

"Not a thing. Mitch splitting some wood for us is payment enough," Julia answered.

"Thank you," Eli said. "Don't be strangers. Come over anytime."

"We will," Carol replied and hugged Eli's neck.

"See you soon," Whit called to them.

†

"I forgot to show you something earlier today," Whit said, pulling out her phone. She showed Eli two pictures of brand samples she had custom created. "What do you think?"

"I like this one the best," Eli answered. "The detail in the wolf is perfect."

"My choice, too," Whit said. "I also got an email confirming our appointment for the artificial insemination on

Thursday after we return from our honeymoon. I hope that's not too soon for you."

"Not at all." Eli smiled. "I can't wait to have a little one running around here."

"Me, too. I'm really looking forward to us becoming parents. I think we'll be great."

"We'd better get some lovin' in before then. Two-hour feedings and diaper changes will take some getting used to."

"So, let's start tonight," Whit coyly said, reaching for Eli's hand.

"I'm all for that." Eli smiled and followed Whit upstairs.

CHAPTER EIGHT

Mark was floored when he pulled into the yard and saw the fence surrounding the garden plot. He could hear the drone of the sander coming from the forge when he stepped from his truck. Mark checked his watch and knew it was too early for Mitch to be home. He entered the cave and saw Eli sitting at the sander, cleaning metal. Cruz jumped up and rushed to him.

"Hey, baby girl," he said and stroked her head.

Eli felt Cruz's movement and looked up to find Mark smiling at her. "Well, damn. I was hoping to get this last piece done before you arrived."

"You cleaned it all?" Mark's eyebrows shot up with surprise.

"This is the last one, and I've got about three more minutes on it."

"I'm going to carry my bag inside. Come in and have a cold one with me, and we can catch each other up on current events."

"I'll be right there. Oh, you have a new daughter. The last I checked, Tink was looking out the front door. She sits there when it's close for Mitch to come home. I can't wait for you to meet my three new boys this weekend."

"Get busy, and you can tell me all about it."

Mark grabbed his bag and walked to the front door. Green eyes blinked at him and dashed away as he opened the door. He placed his bag in the hallway and walked into the room.

"Come here, Tink," Mark called. As he took a seat at the table.

Tink peeked around a chair to study him. "It's okay. I'm your grandpa," Mark said with a chuckle.

Tink eased toward him, and Mark bent over to pet her. "That's a good kitty," Mark praised as the room filled with a purring sound. Tink had climbed into his lap when Cruz and Eli entered.

"I see you found Tink, or did she find you?"

"It was a mutual discovery." Cruz and Tink were nose to nose until Cruz licked her in the face. "That was sweet, Cruz."

"They get along well. You ready for a cool one?"

"Yes, please," Mark answered. "You all have been busy."

"We have. We've managed to get a lot done. Was your trip successful?"

"I hope Laura can stay firm with him. I thought he would cry when he went to the barbershop, and Brad did cry when he surrendered his electronics. They are safely stored in my gun cabinet, and I'm the only one with access."

"How will that work if you're here and he earns something back?"

Mark raised his phone. "Technology, Sis. I can unlock it from here while Laura removes an item."

"That is clever. How was Brad's behavior when you left?"

"He was dog tired after I worked him at the church on Saturday and at the house on Sunday. He goes directly from school to the church until he finishes striping the parking lot."

"So, he seems to have gotten the point?"

Mark sighed. "I can only hope. Laura is ready to pull him from school to send him up here, but I convinced her to let him finish out the year."

"That's good, at least."

Mark chuckled. "She's learning quickly that her mama drama doesn't help. She's got to be firm with him and not give in to his whining." He took a long drink. "Man, I needed that. So tell me what all you've accomplished since I've been gone."

Eli saw Mitch's truck pull up in the yard. "I think I'll wait and let Mitch update you."

Mitch walked inside and saw Tink in Mark's lap. "Don't even think about stealing my cat."

"I missed you, too, Son. Eli waited for you to drag in before telling me what all you've been doing."

Mitch leaned down to hug his dad. "Welcome home. May I have a beer with you?"

"Yes. Grab me another while you're at it, please."

"Aunt Eli?"

"I'm good, thanks."

Mitch joined them at the table. "We've got the fence built for the garden and the irrigation set up, but I guess you could see that."

"I didn't see the irrigation, but that's awesome."

"We've got all the steel cut and most of it clean."

Eli cleared her throat. "I was cleaning the last piece when your dad snuck up on me."

"Eli supervised me while I got three more welds done for ax heads."

"He did a very nice job on them, too."

"Whit, Eli, and I gathered some hickory and beech branches that came down in the storm, and we've got them cut and planed ready to be ax or knife handles. I cooked some awesome steaks for Jessie and the aunts." He looked at Eli. "Seems like we did more than that."

"Your tiny home," she prompted.

"Oh yeah, we picked out and ordered my tiny home. We will add a cat house next to it with access for Tink to come and go between the house and outside. We need a septic system, but Whit will walk me through setting up my solar panels and water."

"That should prove interesting."

"We adopted Tink, and Eli gets three boys this weekend after they are altered."

Eli chuckled. "You're going to love them. Bip, Bop, and Boop. Three brothers someone left in a cardboard box at the clinic. They are so loving."

"Dang, they sound perfect for here if we had a barn. Your mom would flip if we had them all in the house."

"About that," Eli said. "Whit will draft plans if you'll just give her the size. She's all gung ho about building it."

"I'm impressed with how much work you did quickly. You went to school every day?"

"Every single one." Mitch grinned. "Whit and Eli even helped me order a tux for Jessie's prom."

"I didn't get much of a look at the forge. Do you want to show me what you've done?"

"Sure, Dad. Come on, Tink."

"She goes outside?"

"Tink follows Mitch everywhere he goes." Eli followed them from the house.

†

Mark picked up the stacks of steel Mitch had welded. "You did a beautiful job, Son. I've got enough steel to keep me busy for months."

Eli pulled out her phone. "I don't think I showed you this, Mitch. She showed them the brand she could use with her wood burner."

Mark took her phone. "Damn, I love that."

"You did good, Aunt Eli," Mitch said.

"Nope, Whit designed it for us. It should be here tomorrow."

"Where are the handles?"

"They are all down in my workshop. We didn't want to crowd the forge with supplies. Come on, and I'll take you to see them. Mitch, you want to ride down with us?"

"Go ahead. I need to feed Tink. I'll meet you there soon. Whit will be calling us for supper in a few."

Mark hugged Mitch. "I'm proud of you, Son."

"Thanks, Dad. We can stay busy until it's time to plant the garden."

"Probably long after that, too."

CHAPTER NINE

Eli paced the hall of Mark's home. "I can't believe today has gotten here so quickly." She fidgeted with the cuff links Mark had loaned her.

"Just relax. The ceremony will be over before you know what hit you," Mark teased. "The butts are on the smoker, and the side dishes are ready. Laura texted me that the wedding cake was delivered, and it was beautiful."

"I just hope it tastes good," Mitch joked.

"Who said you were getting any?" Eli asked.

The look of shock on his face helped Eli relax.

"Carol's taking pictures, right?" Mark asked.

"Yes, and Doc Loren is, too. We should have some good ones."

"This is going to be a fabulous day, Sis. I couldn't be happier for you."

"Thanks for standing by me. I may need your support if my knees go weak."

Mark chuckled. "Maybe you should have asked Mitch, then."

"If you let me fall, I know Mitch will get me up."

"I sure will," Mitch said and flexed his muscles. "I'm going to check the meat. I guess I will see you soon."

Mark nodded. "I'm not sure I've ever attended a wedding where we enter on a Gator, but it's too damn far to walk in these shoes."

"You can change and put something comfortable on," Eli said.

"No way I'm going to risk the wrath of Laura. I've got some sneakers in the back of the Gator. I'll slip into them afterward. You look nice, by the way. I didn't realize you cleaned up so well."

"I've gotten so used to work clothes. Dress slacks feel weird."

"Whit may take a look at you and want to marry you more often," Mark teased. He walked over to his liquor cabinet and poured two shots of Jack. Mark handed one to Eli. "To the best sister ever. I love you."

"I love you, too. Thanks for being here."

"I've never been so happy, and it's all thanks to you. You have given us the perfect home, and I can work all day doing something I enjoy." Mark's phone pinged with a text. He looked at Eli. "All the guests have arrived, and Mr. Henry is ready for you. Do you need another shot?"

"No, I'm good."

"Pop this in your mouth so you don't taste like whiskey when you kiss Whit." Mark tossed her a mint.

Mark swung the door open, and they stepped into a beautiful afternoon. They climbed into the Gator, and Mark drove them carefully down the mountain.

Eli's eyes widened when she saw the friends and family gathering for the wedding. Flowers graced every table, and Cruz even wore a corsage as she trotted over to Eli. Eli stepped out of the Gator and walked through the small crowd, greeting their guests. When she reached the arch where the ceremony would take place, Mr. Henry was waiting.

"Are you ready for this?" he asked.

"Yes, sir, I am," Eli replied.

"Let's get ready to greet your bride then," Mr. Henry said, turning back toward the house.

Seeing Whit dressed in white slacks and a blouse took Eli's breath. The smile on Whit's face radiated her happiness as she carefully stepped down the front steps and walked, holding Mitch's arm, across the field. Mitch was wearing black dress pants and a white dress shirt.

"Who is that with Whit?" Eli whispered to Mark.

"He wanted to surprise you," Mark whispered back. "Have no fear. He will be changing to help me cook."

When they approached, Eli reached for Whit's hands and stared into her beautiful eyes, falling in love with her again.

Mr. Henry welcomed the guests and performed a beautiful service. Eli had a moment of panic when Mr. Henry asked for the rings. Eli patted her pockets and found them empty. Mark tapped her shoulder and handed her the box with the matching bands that Julia had made for them. The crowd laughed softly as Eli took the box.

Eli and Whit had each written short vows, and when Mr. Henry finally announced, "You may kiss the bride." The crowd cheered. Eli pulled Whit close and kissed her tenderly.

"Ladies and gentlemen, please welcome Whit and Eli Fortner."

Eli was surprised by his announcement. Whit had initially planned to maintain her last name. Her surprise must have registered on her face when she looked at Whit.

Whit smiled. "I wanted to be completely yours," she whispered. "Let's go greet our guests."

"Thank you, Mr. Henry, for performing our ceremony," Eli said as she hugged him.

"It was my pleasure to do the honors for you and Whit. I wish all couples that marry had the love you two share."

"Thank you. I've never been happier." Eli grinned. "Are you ready for some Fortner BBQ?"

"I'm surprised I could conduct the ceremony. My mouth has been watering for the last half hour."

"Let's go see what we can do about that."

Mark and Mitch rushed into the house to change clothes and pulled the meat from the pork shoulders.

Eli walked over to Mitch. "That was a pleasant surprise. You looked very handsome."

"I needed to practice walking in dress clothes for Jessie's prom," Mitch teased.

"Regardless of your motivation, thank you for escorting Whit."

"Thank you for everything," Mitch said as Eli could swear there was a tear in his eye. "I hope you made a big batch of the Bama white sauce."

"Don't ya know it," he answered.

Evan and Erin walked over. "Congratulations," Evan said.

"Hello, stranger. Thank you for coming. It seems like ages since you've been here."

"I've missed you and this place. Mitch has been keeping me up to date on everything. The forge sounds exciting."

"Mark and Mitch are doing so well. I help with the handles, but they do most of the work."

"Maybe we could sell a few in the store," Evan suggested.

"That's a possibility if they can stay ahead of their orders. Mitch's Viking axes are gaining popularity, too."

"Maybe when I'm home for spring break in a couple of weeks, I can watch them work and possibly get some fishing in."

"Mitch has been dying to wet a fly," Eli answered.

"Are we talking fishing?" Brad asked when he walked up.

"Yes, I want to do some on spring break," Evan answered.

"Maybe if you're out of the doghouse by then, you can fish, too," Eli teased.

"I sure hope so," Brad said. "Dad has been wearing me out. If I make one more pass over that garden with the tiller, I think I'll scream."

"Some lessons you have to learn the hard way." Eli shrugged.

"I know. I brought it all on myself." Brad smiled. "Congratulations, Aunt Eli."

Hayden walked over to Brad. She ran her hand through his hair. "I kind of like it short."

"I'm getting used to it. Mom says I spend less time getting ready in the morning."

Eli chuckled. "How have you been, Hayden? It's been a while. Have you gotten taller?"

"I seem to have hit a growth spurt," Hayden replied. "I got my braces off, too." She smiled at Brad.

Mitch broke out laughing. "I guess you two can start kissing now and not get locked up."

"Very funny, Bro," Brad said.

Eli noticed Hayden's blush. "Don't pay them attention. Sometimes they act like little kids."

"I should be used to their teasing by now. Congratulations. You and Whit look great together."

"It's been quite a journey, and it's just barely begun." Eli smiled. "I hope we'll see more of you this summer."

Hayden shot a glance at Brad. "I think you will. We often talked until his mouth got him in trouble."

"I think he's learned his lesson. I think you and the others are a good influence for him, and I hope we can have some fun this summer."

"Ladies and gentlemen," Mark called out from the front steps as he struck a fork against his glass. "Before we embark upon a glorious feast, I propose a toast." He looked at Whit and Eli.

Eli felt Whit's hand slide into hers with a gentle squeeze.

"To the best two sisters, a man could ever ask for. I wish you never-ending love, happiness, and prosperity. We all love you and appreciate what you do for us all. Cheers."

"Cheers" rang out through the small crowd.

"Now, let's grub." Mark chuckled. "Whit, Eli, will you be the first to dine?"

Eli led Whit to the beginning of a long buffet line.

"Mr. Henry, will you bless this food and everyone here today?" Eli asked.

"I'd be honored." Mr. Henry bowed his head and blessed the food and the friends and family who were about to feast from the bounty the lord provided. "Amen."

Eli smiled and handed Whit a plate. "My love, will you go first?"

†

Once everyone had finished eating, Mark stood. "The ladies will open gifts, and then we will share that beautiful cake with them."

Eli was surprised by the various heartfelt gifts they were given, but the last box made her laugh out loud. It was from Mitch, and he had taken pride in wrapping it himself. Eli carefully peeled back the paper and laughed when she pulled out a first aid kit. "Hopefully, this won't be used much, but thank you, Mitch."

"You're welcome, Grace," Mitch replied.

Laura jabbed him in the ribs. "Hush," she said a bit too loudly.

After cake and pictures, Eli and Whit went inside to change into something more comfortable. Music was playing, and several couples were dancing when they

151

returned. Eli turned to Whit just as a slow song began to play. "Mrs. Fortner. May I have this dance?"

Whit chuckled as she took Eli's hand. "You know we've never danced?"

"I just realized that, too," Eli whispered in her ear. "So, I apologize in advance if I step on your toes."

Whit smiled and kissed Eli sweetly and pulled her close.

Eli grabbed Whit's hand when the next song had a fast beat. "We need to sit this out and let the youngins show their moves."

Whit and Eli mingled with the crowd showing their appreciation for their friends joining the celebration. Mr. Henry and Flora were the first to depart as the sun began to fade. "We hate to leave, but these old eyes aren't what they used to be," Mr. Henry said.

"Thank you for the lovely service and all your homemade goodies," Eli told them. "We will definitely have more cookouts this summer."

"I wouldn't mind coming out to fish if that's alright?"

Eli placed her hand on his shoulder. "Mr. Henry, do I need to remind you that you don't need an invite? Any of these boys will fish with you anytime you're ready."

The boys loaded the tables and chairs onto the trailer to return to the rental place as the crowd began to wind down. When only Whit, Eli, Mark, and Laura were left sitting around the fire pit, Mark looked at Eli. "I think it was a beautiful day."

"It couldn't have been more perfect," Whit said.

"When are you heading out in the morning?" Laura asked.

Eli looked at Whit. "Fairly early. We are both excited to see the Outer Banks."

"May we send you off with full stomachs? Mark has been bragging about his breakfast burritos since we arrived," Laura said.

"Those are too good to pass up," Whit answered. "Eightish?"

"Perfect," Mark answered.

"I hope you will eat some of these leftovers. They are too good to waste," Eli said.

"That won't be a problem. Your house sitter has organized a gathering tomorrow night. That should take care of most of them. Anything else we'll stick in the freezer," Mark stated.

"That sounds good," Eli said. "Everything was delicious."

"I think it turned out well today, and you couldn't have ordered better weather," Mark replied.

"Honey, I think it's time for us to go home and let these newlyweds decompress from the day's events," Laura told Mark.

"Decompress. Is that what they call it now?" Mark teased. "Have a great night, and we'll see you in the morning."

"Good night, and thanks again for everything."

Mark wrapped Eli in a hug. "I'm so happy for you. Both of you," he said and pulled Whit into the embrace.

"Come on, you big teddy bear, before you start to cry," Laura teased.

Eli chuckled. "We'll see you in the morning."

Eli watched them disappear into the night and turned back to Whit? "Are you ready to call it a night?"

Whit nodded and closed the lid on the fire pit. "It's been a long but perfect day. I just want to snuggle next to you and relax."

†

Eli lit a candle beside the bed. She was lying on her back with Whit's head on her shoulder. Eli lifted her left hand to admire the wedding band. "Julia did a remarkable job on these."

"Yes, she did. I love how the diamonds sparkle, but they aren't exposed. We both use our hands a lot, and anything set outside of the band would have become an issue."

Eli kissed the top of her head. "What if we got a nice set of silicone rings for working in the garden or other projects and kept these for social occasions?"

"That's not a bad idea, but I want to wear them every day. I'll order a set for when we start to garden." Whit stifled a yawn.

"Tired?" Eli asked. "Me, too."

"We won't be rushed by anything in the Outer Banks. We have a week to relax and enjoy one another without any responsibilities."

"I am so looking forward to long walks on the beach with you," Eli said.

"I know the house has a full kitchen, but I'd love to take advantage of the fresh seafood for dinners," Whit said.

"That's not a problem at all. We can stock it with items for breakfast and a few lunches and eat at a different restaurant every night if that's what you want."

"Or the same one repeatedly if we find one we like." Whit chuckled.

Cruz whimpered in her sleep. "She must be chasing rabbits."

"I don't envy your conversation with her when you load our suitcases, and she doesn't get to join us," Whit said.

"She will survive," Eli promised. "You're right, though. It will be hard on both of us. The first time we've been apart since we moved up here. I promised I'd never leave her again."

"I'm sure the house probably has a pet policy," Whit said. "Bring her if you want."

"No, I'm sure that with having Mitch stay here, she'll be fine. Mark will have her with him in the forge all day, too. She probably won't even miss me."

"I seriously doubt that," Whit replied. "She loves you almost as much as I do. Blow that candle out, and we'll be on a grand adventure together when we wake."

"Good night, Mrs. Fortner," Eli said. "I love you."

"Most," Whit whispered in the darkness.

✝

Cruz was attached to Eli like a second skin the following day as she loaded their bags in the back of the truck. Eli knelt down beside her and took her head in her hands. "I will be gone for a little while, but Mitch and Mark will take good care of you. I promise I will be back."

Cruz licked Eli's cheek.

"I love you, too, baby girl. Let's go see Mark and the boys." She opened the back door for Cruz to jump inside.

Whit could see the tears in Eli's eyes. "Are you sure you don't want to bring her?"

Eli shook her head. "The boys will take good care of her."

Eli turned the key and drove to Mark's.

"Good morning," Mitch called out from the deck. "Y'all have great timing. We are nearly done cooking."

"We planned it like that," Eli teased as she opened the door for Cruz.

"Have you had the talk with her yet?" Mark asked as they walked onto the deck.

"Yes, I promised her you and Mitch would take great care of her while we're gone."

Mark nodded. "You know we will."

"Those look delicious."

Mark smiled. "Go inside and pour your drinks. We'll be right behind you."

Eli and Wit walked into the kitchen.

"Do ya'll want to start with coffee, juice, or both?" Brad asked.

"Both, please," Whit responded. "Good morning, Tink," Whit said as she stroked along the cat's back. "What do y'all think of Mitch's new buddy?"

"She's sweet and follows him around like a puppy," Laura said.

"He's so excited to be getting his tiny house," Brad said.

"It will be here soon. The septic tank and electricity will be installed next week," Eli stated as Mark and Mitch entered carrying a large tray of burritos. "Don't forget that, Mark."

"The septic company and electrician are coming to hook up Mitch's homesite this week."

"I don't plan on going anywhere, so it should be fine. Do both of them know the location?"

"Yes, I left checks for both contractors on the counter. Bring them up for your dad, please," she asked Mitch.

"No problem. I'll get the checks when I go down to feed everyone."

"Please do not let Bip, Bop, and Boop into the house. It's like a Nascar race for them."

"Got it. Anything else I need to know," Mitch asked and took a bite of burrito.

"I think it goes without saying, no wild parties," Eli teased.

"Mom and Dad will be there to supervise tonight. I just thought it would be fun to get everyone together and eat some of those leftovers."

"Stay out of the wedding cake. That section is for our first anniversary," Whit warned.

"You heard the lady. If you want to live to see next year, stay outta her cake," Eli replied.

"Got it," Mitch said. "There's a plethora of other desserts to choose from."

"What did you just say?" Laura asked.

"I said there was a plethora of other desserts to choose from. Why?"

"That's a mighty big word for you, Son," Laura teased.

"Whit taught me," Mitch said with a wink to Whit.

†

After breakfast and a final bathroom break, Whit and Eli walked out to the truck. Cruz ran after her and kissed her cheek.

"I'll be back soon. You be a good girl while I'm gone."

"Come here, Cruz," Mark called to her.

Cruz ran to Mark and sat beside him, "Go ahead, I've got her," he said, placing a hand on her collar.

"We'll see you next Sunday." Eli climbed into the truck.

"Have fun and enjoy your time together," Mitch said.

"We will," Whit replied.

Mark raised his hand. "Be careful."

"See you in a couple of weeks," Laura said.

Eli nodded. "Yes, you will."

She put the car in drive and drove to the highway. "We will have a busy few weeks when we get back. Our doctor's appointment, Mitch's prom date, and then his graduation in Montgomery a few weeks later."

"It's probably a good thing we are getting this time together," Whit said. She entwined her fingers with Eli's.

"Yes, it is. Outer Banks, here we come!"

"I know it's going to be a long drive, so let me know if you want me to share some of the driving."

"I think I'm good. You know I'm a horrible passenger."

"Yes, love, I remember, but it will take eight hours to get there even if we don't hit a snag."

"Doesn't matter as long as I'm with you," Eli told her.

CHAPTER TEN

As they drove east across the state, the scenery shifts were gorgeous, but the day was growing long. Eli was glad to read the sign for only ten miles remaining to their destination.

"Could you survive on pizza, sodas, and a hot tub tonight? We can shop and play tourist tomorrow."

"That sounds lovely to me. Especially the hot tub. I'm stiff from the ride, so I know you must be. There wasn't much opportunity to set your cruise control today."

"I could use a good soak," Eli admitted. "I may have to break down and let you help with the drive home. That's six days away, so I may change my mind again." She smiled at Whit. "Will you see what you can find for pizza and put in an order?"

"I'm on it," Whit replied, tapping away on her phone. "The spot should be ahead on the right. Pizza will be hot in ten."

"Perfect," Eli said. "Let me know where to turn. I've got my GPS programmed for the beach house."

She was surprised by how light the traffic was, but she thought it might still be early in the tourist season, which was okay with Eli. Less traffic on the road and fewer people on the beach.

"There." Whit pointed out the small pizza joint, and they pulled in. "I'll be right back," she said, leaving the truck.

Eli looked at the GPS. Only two more miles to reach the house. She lowered her window and listened to the sound of the surf pounding against the shore. It reminded her of Pensacola, but she doubted the sand or water would be as beautiful. The sugar-white sand and emerald waters were hard to beat. She would ensure Whit got to see for herself before the end of summer.

Whit returned carrying a large box with a bag holding drinks, plates, and napkins.

"Were you hungry?"

Whit smiled. "I was channeling my inner Mitch. Besides, leftover pizza will be good for lunch."

"That is a good point." Eli rolled up the window. "I was enjoying the sound of the surf. It nearly lulled me to sleep."

"I won't let you face plant into your pizza," Whit joked.

"I'll be good once we arrive and I can stretch my legs. Damn, that pizza smells good."

Eli turned her blinker on and pulled into a small driveway.

"Oh, my goodness. This is beautiful," Whit said.

"You didn't think I'd rent a beach hut for our honeymoon, did you?"

"No, but this is gorgeous from the outside."

"I hope the inside pictures were accurate," Eli said. "I'll get the bags if you bring the food."

"What's the code?" Whit asked when they reached the door.

"One one four three," Eli answered.

When they entered the house, Whit gasped. "This so beautiful, Eli."

Eli followed her inside, carrying the bags, and kicked the door closed behind her. "Yes, it is. Put the pizza down, and let's take a tour."

Whit placed the pizza and supplies on the kitchen counter. All the appliances were stainless steel and a cook's dream. "Almost as nice as ours." Whit grinned as she took a bag from Eli.

The house was only one bedroom and bath, but the amenities were luxurious. The master bath had a large garden whirlpool tub, a separate walk-in shower with dual shower heads, and a private toilet area complete with a bidet. "Ooh, la la." Whit chuckled.

The bedroom was next. It was massive, with a large king-sized bed and a door exiting onto the front deck. The deck comprised a four-person hot tub, an outdoor shower, and a sunbathing area. The balcony allowed for a beautiful view of the beach.

"This is gorgeous," Whit said.

"Let's eat, and then we can try out that hot tub," Eli suggested.

✝

Thick cotton robes hung on the wall just inside the bedroom. Eli and Whit undressed and pulled on a robe.

"These are so soft," Whit said as she tied the belt and walked into the bathroom for two thick bath sheets to wrap around their bodies. She reached her hand to Eli. "Let's go soak."

Whit placed the bath sheets on a small table, and they draped their robes over a chair before stepping into the steamy water.

"This feels heavenly," Eli said as she submerged her body. She slicked the wet hair back on her head. She reached out her hand to Whit and helped her into the tub.

"This does feel nice." Whit sat next to Eli and felt the pulsing of a jet against her back. "Oh, that's the perfect spot," Whit cooed.

"I agree," Eli said as she draped her arm across Whit's shoulders. "This is precisely what we needed after a long drive."

Night had fallen, and Eli could see the whitecaps as they rushed to shore. The moon hadn't risen, so the white glowed against the water. "Beautiful view, too," she said, nodding toward the beach.

"I had forgotten how beautiful the beach could be," Whit said as she snuggled into Eli. "This is perfect."

"Ours for the next six days," Eli replied.

Whit laid her head against Eli's arm. "I will cherish every moment."

Eli kissed the top of her head. "We have no designated schedule. If you want to stay in bed until noon, that's what we'll do. This is the first of many trips I hope to share with you." The water was doing an excellent job of relaxing Eli's stiff body. The jets and the surf pounding threatened to lull her to sleep.

Whit glanced up at Eli and saw the peaceful look on her face. "Are you ready to rinse off and stretch out on that bed?"

"Yes, I believe I am." Eli smiled.

Whit stepped out of the tub and turned on the outdoor shower. She was surprised to immediately feel warm water as she stepped into the flow and reached for Eli. They rinsed off quickly and dried their bodies with the bath sheets before slipping into the thick robes to return inside. Whit took the towels into the bathroom and hung them to dry.

Eli had pulled back the linens and removed her robe when Whit returned. Whit took the robe and hung it beside hers. "That looks so inviting."

Eli slipped between the sheets and reached for Whit. Whit turned off the lamp and climbed in beside Eli.

They were satisfied to entwine their bodies and share several long kisses. Whit knew Eli was tired from the drive. "Let's rest tonight and begin our adventure tomorrow."

Eli pulled Whit close and listened to her soft breathing as sleep overwhelmed her.

†

The soft caress of Whit's hand across her stomach woke Eli with a smile. "Good morning," Whit said.

Eli could see the excitement in Whit's eyes as she leaned in for a kiss. Whit's hand teased her breasts, gently squeezing her nipples, bringing them to full attention.

"That feels good," Eli whispered between kisses. She could feel the burn of desire in her stomach and wetness seeping from her core.

"I want breakfast in bed, and then we can shower and take a walk on the beach."

"Perfect," Eli replied as she moved Whit's body on top of hers.

Whit kissed her way down Eli's body as her fingertips teased her soaked entrance. Eli lifted her hips, but Whit lifted her fingers, enjoying Eli's reaction to her teasing.

Eli felt blood rushing to bring her clit to a sensitive, swollen mound. Whit's warm breath on her skin made Eli's body beg for more contact. Eli felt Whit's tongue slide down the crease between her trunk and thigh, making her quiver with anticipation. "Yes, please," Eli whispered as Whit's warm mouth enclosed her throbbing clit, and two fingers slipped inside her wetness. Whit's fingers caressed each sensitive spot inside her until Eli felt she would explode. When Whit's lips closed around her clit, Eli's body erupted with sensation, and she groaned loudly.

"Oh, yes, baby," Eli pleaded.

†

Whit loved the way Eli's body responded to her. She carefully removed her fingers and replaced them with her tongue.

"Oh, dear lord." She heard Eli groan.

That was the perfect urging of her tongue as she lapped the juices which poured out of Eli, coating Whit's face. She moaned with the earthy flavor of Eli's arousal sending vibrations through Eli's body.

"Hell yes," Eli groaned loudly.

Whit could feel Eli's body tremble and knew a second climax was imminent. "Come for me, baby," she whispered and ran her tongue down the length of Eli's entrance.

†

The sound of Whit's voice filled with arousal was Eli's undoing. She gripped the sheets as her hips writhed with pleasure. "Yes, baby," Whit whispered across her skin.

Eli was spent. That was the most intense lovemaking they had shared since they first met. She struggled to catch her breath and reached for Whit. Whit dragged her tongue up Eli's body, kissing each breast tenderly before arriving at Eli's mouth.

"That felt incredible," Eli said as her fingers wove through Whit's hair.

"I thought so, too," Whit said with a grin. "That second orgasm pushed me over the edge, and I came with you."

"You can wake me like that anytime," Eli purred.

Her hands caressed down Whit's back, and her hands filled with Whit's cute ass. Eli gave them a gentle squeeze. Whit's hip began to grind into Eli's body as their mouths joined in a fevered kiss. Whit broke the kiss for a breath, and Eli slipped a hand between them, entering Whit deeply in one stroke. Whit growled, and her hips thrashed wildly against Eli's fingers until she collapsed in a heap on Eli's chest. Eli eased her fingers from Whit's body and embraced her tightly. "I love you so much."

"I love you, too," Whit answered.

They dozed for another hour, their bodies spent from the lovemaking.

When Eli woke, she found Whit smiling at her. "I think we'd better leave this bed and hit a shower if we plan to leave this house today."

Eli chuckled. "Unless you want leftover pizza, we need to find a store sometime today and scout a place for dinner."

Whit rolled off Eli and sat up in the bed. Eli smiled at her. "My hair is a mess, isn't it?"

"Yes, but I love every inch of your soft curls."

"Let's go, Romeo. Our shower is waiting."

Eli followed Whit into the bathroom for a leisurely shower.

†

Eli bent down for a small bucket as they left the deck heading to the ocean. It was still early, and there didn't seem to be anyone on the beach as far as her eyes could see. "Which way?" she asked Whit.

"Let's go right. There doesn't appear to be any structures for some time."

Eli took Whit's hand as they began strolling down the empty beach. The water was cold as it raced across their bare feet, but neither seemed to mind. Whit bent over, looking at several shells, while Eli pointed her phone to the horizon. The sun had advanced above the water and graced them with beautiful rays of orange and yellow as they reflected off the glassy-surfaced water. Tiny breakers reached the shore, but Eli was confident they would grow once the offshore winds came alive for the day. Several fishing and shrimp boats sailed toward the sun as they began their long days.

"They are going to catch our dinner," Eli said to Whit as she stood and gazed after the boats.

Whit chuckled. "We definitely need to eat something before we go grocery shopping. My pizza is long gone."

"We will have a late breakfast or early lunch when we finish our walk," Eli promised.

Whit looked inside the bucket Eli carried. "We got a few nice ones this morning."

Eli smiled at her wife. "Is that your gentle suggestion we go for breakfast somewhere?"

Whit nodded. "Yes, please."

They turned back toward the beach house and rinsed their feet before entering. "Let's slip on some shoes and go grub."

"I could eat some of Mark's breakfast burritos," Whit said as she climbed into the truck.

Eli chuckled. "I don't know if we can find those, but we can look." Eli closed the truck door behind Whit.

†

Eli drove back through town, passing T-shirt shops and fast-food restaurants. Whit pointed to a sign ahead. "Country breakfast sounds good to me."

"Me, too," Whit answered.

Eli turned into the parking lot and found a spot near the end of the building. "It must be good to be this crowded on a Monday morning," she commented.

They were greeted by a hostess and led to a table with a beautiful view of the beach. "Is this okay?"

"Perfect," Whit replied.

"If that sun bothers you, I can close the blinds," the hostess stated.

"No, it's such a beautiful view," Eli said.

"Janet, your server, will be with you in just a minute," the woman said as she handed them menus. "Can I start you off with coffee or something else?"

"Coffees would be great," Whit answered.

Eli opened the menu.

Whit leaned toward Eli. "Did you see the size of those pancakes? I swear they were basketball size."

"They did look good. Omelets but no burritos," Eli reported. "I'm torn between pancakes and waffles."

"Too many choices," Whit groaned.

Janet brought two coffee mugs and a carafe to the table and poured their drinks. "Good morning, ladies. Are you ready to order, or do you need a few minutes?"

"I'm ready," Eli said. "I'd like the pecan pancakes with ham."

"Short stack or full? A full stack is four, short is two."

"Better stick to short then. They look huge."

Janet turned to Whit. "You, miss?"

"I'll go with a short stack of blueberry pancakes, also with ham and a large glass of apple juice."

"Make that two juices, please," Eli added.

"Absolutely," Janet replied. "I'll have this right out for you."

Eli sipped her coffee and reached over to hold Whit's hand. "What a beautiful morning."

"We couldn't ask for better."

They stared across the water until Janet delivered their meals with various syrups. "Is there anything else I can get you?"

"A recommendation for a good seafood spot for dinner," Eli said.

"I like two places. Rusty's and the Diamond," Janet said. "You can't go wrong with any of them on the island, but those are my favorites. Tell them I sent you, and you'll get a free dessert. Both serve Key lime pie and bread pudding to die for."

"Thanks, Janet. We will try both of them," Eli said.

Janet nodded. "I'll be back to check on y'all."

"Damn, this looks good," Eli said as she drizzled syrup over the pancakes.

"The ham steak is awesome, too," Whit said.

"We will be waddling through the grocery store if we eat all of this," Eli warned.

Whit sighed. "I don't think we stand a chance of that. Mitch probably, but not us."

"I hope everything is going well at home," Eli said between bites.

"Mark would call us if there were any issues they couldn't handle. Relax and have fun," Whit told her.

Janet brought a fresh carafe of coffee. "Is there anything else I can get you?"

Eli looked at her plate. "No, but please remind us to split an order next time."

"You made an impressive dent in the short stack," she told Eli. She grinned at Whit. "You, not so much."

"I enjoyed every bite, though." Whit smiled at her.

"That's all that matters. I'll bring your check in a few, but take your time and don't rush out."

Eli chuckled. "I don't believe I will rush anywhere after that meal."

Janet smiled and returned to the counter.

"That was a great breakfast. We will definitely come here again before we leave," Whit said.

"Maybe every day?" Eli joked.

"I wouldn't have a problem with that. We could just buy some lunchmeat, drinks, and snacks and eat out for breakfast and dinner."

"That works for me," Eli said, handing Janet her credit card.

†

Eli plucked a local tourism guide from a rack when they left the restaurant. She thumbed through the magazine as Eli drove in search of a grocery store.

"Hey, they have a tour to see the wild horses," Whit said excitedly.

"Call and book us a spot tomorrow," Eli said as she spotted a grocery store. "They have whale-watching tours, too, but we may be too early to see them, and the Atlantic gets rough this time of the year."

"Yeah, I thought of a deep sea fishing trip, but thankfully Mark talked me out of it. I will take you fishing in Destin after we attend Mitch's graduation in May."

"Do you think Mark and the boys would enjoy a fishing trip? Never mind, I don't know what I thought to ask that. They'd love it."

Eli put the truck in park. "Yeah, they would. Laura can shop at the outlets. I doubt she would step onto a boat."

"Outlets?" Whit asked.

"You can shop with Laura if you want."

"Heck no, I want to fish."

"My home is an hour away, so maybe we'll find a house for the weekend. You can shop to your heart's desire. After we fish."

†

They purchased their supplies and drove back to the house. "Go stretch out on the deck in the sun, and I'll join you in a few minutes," Eli said as they placed bags on the counter.

"You sure?"

"Go. It won't take me long."

Whit picked up the magazine and walked out to the sun deck. She was flipping through the restaurant section when Eli arrived. "This Outer Banks Boil place looks good, too, if it's open. It's a seasonal spot."

"Call them and see if they are open yet," Eli said, kicking off her shoes and stretching out next to Whit.

Whit listened to a recorded message and smiled. She tapped a few keys and then spoke, "Fortner, a party of two for six o'clock Friday." She ended the call and looked at Eli. "They open up mid-week. I thought it best to give them a night or two to knock the rust off."

"Good decision," Eli said. Her eyes trailed a jet headed north. She turned to Whit. "Have you ever been to Alaska?"

Whit shook her head. "No, but I've always wanted to visit."

175

"Maybe that should be our next adventure this summer," Eli said.

"That would be fun," Whit replied.

†

Whit and Eli enjoyed a week of waking up to make love before enjoying the day together. They did the wild horse tour, toured several lighthouses, and ate more than their fill of fresh seafood. Sunday morning, Eli packed their bags in the truck, and after stopping for a final breakfast with Janet, they were on their way home.

"That was a great time," Eli said as she smiled at Whit.

"Yes, it was, but I'm happy to be heading home. I would have to buy a new wardrobe if we stayed much longer. That was great food."

"I'm positive it won't take long to work all those calories off when we get home." She chuckled. "I'll probably have to play ball for two hours every day to compensate for being gone so long."

"Call Mitch and tell him we're about two hours out if he wants to return home this afternoon."

"Hey, you two," Mitch answered.

"We're about two hours out," Whit told him.

"That's cool. Dad and I have been in the forge all day while Cruz and Tink have been curled up. She's really

176

missed you. I'll feed up and have dinner with Dad. Will y'all be back in time to eat with us?"

Eli looked at the clock. "If you make it after seven."

"That won't be a problem. I'm cooking Hibachi chicken and steak with fried rice and veggies on the grill."

"Sounds delicious," Whit said. "We'll see you soon."

"Drive safe. Love y'all."

"We will. Love you, too," Eli answered.

"I'm glad Mark and Mitch are working together. It seems to be bringing them closer," Whit noted.

"Yeah, they make a good team now that Mark realizes Mitch has some skills in the forge."

"All he needed was a chance. I wonder how far Brad got on his list of chores before they left for home yesterday." Whit chuckled.

"Mark planned to work him hard, so we'll see."

†

The sun was fading quickly when Eli pulled into Mark's yard. She could see a pile of rocks and a freshly tilled garden plot.

"Brad was very busy." Eli smiled at Whit.

"I'd say so. That's a lot more rocks than I thought would be there."

The glow from the forge lit the cave, so Whit and Eli walked toward it. Cruz must have seen the flash of headlights and she flew out of the cave, nearly knocking Eli down.

177

"Whoa, easy, baby girl," Eli said as she hugged the excited dog. "I told you we'd be back."

Mitch stepped out of the forge. "It is them," he hollered back to Mark. "You made good time."

"I was excited about you cooking," Whit said as she hugged Mitch. "How did everything go?"

"Pretty well. Cruz didn't want to eat for a day or so, but Dad finally convinced her to eat with a breakfast burrito. After that, all was good."

"Welcome home," Mark said when he stepped out of the cave.

"Thanks," Eli said and hugged him. "It sounds like y'all have been busy. That's an impressive pile of rocks."

"Courtesy of Brad. Mitch felt sorry for him and helped, too," Mark answered. "I think he was relieved to go home yesterday."

"Did he finish everything you had planned for him?" Whit asked.

"He didn't finish staining your barn, but Mitch and I finished it this morning," Mark answered.

"Thank you," Eli said. "Show us what you've been working on."

"Mitch has made two more ax heads, and we have forged five knife blades this week. I get new orders almost every day."

"I guess I need to get busy on some handles," Eli said.

Mark nodded. "We've used almost everything you've made."

"I can work on them between tilling the garden," Eli said.

Mark shot a look at Mitch. "Tell her."

"Evan and I tilled yours the day after the wedding. We were only going to do a few passes, but the next thing we knew, we had done the entire plot. It looks great, too."

"I guess I can work on handles in the morning then," Eli said.

"Why don't you get showered and ready to cook? I'll finish this blade and come help," Mark told his son.

"We can help, too," Eli said.

"I don't believe so." Mark pointed at Cruz. "Your daughter says you need to play with her." Cruz trotted over and dropped a tennis ball at Eli's feet.

"Go ahead," Whit said. "I'll keep Mark company. I've wanted to watch him forge anyhow."

Eli tossed the ball and walked with Mitch to the house.

"Do you want a beer?" Mitch asked when she sat on the steps.

"Sure." She tossed the ball for Cruz.

"She's not the only one glad that you're home. The septic and electric were installed this week at my home site."

"Are you getting excited?" Eli asked.

"Yeah, I am. I'm gonna shower and start cooking. I could use a gopher if you're not busy?"

"I'll play with Cruz until you get ready to cook."

†

Whit inspected the blades Mark had worked on during the week. "These are impressive."

"I'm feeling much more confident about the process," Mark answered as he placed a steel section in the forge.

Whit noticed Mark was wearing the bracelet on his wrist. "Is that helping with your pain?" Whit asked, pointing to his wrist.

Mark pointed to the leather cord around his neck. "The combination really helps reduce the pain and stiffness. I don't know what those crystals are made of, but they are like magic on pain."

"That's very good to hear. Eli worries when you're in pain."

"I'll be sure to tell her how good they work."

Whit smiled up at him. "You and Mitch seem to be getting a lot done working together."

Mark nodded as he carried the blade to the hammer. "He's grown so much and has a passion and talent for working steel." Mark quenched the knife he was working on and, after inspecting it, placed it on a cooling pad. He switched off the forge. "Let's go see how supper is coming.

I'm hungry." He put an arm around Whit's shoulders. "Was it a good trip?"

"It was, but it's good to be home," Whit answered.

CHAPTER ELEVEN

Eli and Whit spent the next three days in the workshop, preparing handles for Mitch and Mark's blades. When they broke for lunch on Wednesday, Eli looked at Whit. "Are you nervous about tomorrow?"

"A little, but more excited than anything. We will create a child. Are you okay?"

"Yeah, probably more nervous than you," Eli answered. Her eyes grew wide. "You must be hungry. That's a lot of sandwiches," Eli teased.

"I thought we would pack a picnic basket and join Mark for lunch. You know he won't break for lunch on his own."

"That's true. Mark's working hard on all those new orders."

"Why don't you get a Gator and collect the finished handles to deliver? When you return, I'll pack the basket, and we can force him into a break."

Eli leaned in to kiss Whit. "I'll be right back to carry the basket out for you. Love you."

"Love you, too." Whit picked up half a sandwich and handed it to Eli. "I could see you eyeing them," she teased.

Eli took the sandwich and walked to the barn. The brothers Bip, Bop, and Boop were the first to greet her in the barn. At least, that's who she thought they were. All the black cats were starting to blend together.

"Good morning, my babies," Eli called to them. She checked their food and then drove to the workshop. Eli was collecting the handles when a thought hit her like a ton of bricks. *Tomorrow is the big day. If all goes well, we could have a baby soon.* Her eyes scanned the equipment in the workshop. *I won't start anything until we know, but I'd like to make our baby a cradle. I don't want to jinx things, though.* Eli smiled at the thought. "I'd better start searching patterns," she said as she picked up the bundle and loaded them in the Gator. She looked up to find Whit standing on the porch waiting for her with Cruz by her side. *So beautiful.*

†

"Time for a break," Whit announced when they arrived at the forge.

Mark looked up and smiled as they approached. "I hope you have extras. This is Mitch's early day. He should be home any minute."

"I planned for that." Whit smiled. "I even made a bigger batch of brownies."

Eli placed the picnic basket on a workbench and handed Mark the bundle of handles.

"Oh, wow, these look great," Mark said as he inspected them.

Eli began unfolding chairs as Whit started making plates.

Mark helped Eli with the chairs. "Are you excited about tomorrow?"

Eli nodded. "Anxious, too, about becoming a parent."

"You two will make great parents," Mark told Eli. "I have no doubt about that. How is Whit feeling?"

"A little nervous, too," Eli answered.

Mark looked up to see Mitch pulling into the yard. "I'd better grab another chair."

†

Whit and Eli returned home and put away the picnic supplies. "That was fun," Eli told Whit. "What should we do this afternoon? I'd like to take you to the diner for an early supper."

"That sounds good. Why don't we list crops we want to grow this spring? We can get with Mark and see what he wants to grow and make our supply orders. We are still a few weeks away from being able to plant, but I'd like to be ready."

"My mouth is watering already." Eli wrapped Whit in a hug. "We need to work on some jelly soon, too. The boys almost wiped us out of apple cinnamon while we were gone. Maybe we can get the supplies, and you can make some while I work on tilling your garden plot."

"I can do that. You are going to baby me after tomorrow, aren't you?"

"Probably, but not intentionally," Eli said.

"Please trust me to tell you what I can do," Whit replied. "I need to still feel a part of our home."

"I will. I'm sure you will remind me often," Eli said and kissed Whit.

Whit chuckled. "I want you to do something for me later this week. We need to let the hens into the garden to rid us of bugs before planting. They can enjoy a few juicy worms as dark as the soil looks."

"I am excited to see plants growing again," Eli admitted. "We can empty the compost bin to be tilled in, too."

"You are beginning to sound like a regular farmer," Whit teased.

"What can I say? I have a great teacher. Are you up for some coffee?"

"Sure. You start some, and I'll grab a notepad for our list."

"Corn and lots of it," Eli called out as she poured the first cup. "I am so spoiled on street corn and your creamed corn."

"I did notice the jars of creamed corn were the first to be emptied over the winter. Hopefully, we will plant some in all three plots to give us plenty. Mark can grow street corn, and we can focus on refilling our pantry."

†

"We need more okra this year, too," Eli said as they climbed into bed.

"Good Lord, are you still thinking about the garden?" Whit teased.

"I am so ready for some of our home-grown veggies."

"I hope you don't dream about them all night. We have to be up early in the morning."

"I've already got Mitch coming by on his way to school to feed the animals, and we can drop Cruz off before we leave. She and Tink are becoming good friends and enjoy spending time with Mark at the forge."

"So, wake up, shower, grab a coffee, and go?" Whit asked.

"Yes, we can stop for breakfast in Asheville before our appointment."

"I'm not sure I'll be able to eat," Whit replied.

"We will have a good lunch if you aren't up for breakfast."

"That may be safer all around." Whit smiled.

†

Eli closed the door behind Whit and opened a back door for Cruz. "Load up. You're spending the morning with Mark."

Cruz jumped into the back seat, excited to go for a ride.

Mark walked out to the truck for Cruz. "Good luck today, and I'll see you later."

"Thanks, Mark. We'll be back soon."

Eli pulled away and drove to Asheville.

Whit held her hand the entire trip.

"How's your stomach? Want some breakfast? We have time."

"Maybe some toast and apple juice. No more coffee. The acid has my belly rolling."

"That's easy enough to find." Eli pulled into a breakfast shop not far from the doctor's office.

Whit eyed the cinnamon rolls as they walked past the counter. "Maybe I'll change my mind and have one instead."

187

"Two cinnamon rolls and apple juice, please," Eli ordered.

"Those were delicious," Whit said when they finished eating. "Should we take some to go?"

Eli smiled when the waitress returned. "Will you box a dozen and add it to the bill?"

"Sure will." The waitress smiled.

†

Eli and Whit waited for the doctor in the treatment room. "There are a few things we need to check before we can get started. We need a blood test and ultrasound to ensure you are in the correct ovulation phase. We are on schedule, but I want to be positive."

The doctor looked at Eli. "Do you want to be present?"

"Yes, I do."

He looked at Whit. "Do you consent?"

"Yes, I want her by my side," Whit answered.

"I figured as much, but I have to ask by law. By the way, congratulations on the marriage. I see you are both sporting some new jewelry."

"Thank you," Whit replied. "We just got home from a honeymoon in the Outer Banks Sunday."

"Beautiful," the doctor said as the nurse drew a blood sample and he performed the ultrasound. "The ultrasound looks good, and I'll have the blood test results in just a few minutes. Relax, and I'll be back as soon as possible."

Eli finished wiping away the excess jelly from the ultrasound and took Whit's hand. "All clean again. That does remind me we need to get supplies for jelly."

"You are so not right, Eli Fortner." Whit chuckled.

"Well, that stuff is just like jelly." Eli shrugged. She was happy to hear Whit laugh. She was trying to keep her relaxed.

The doctor walked back into the room. "We are good to go if you're ready."

†

"Relax a few minutes before you get dressed."

Eli was surprised the procedure was done so quickly. "Any special treatment or precautions?"

"No marathons and limit physical activity the next few days. No lifting anything over ten pounds. Rest if you can, but I can bet you will be a challenging patient," he told Whit.

"My nephew graduates from high school in Montgomery in a few weeks. Any problem with the travel or possibly offshore fishing?"

"I don't see a problem with either of those as long as Whit feels good."

"I can always shop with Laura while you and the boys fish," Whit said.

"Trust Whit to tell you what she can and can't do. Have a great time, and I'll see you in a month."

"Thanks," Eli said as she picked up Whit's clothes.

"Oh, no hanky panky for a few days either," he teased Eli.

"Got it," Eli said with a blush.

She helped Whit get dressed, and they started for home.

†

Eli merged onto the interstate. "Will you stop that?" Whit asked.

"What?"

"Driving like an old lady. You never go this slow. Drive us home. I'm not a delicate piece of blown glass that will shatter if you hit a pothole."

"Yes, dear." Eli smiled and reached for Whit's hand.

They rode along in silence for a few minutes. "How did it feel? Was it painful?"

"No. Not at all," Whit answered. "It was so quick I hardly felt anything besides a little pressure."

"Good." Eli lifted her hand to her mouth and kissed it. "Love you."

"Love you more."

Eli shook her head. "Most."

†

"I'm hungry. Could you eat some livers and wings?" Whit asked.

"I will never pass on those. Do you want to call an order in?"

"Sure. Do you mind if I get enough for Mark?"

"Better make it a triple order of livers. Mitch will pout if we don't save him some."

"I'll call Mark and tell him not to eat lunch yet."

"That's good, and just place any order you want," Eli said.

"That's great news," Whit said while chatting with Mark. "Yes, I feel good, but you know your sister will keep me on the couch for a few days. I will go slow. We'll see you in about half an hour. Tell Mitch congratulations."

Whit looked at Eli. "Mitch had a final exam in one of his classes this morning and thinks he aced it. So he's already at home."

"Call a big order in for us then," Eli stated.

†

"We're heading home to stretch out on the couch," Eli said when they finished eating. "I'll be in the workshop tomorrow to work on more handles."

"I'll come down later and feed the animals, so you can keep an eye on Love Muffin to keep her out of trouble."

191

Whit laughed and punched Mitch in the arm. "I haven't heard you call me that for a long time."

"You sure don't punch like a girl," Mitch said, rubbing his arm.

"We still have a few handles if you need to take a few days off," Mark said.

"No, she won't," Whit said. "I can join her in the workshop so she can keep an eye on me. She's worse than I am about being cooped up inside."

"I've got a comfy chaise lounge you can stretch on if you want to join us at the forge," Mark offered. "Wonder boy has one other test, and he's done for the semester."

"That's great news," Whit said. "Have you enrolled in another semester yet?"

"I want to take the summer off from school and work with Dad. Maybe hike another short AT section with Brad if he survives the school year."

"Do you plan to transition him up here next year?" Eli asked.

"Laura and I are still discussing that. She wants him to finish there, but I'm not sold on the idea yet."

"You still have plenty of time to decide. I'll see you when you come down to feed the animals," Eli told Mitch.

"Call if you need anything," Mark said.

Whit climbed into the truck. "What about the cinnamon rolls?"

"I'll send half home with Mitch when he comes to feed."

"Gotcha," Whit said as she moved the bag from Cruz's prying nose.

†

Whit curled up in Eli's arms on the couch, and they fell asleep. They had been up early, and while it was exciting, the day had also been emotionally draining. Cruz rushed to the door when she heard a noise on the porch.

Mitch had stomped his boots off on the porch before entering the cabin. "I'm sorry I woke you," he told them as he stepped inside. "You did say to check in, though."

"That's okay. It was a long day, and we drifted off."

"Dad has gone for pizza and should be here in a few minutes. Everyone is fed in the barn, so these house critters need to be fed."

"I can get them," Eli said as she turned to slide into her boots.

"I got them. You can set the table with fine china. You have any Dew?"

"I think there's a couple and some fresh tea in there."

"Dew for me, please," Mitch answered.

"The prom is tomorrow night, isn't it?" Whit asked.

"Yeah. I picked up my tux after school today."

"Will you want some help getting gussied up?" Eli asked. "I can send Whit up if you do."

193

"Naw, Dad said he would help me."

"Be sure to send us some pics of you and Jessie."

"I will," Mitch promised.

†

"Do you have any plans for the weekend after graduation?" Eli asked Mark and Mitch.

"To drive back here on Sunday," Mark said.

"Would you mind a side trip?"

"Depends on where it takes us," Mitch said.

"We were thinking a weekend in Destin after graduation would be nice. We could do some offshore fishing, and Laura could shop the outlets."

Mark looked at Whit. "Are you going to be up for that?"

"If not, I'll shop with Laura," Whit answered. "However, I want to make it known upfront that if the procedure is successful, I will not be treated like something fragile."

Mitch's eyebrows shot up. "I read that loud and clear."

Mark smiled. "You may need to remind us repeatedly, but we will try our best. Please know that it's only because we love you and want to take care of you."

"I know that, but I don't want to feel like I'm a burden to anyone. Women have babies every day."

"Not our women," Mitch said. "You're special to us and could never be a burden."

"Thank you both. It means a lot to me."

Mitch shot Eli a grin. "I sure hope you can bake brownies if Whit gets morning sickness."

"I was baking them before you were born, even if they aren't as good as Whit's."

"I assume Brad will be here over the summer. He got pretty good at baking last summer."

"Much to his mother's chagrin." Mark chuckled. "He's constantly baking stuff she's trying to avoid."

"Do you want me to come down and feed for you the next few days?" Mitch offered.

"No, I think we've got that handled. We need you to come up with a list of vegetables you want to plant. Whit's getting an ordering list together. We plan to let the hens do some free-range foraging in our plot for a week or so."

"I can't wait until we can plant." Mark rubbed his hands together.

"I can imagine you and Eli both in the garden measuring growth daily," Whit teased.

"That is a possibility," Mark agreed.

"Thanks for the pizza. Mitch, will you drop the boxes in the compost bin for me? I almost forgot." Eli handed Mark a container with six cinnamon rolls. "They were so good at breakfast we brought some home."

"Thanks. I know what we'll be snacking on later." Mark grinned.

CHAPTER TWELVE

Whit and Eli pulled into the casino parking lot to check into the hotel. Mitch had offered his bed, but Eli told them she'd already booked a room for two nights at the casino.

"What time are we supposed to meet for dinner tonight?" Whit asked.

"At six. Why?" Eli placed their suitcase on the stand. "You want to gamble a bit?"

Whit nodded. "If that's okay. I've only been in one casino before."

"Sure, let me unpack, and we will go. Our clothes are all set for tomorrow, so we have three hours before we meet them at the restaurant."

"That will give us time to play a bit, and if we're not lucky, we can kick back and relax."

"You do realize you are talking to Eli Fortner, the luckiest woman alive?"

"Because you won the lottery?" Whit asked.

Eli shook her head. "No, because I hit the jackpot with you."

"That is so sweet." Whit pulled Eli in for a kiss.

"Come on, let's play," Eli said, leading her to the elevator.

They walked into the casino and started looking for machines that looked interesting. They found two on a back wall, several chairs apart. "Good luck," Eli said.

"You, too," Whit answered.

Eli slipped a fifty-dollar bill into a machine and began playing. She hit a few small pots and stayed even with what she had spent.

"Come on, come on. Yes!" Eli heard Whit call out.

Lights began flashing, and a siren blared as she hit a large jackpot. Eli smiled at her. "How much?"

"I don't know. It's at eight thousand and still growing."

"Damn, you go, Whit."

Eli cashed out of her machine and walked over to Whit as a casino worker approached. "Congratulations. That's the highest payout so far today."

Eli's eyes drifted to the payout line. "Ten thousand? That is fantastic."

"How would you like the payout?" the attendant asked.

Whit looked at Eli. "We are guests here. Can you bank it here until we check out Saturday morning?" Eli asked.

"We indeed can. I will need you to follow me to fill out some paperwork. A win this size, and Uncle Sam wants his cut immediately."

"You want me to join you?" Eli asked.

"No. I've got this. Keep playing, and I'll be back soon."

Eli returned to her seat and placed the paper receipt into the machine with her balance of a little over fifty dollars. She was so happy for Whit that she didn't realize she was hitting small pots. Her fingers pressed the button without thought. When she looked up and saw her balance, Eli cashed out quickly to prevent exceeding the limit for immediate tax payout. The ticket was printed out for two thousand dollars. She slipped it into her pocket and placed a twenty in her machine.

Eli built up the winnings to a thousand before the machine started taking it back. At nine hundred dollars, she cashed out. She placed the second ticket in her pocket. Eli contemplated adding another twenty to the machine when

Whit returned, her smile beaming. "Hey, lucky lady," Eli said. "All taken care of?"

"Yes, ma'am. Do we have a little more time?"

"We have plenty of time. Go hit another big one," Eli teased.

"I probably shouldn't, but I'll play this dollar machine behind you. I'll only play fifty, and once that's gone, I'm done."

"If you're feeling it, play on, baby girl." Eli settled on the seat next to Whit and placed a ten in the machine. Why not?

On Eli's second spin, she won fifty free spins. "Here we go." Eli sat back on the seat and waved a server down. "Do you want something to drink?"

"A bottle of water and a coke, please," Eli requested. She watched her two-dollar investment grow to two hundred with thirty spins left. "Keep growing, baby," Eli said as she paid the waitress for the drinks.

"Wow, you've got a nice one growing." The waitress pointed at Eli's machine.

The balance grew on nearly every spin until the last spin stopped at just under three thousand. "That's it for me." Eli sipped her drink and watched Whit. She was having so much fun she was almost disappointed when Whit looked at her.

"I guess we'd better get going before we're late."

"I'm going to the valet station to get the truck pulled around, then I need to cash out. I'll be right back."

Whit played the last of her fifty and was surprised when Eli came over to her.

"Let's cash out and go."

Whit only had a small ticket to cash out, so she watched Eli feed the machine one ticket, then another, and one final one. "That's almost six thousand dollars," Whit whispered.

"I know," Eli whispered, handing Whit a stack of one hundred dollar bills. "Stick those in your bag, please."

Whit tucked them away as Eli slipped the rest into her pocket.

†

They pulled up at Mitch's favorite sushi place, and Mark pulled in next to them. "Dinner is on me," she told Mark. "Whit and I both did well at the casino tonight."

"Why are you here then?" Mark asked.

"To eat with the best family in the world," Eli answered. "Hey, Laura."

Brad started to hold his arms out to hug Whit and stopped. "Go ahead, Whit won't break," Eli told him.

Eli pulled him into a hug. "About time for a cut, isn't it?" she ruffled his hair.

Brad shook his head. "Dad is letting me grow it back out. I've got all my grades up and will make it to my senior year."

"Congratulations."

"Well done, Brad," Whit added.

"Order us some good sushi," Eli told Mitch.

They ate a delicious meal, and Eli pulled out a stack of one hundred dollar bills to pay for the check.

"I guess you were lucky today," Mitch said.

"I'm small fry compared to Love Muffin. She hit a big one."

"How much?"

"Ten thousand, but Uncle Sam will get his cut off the top," Whit answered.

"Damn. How much did you win, Aunt Eli?" Brad asked.

"Almost six, but mine were in smaller payouts, so Uncle Sam didn't bite me."

"Are you going back tonight?" Mitch asked.

"I don't think so," Whit said. "I think we should count our blessings and be done."

"Probably not a bad idea. So many get greedy and play it right back to the casino," Laura reported.

†

"Everyone is off tomorrow for the big event, so come out when you're ready. We can have some Mexican after the ceremony. My treat, though," Mark said.

"That sounds good. We're all set for Destin and can check in at eleven tomorrow. Our fishing trip is scheduled at seven Sunday morning," Eli said.

"I am so glad I'm going to shop. No way I'm getting up that early to come back smelling like fish," Laura said.

"How are you feeling?" Mitch asked. "You're fishing with us, right?"

"Yeah, I feel good right now." Whit smiled. "I don't think that will change that quick."

"We'll sleep in a bit and come out just after lunch." Eli hugged Mark.

"Good luck with that," Mitch said.

"Okay, so maybe until seven." Eli grinned.

"We'll be ready anytime you show up," Mark said. "Drive careful."

†

After dropping the truck at the valet, Eli and Whit returned to the casino. "Dinner was great, but I could go for something sweet," Whit said.

"Let's go see what we can find. We can scout a spot for breakfast, too," Eli said.

Eli pointed to an éclair. "I'll take two of those and a carton of milk."

Whit scanned the baked selection. "May I have two of those cinnamon rolls and milk?"

"That's my favorite, too," the woman working the counter replied. "For here or to go?"

"Let's take them to the room," Whit said.

"To go, please."

"I'll add forks and napkins. Would you like straws or plastic cups for the milk?"

"Straws will be fine," Eli answered, giving her the money for their goods.

"Congratulation on your big win, too, by the way," the woman told Whit.

"Thanks," Whit replied. She wasn't sure how the lady knew about her jackpot, but she figured out the answer when they entered the lobby to catch the elevator. Hanging on the wall was a poster with her holding an oversized check with her winnings.

"I didn't realize I was accompanied by such a celebrity," Eli teased.

"Ha, did you notice it was the amount before Uncle Sam took his cut?"

"I did, but it's still a great return on your bet."

"I am not complaining at all," Whit said.

"Stand by it and let me snap a photo to send to Mitch. He'll get a kick out of it."

Whit smiled, and Eli snapped the pic.

"Got it," Eli said and sent it to Mitch.

They took their baked goods out to their balcony overlooking the river. "This is a great spot. Cheers." Eli lifted her milk bottle to Whit.

Whit lifted hers and took a bite of a cinnamon roll. "Oh my goodness, this is heavenly."

"As good as Asheville?"

"No, but close enough to satisfy me until we go back."

"That river sure sounds peaceful, doesn't it?"

"It does, but it makes me miss home," Whit admitted.

"We'll be home in a few days. I'll admit, I miss it, too," Eli said as she picked up their trash.

†

Mitch was handsome when he removed the cap and gown. Laura beamed with pride when he handed her his diploma. "I know there were plenty of days you never thought I'd make it this far, but here we are."

"I'm so proud of you, Son," Laura said.

"Thanks, Mom."

Mark held out his hand. "I'm proud of you in so many ways," Mark said and pulled Mitch into a hug.

"Way to go, Bro," Brad said.

"Your turn next," Mitch told Brad. "If I can do it, so can you."

Brad nodded his head. "I will. I know I've got to clean up my act if I plan to walk."

"You got this." Mitch bumped shoulders with him. Let's go eat," Mitch said. "I'll ride with Aunt Eli in case we get separated."

†

"I think we'll roll out early in the morning," Eli said. "Maybe grab some groceries for breakfast and snacks."

"We can eat some seafood fresh from the Gulf," Mark said. "Hopefully, we will have freshly caught fish for supper on Sunday. I haven't been fishing in years."

"I think we'll have fun," Eli said.

"Would riding with Aunt Eli in the morning be okay?" Mitch asked.

"Okay with you, Eli and Whit?" Mark asked.

"Fine with us. Do you want me to pick you up?"

"Naw, I'll drop him off while Laura and Brad wake up," Mark teased.

"Okay, we'll see you in the morning then," Eli said.

Eli opened the door for Whit. "Your sweet tooth acting up tonight? There's a Krispy Kreme donut shop on our way."

"Never had them. Good with me as long as they have cinnamon rolls." Whit laughed.

"They have a bit of everything," Eli said. "I've seen them in some grocery stores, but there's nothing like pulling up to see the 'Hot Doughnuts' sign lit."

"Let's go," Whit said.

†

"What did you think of your first Krispy Kreme adventure?"

"You weren't kidding when you said they had a bit of everything. The cinnamon twists were good, but the freshly cooked glazed melted in my mouth."

Eli smiled. "They have them in Destin, too, so maybe we'll pick up a couple dozen."

"I bet Mitch and Brad could eat a dozen alone," Whit said.

"That's a good possibility."

"What time do you think Mitch will show up in the morning?" Whit asked while they drove to the casino.

"He's used to getting up early, so I'd bet by seven," Eli said.

"We must go to the cashier tomorrow to pick up your winnings and eat breakfast."

"Why don't I invite Mitch and Mark to breakfast?" Whit said.

"Go for it," Eli said as they approached the casino.

Whit chuckled. "Mitch says they will be here between six thirty and seven."

207

CHAPTER THIRTEEN

The weekend in Destin went by quickly. They caught enough fish for supper and had some to take home. Mark and Mitch grilled them to perfection. Whit was helping Laura in the kitchen while Eli and the boys shared beers on the deck.

"This was a great idea," Mark said. "I hope y'all enjoyed it as much as me."

"Lots of good memories," Eli said. "I haven't been offshore fishing since Dad was alive."

"I've only been once or twice. I can't believe Whit outfished us all and reeled in that monster grouper," Mark said. "That smile on her face was priceless."

"It will certainly be hanging on our walls soon," Eli said. "Will you and Mitch stay an extra day or two?"

"No. We talked about it but decided we'd go home. Orders are piling up again."

"That's a good problem to have, Mark," Eli said.

"Yes, it is. At this rate, we'll need to make a junkyard run for more springs."

Eli chuckled and lifted her hands. "I have two good hands this time."

"Maybe we'll take a run next weekend."

"Sounds good. I think Whit and I will put that garden tub to use upstairs. We'll see you for breakfast?"

"I think we've got enough eggs to have a decent breakfast," Mark said.

"That works for me," Eli said. "Goodnight, guys. Thanks for cooking a great supper."

"It was good," Mitch said. "See you in the morning. Love ya."

"Love y'all, too," Eli answered. She walked inside and hugged Whit from behind as she talked with Laura.

"Would you mind if I steal my wife? We need to try out that garden tub upstairs." Eli kissed Whit's neck.

"That does sound good," Whit replied.

Eli spun her around and took her hand to lead her upstairs. "We'll see you in the morning for breakfast."

"Have a good night," Laura said.

†

Whit had already left the bed the following day when Eli woke. She could hear the shower running in the bathroom. She relieved her bladder and slipped into the shower with Whit. "Are you okay?"

"Yeah, I woke up nauseated this morning and decided to shower to see if that would help."

"Maybe a bagel or some dry toast will help," Eli said.

"I hope so," Whit said with a weak smile.

They dressed and packed their bags. "I'll get Mitch to come up and get them," Eli said. "Let's go see what Mark's dishing up."

They walked down, and Mitch stood in front of the toaster, making toast. "One slice naked, please," Eli requested.

Mark was handing Laura the milk, and Eli saw a look pass between them.

"You a bit queasy this morning?" Mark asked with concern.

"Yeah, my stomach woke me up this morning," Whit answered.

Again a look passed between Mark and Laura. This time Mark grinned when he looked at Whit. "Congratulations."

"What?" Eli asked.

"It sounds like classic morning sickness," Laura said.

Eli looked at Whit. "We're pregnant?"

"At least I am," Whit said with a laugh.

Whit noticed the drop in Eli's face when she made the comment. "I think we are, but you can have this part."

"I would if I could, baby," Eli said.

"Hopefully, it won't last long and will stay mild," Laura replied. "Get ready for the cravings to hit."

Eli burst out laughing. "Cinnamon buns. She can't get enough of them."

Whit nodded. "That's true, but even that doesn't sound good right now."

Mitch handed her a piece of dry toast on a plate. "One naked slice."

"Thanks, Mitch."

"Could I talk you into carrying our bags out to the truck?" Eli asked.

"Sure thing. Let me finish the toast."

"Go ahead, and I'll keep it going until you return." Eli handed him the keys. "What's on the menu this morning?"

"I'm making some SOS using the leftover milk, bread, and lunchmeat."

"That's cruel," Whit said. "I love your SOS."

"Do you want to try some before I add the seasoning?" Mark asked.

"I want to, but I'll pass for now. I'll take you up on some as soon as this morning sickness ends. With cinnamon rolls," Whit teased.

†

Whit dozed off and on during the ride home, but the nausea was held at bay. Eli stopped for gas and went inside for a ginger ale and saltine crackers. "These should help if your stomach is still queasy."

"Thanks. I'm sorry I'm napping and not much company on this trip."

"Darling, I traveled solo for years, so it's not a problem. I'd rather you rest and relax."

Whit frowned. "I still feel guilty. I preach to you about not being fragile, and yet here I am."

Eli reached over and took Whit's hand. "Your body is going through changes, and it needs rest. Listen to what your body tells you."

When they were thirty minutes from home, Whit looked at Eli. "Will you stop at a drugstore?"

"Sure. Do you need something?"

"It may be premature, but I'd like to do a pregnancy test. Will you go in and get one?"

"I sure will." Eli smiled.

†

Eli walked inside straight to the pharmacy section when they stopped at the store.

"May I help you?" a young pharmacist asked.

"I need to know the most accurate pregnancy test," she explained.

The young woman walked through the door and escorted Eli to the correct aisle. "This one comes highly rated."

"Thanks. We think my wife is pregnant and want to test before returning to the doctor."

"Can't wait, huh?" The woman smiled.

"We're just a bit excited," Eli said. "May I check out back here?"

"Sure, let's get you set." She rang up Eli's purchase and slipped it into a bag. "Good luck." She smiled.

"Thank you," Eli said. Eli was so excited she felt like she was floating. *Who knew buying a pregnancy test could be so exciting?* She climbed back into the truck and handed the bag to Whit. "Here we go."

Whit read the instructions on the package several times as they drove the last few miles home.

"Is it okay to stop by for Cruz on the way in?"

"Sure. We can thank Carol and Julia for watching over the zoo."

"We do have quite the collection."

"I wouldn't trade any of them." Whit smiled as she took Eli's hand. "I love our family."

✝

Eli pulled up at Whit's cabin to find Carol and Julia sitting on the porch surrounded by animals. Cruz rushed to

Eli, and Oscar and Walter began purring as soon as Whit bent down.

"Welcome home," Carol said. "Everyone's been fed for the night. We weren't sure when you'd make it home."

"We should have called," Eli said.

"Nonsense, I haven't laughed so hard in ages as we watched those kittens play. I get a kick from them coming down that slide, and Molly is quite the character. We fed Tink and emptied her litter box. I think she's missing Mitch."

"They shouldn't be but an hour or two behind us," Eli said.

"Was it a good trip?" Julia asked.

"It was." Whit chuckled and pulled out her phone. "I was lucky this trip." She showed them the picture of her casino win and the giant grouper she caught. "I caught the biggest fish, too."

"Wow, maybe you two should vacation more often," Carol suggested.

"We had a great time and did well at the casino. Mitch graduated, and we had a fun time at the beach."

"Did it make you miss home?" Carol asked.

Eli grinned. "Yes, this one. It was a nice getaway, but we are ready to be in our own bed."

"Well, go and get unloaded. We can catch up later."

"Dinner at our place tomorrow night?" Eli asked.

"Sounds great."

"Thank you both for caring for our crew," Whit said. "Boys, are you coming home or going to visit for a while yet?"

Oscar and Walter pranced across the yard and headed for the bridge.

"I guess that answers that." Julia laughed.

"We'll see you tomorrow," Eli said. "Come over when you're ready."

"Will do," Carol said. "The mail is on the table."

"Thanks," Eli said, opening the door for Whit and Cruz. "Let's go home, girls," she said when she climbed inside.

Eli dropped Whit and the bags on the porch before she parked the truck. "I've got the suitcases if you're ready to test."

"This one only takes three minutes," Whit said. "I thought for sure we'd be pacing for fifteen minutes."

"Three will still seem an eternity," Eli said. She picked up the suitcases and carried them upstairs behind Whit. She placed them on the end of the bed and sat, waiting for Whit to return from the bathroom.

Whit held the test and started the timer on her watch before sitting next to Eli. It was barely two minutes before the pink lines began to form. They watched as the lines grew thicker. Eli turned to Whit. "You will make the best mom a child could have."

"Correction, we will make the best moms," Whit told Eli.

Eli sat staring at the results for several minutes. "We are going to be parents." She finally grinned.

"Yes, we are." Whit leaned into Eli and kissed her. "I forgot to bring my ginger ale and crackers up when we came. Will you get them?"

"Sure, I'll be right back."

Whit laid the test on the nightstand beside the bed and took a picture. She was tempted to send it to Mark but decided Eli should share the news. She plugged in her phone and walked to the dresser. When they went, she had forgotten to wear the amulet to Mitch's graduation. Eli was walking into the room when Whit picked up the necklace. It flared and glowed brightly as she slipped it over her head.

"I've never seen it that bright," Eli said as she placed the drink on the table. "Mine is glowing, but nothing like yours."

"I can't believe I forgot it when we went to Montgomery. I felt naked without it."

"It seems delighted to be around your neck again," Eli said. "Are you ready to dress for bed?"

"Yes, please, I want one of your sleep shirts," Whit said.

After changing into nightshirts, Eli pulled back the covers. When Whit climbed into the bed, Eli couldn't resist picking up the test to look at the two pink lines. Her face was beginning to hurt from smiling so hard.

"Come hold me," Whit requested.

Eli laid the test back on the table and walked around the bed. She climbed in and reached for Whit. "We're going to be parents. I didn't ever think I'd be saying that. Thank you."

"Thank you for loving me," Whit said.

Eli kissed her goodnight and chuckled. "Moms," she whispered.

†

Whit snuggled into Eli. She didn't have to look at the gem around her neck to know it was glowing. She could feel the warmth on her skin and felt her body fill with energy. Somehow she knew that her morning sickness would disappear now that she wore the amulet. It was somehow protecting her and the child she now carried. Whit dreamed of her mother and grandparents and woke feeling refreshed and energized.

CHAPTER FOURTEEN

Whit was watching Eli sleep. *She looks so peaceful. We'd better get as much sleep as possible before the baby arrives.* Whit didn't realize she laughed out loud until Eli startled awake.

"Is everything okay?" Eli looked at her with panic in her eyes.

"I'm sorry. I didn't realize my inner laughter was so loud," Whit apologized.

"That's okay, but what's so funny?" Eli asked. "The sun is barely up."

"I watched you sleep so peacefully, and I laughed, thinking we better get all the sleep we can over the next few months. I didn't mean to wake you."

"That's okay. I was scared something was wrong."

"Quite the opposite. I feel great and energized this morning. You may think me crazy, but I think the amulet has something to do with it."

"Not crazy at all. Especially the way it flared when you picked it up last night. We both know it's shown some healing powers in the past."

"I want some of Mark's SOS. Do you think he's up and will cook me some?"

"There's only one way to find out." Eli picked up her phone and dialed Mark. "Your sister-in-law wants SOS. Do you have the ingredients to make her some?"

They could hear Mark chuckling. "I sure do. We even stopped last night to purchase some cinnamon rolls, so come on up when you're ready."

"We'll be there soon," Whit called out.

"Okay, I'll get Mitch up and get started."

"Thanks. Love you, Mark," Eli said.

"Love you, too. Get your butts up here."

"See you in a few. Bye." Eli turned to Whit. "Do I have time to dress and brush my hair and teeth?"

"Yes, silly. Just don't primp," Whit teased.

"Wow. Okay. Let me hop right to it." Eli kissed Whit and left the bed.

Whit dressed and joined Eli in the bathroom. "Do you want to feed the animals on the way up?"

"That probably won't hurt and will take just a few minutes. You can get the Gator while I feed the critters. Have you given any thought to supper tonight with Carol and Julia?"

"I thought I would come back after dinner and make a couple trays of lasagna while you work with the guys."

Eli stopped mid-stroke with her toothbrush. "You feel that good?"

Whit nodded. "Yeah, I do."

"That's fantastic." Eli kissed Whit. "I'll see you in the barn in a few. Come on, Cruz," Eli called.

†

Mark and Mitch were busy in the kitchen when they arrived. Mark stirred the mixture in the frying pan while Mitch made toast. "There's coffee in the pot and cinnamon rolls on the table if you want a snack. It won't be much longer for breakfast."

"Do you guys have plans for dinner tonight?" Whit asked. "I'm going to make some lasagna. Julia and Carol are coming for dinner, and we'd like you to join us."

"I love your lasagna," Mitch said.

"Is there something we can bring?" Mark asked.

"More of these if you have them," Whit teased as she took a bite of the pastry.

When they were all seated around the table, Whit looked at Eli. "I believe Eli has something to share with y'all."

Eli nearly choked on the bite of food in her mouth. She swallowed and drank some juice. "Are you trying to kill me?" she teased.

"Hardly," Whit replied.

"Enough already. Tell us the news," Mark grumbled.

"You are going to be an uncle," she told Mark, "and you a cousin."

Mark grinned. "You're pregnant?"

"According to the test she took last night, yes." Eli beamed with excitement.

"We'll confirm by the end of the week when I go for my next appointment." Whit radiated as she told them the news.

"Congratulations, you two," Mark said.

"Thanks. We're just a bit excited," Eli replied.

"I can tell. You never call me before the sun comes up for breakfast. How's your stomach this morning?" He smiled at Whit.

"Ravenous," she replied after swallowing. "No nausea this morning. It was weird when we got home last night. I had forgotten to wear my amulet when we left to come and watch you graduate. When I picked it up and put it on last night, it flared and was bright."

Mark lifted his hand. "I can attest to the gem's healing powers. I haven't moved this well for years."

"That's pretty awesome."

"I look forward to having a little one around to spoil," Mitch said.

"It will be good practice for you if you want to have kids someday," Eli said.

"That's true, but years down the road." Mitch grinned and poured more juice.

"What's the plan for today?" Eli asked Mark.

"Mitch and I will work on a few blades to go with your beautiful handles. We are getting a bit low on wood, so we may need to ride up to the top."

"Why don't you let us do that?" Whit suggested. "We can gather some limbs, and Eli can start on them while I create the lasagna for tonight."

"That works for me," Mark answered. "I bet there are still limbs down from the winter storm that came through."

"Probably," Eli answered.

"I can put together some egg salad for lunch. The ladies were busy laying while we were gone," Whit added.

"Now we're talking," Eli said.

"I guess we have a deal then. Dessert?" she asked Mitch.

"Will you make a coconut cake?"

"Only because I love you," Whit replied.

"I love you, too," Mitch said. "Are we still going to the junkyard this weekend?"

"I'd like to," Mark answered. "Do you have plans?"

"Evan will be home, and we thought we might do some fishing."

"I can go help your dad," Eli offered.

"Nonsense. Tell Evan to come out early, and y'all can fish when we return. With three of us working, it won't take long."

"That works for me, and I'm sure Evan won't mind."

"I'll go ahead and whip up a batch of hush puppy mix to go with the fish you catch. If you get a bunch, Whit and I can take some filets to Mr. Henry and Miss Clara with some of the mix."

"He's even mentioned coming out to fish," Whit reminded her.

"Why don't we go ahead and invite them out then?" Eli said. "Mr. Henry can fish with y'all, and later, we can feast together."

"Oh, yeah. Miss Clara's baked beans and potato salad are the bomb," Mitch said.

"I bet Julia and Carol would join us and bring some salads or desserts," Eli said.

"Julia's banana pudding is off the chain. Almost as good as Mom's, but don't tell her I said that."

"Speaking of your mom…when will Brad be coming up for the summer?"

"Another week of peace and quiet," Mitch answered.

Eli smiled. "I got an email this morning. Your tiny house will be delivered next week. Have you given thought to furniture? Whit and I thought we would use some of our gambling money to help you get set up."

"Really? I don't have to go to second-hand stores like Mom and Dad?"

"I think we can afford a few pieces. It's a tiny house, so you can't go crazy. We'll need to get you stocked up for groceries and other supplies, too," Eli said. "Let's look at some furniture tonight to get it ordered. I'll let you and Whit create the shopping list. You know she's the queen of start-ups," Eli teased.

"Will you help me?" Mitch asked Whit.

"Of course I will. I love making lists." Whit laughed.

"Are you ready to find some wood?" Eli asked. "You can call Mr. Henry later if we can't catch him today when he delivers."

"Thanks for breakfast. It was delicious," Whit told Mark.

"You're very welcome. I'm glad you had an appetite. Congratulations on the good news."

Whit stood and hugged him. "Thank you."

"Let's roll," Eli said. "I'll need to return to the workshop for a chainsaw."

†

Eli picked up the chainsaw when they parked at the top of the trail. "You up for a short hike to the shelter to see if we can get more hickory and beech?"

"Sure," Whit answered.

They hit the jackpot, and Eli cut the branches into sections small enough to transport. She handed Whit the chainsaw and a few pieces of wood. Whit lifted an eyebrow, and Eli added another short log. "I can come back for another load."

They were approaching the shelter when they saw a hiker coming. Whit smiled at the fast-moving man. "Timeless?" she asked.

"Star Child?" he asked.

"Yes, how are you?" Whit was shocked to see one of her friends from the Appalachian Trail. "I'm sorry, this is my wife, Eli," Whit said. "We met Timeless on the trail last summer."

"Nice to meet you," he said. "Can I help?"

"There's another small stack you could grab," Whit said. "Do you have time to stop for some supplies? I can heat something for a hot meal and send you on your way."

"That sounds great." He followed Whit's direction and returned quickly with the stack of wood.

"Our Gator is just down the trail a bit," Eli explained.

"How have you been?" Whit asked.

"Crazy busy, so I needed a break to hike. How are you? Congrats on getting married."

"Thanks," Whit answered. "We've been doing well. Maverick and his dad have moved up, and Jester will be here in a week for summer break."

"I know he'll be excited. Will y'all hike again this summer?"

"The boys have been discussing it, but I won't be able to go this year."

He cocked his head.

"I'm pregnant." Whit grinned.

"Well, damn. Congratulations. That's great news."

They dumped the wood into the bed of the Gator.

"Hop in," Eli said. "It's not far. She looked at Whit. "Call Mitch and get him to come down for a few. Tell him we have a surprise."

"Will do." Whit called him, and Mitch promised to meet them in a few minutes.

"We've got a laundry room and separate shower building if you'd like to drop some clothes into the wash and take a hot shower."

"You're going to spoil me." He smiled.

Cruz heard the Gator returning and rushed over to follow them home. "My daughter, Cruz," Eli said as she pulled over to the laundry room. "The shower and laundry are there."

"Come over to the cabin when you finish showering. Some chicken and dumplings good for you?" Whit asked. "We've got some trail rations you can pick out, too."

"Thank you so much. I won't be long."

"Take whatever time you need," Whit answered. When they returned to the cabin, Whit asked Eli to put a dozen eggs on to boil while she pulled some frozen chicken and dumplings from the freezer and a can of biscuits. "Timeless is a physician from California. He hikes the AT to relieve stress and walks fast, straight through, with very few stops. I hope you didn't mind me inviting him here."

"Goodness no," Eli said. "I'm glad you recognized him."

"I want to send a few boiled eggs with him. He can eat those on the run and they will be good protein."

"What else do you think he will take?" Eli asked.

"I have no clue. I thought we could open the pantry and offer him some snacks. Probably trail mix and maybe some cookies. He tends to travel light."

Eli heard boots on the front porch and looked out the window to see Mark and Mitch. "Come on in she called out."

"It looks like you got a good load of wood," Mitch said. "Did you need us to unload it for you?"

Whit laughed. "You're never going to believe who we ran into on the trail."

"Smokey the bear?" Mitch teased.

"Timeless," she said.

"You're kidding me?"

"Nope, he's in the shower now, and I'm heating up some chicken and dumplings for him. I knew you'd want to

227

see him, and you know he won't stay long. Only to eat, shower and wash his clothes, and he'll be gone again."

"Is he the one that practically runs the trail? A doctor from California or somewhere?" Mark asked.

"See, he listens sometimes," Mitch teased.

"Yes, he is," Whit replied.

"Will you put those canned biscuits in the oven for me?" Whit asked Eli. "She's boiling our eggs for egg salad, and I'll give him some to take."

"I think I'll put another half dozen on to boil, and you can send those with him."

"What can we do?" Mark said.

"Relax for a few until he gets here," Whit said. "Have you gotten much done this morning?"

"We were just about to start a new blade when you called," Mitch replied.

A soft knock on the door alerted them to Timeless' presence. "That shower was heavenly," he said. "I skipped out on laundry. I'm good for a few days." He looked at Mitch. "Have you gotten taller?"

"Maybe an inch or two," Mitch replied. "I've graduated high school and work with Dad when I'm not in mechanic school."

Mark chimed in. "We have a small forge where we make custom knives, and Mitch makes small Viking axes."

"Take a seat at the table. Mitch, will you get him something to drink?"

"Soda, milk, juice, or water?"

"I would love a glass of milk," he answered.

"Your food is almost heated. Eli is boiling some eggs you can take with you, and you can hit the pantry for whatever you can fit in your pack."

"Thanks so much. My trail mix is running low."

"We've got plenty, some cookies, nuts, and meat sticks if you want," Eli said.

"I knew you said you were from North Carolina, but I never dreamed I'd run into you again," he said.

"We were gathering limbs to fashion into handles for these two." Whit nodded toward Mitch and Mark.

"Would it be possible to see what you're doing in the forge?" he asked.

Eli could see Mitch's chest puff out with pride. "That can be arranged. It's on the way back up the mountain."

Whit placed the bowl of steaming food in front of him with the biscuits as Eli cooled the eggs. "Can you take six eggs?"

"That would be great. Those are easy to eat on the run."

"That's exactly what Whit said." Eli grinned.

"This is delicious," Timeless said.

"She's a great cook," Mitch said. "How did the trail look nearby? Is any trail maintenance needed?

"The shelter just before this one has several broken boards. It looks like a limb came down on it during the winter."

"We had some snow, so that doesn't surprise me. We'll hike over and make repairs when Brad makes it up here. I know exactly which one you're talking about."

"Is that your crown shelter?" Eli teased.

"It is indeed," Mitch replied. He looked at Timeless. "Brad and I did some hiking with some brothers from Georgia. The oldest had some crown royal, which wasn't a pleasant experience."

"He couldn't eat fish for about a month," Whit remembered.

"Yeah, not my best decision, but a good lesson learned the hard way."

Timeless smiled at Mitch. "Those are usually the ones that stick with us the longest."

"Are you going all the way to Springer?" Whit asked.

"Yeah, I figured a few more hard days, and I should be close. You're welcome to bunk here if you need some sleep," Eli said.

"Thanks, but there's plenty of daylight left. I should make two more shelters before I stop for the night."

Eli raised her eyes. "That's a good ten miles."

"Easy ones, though," Timeless said. "I've done this section many times."

Whit packed the remaining biscuits while Eli placed six eggs in a Ziplock bag when he finished the meal. "Come take a look to see what else you can carry."

He picked out some trail mix, cookies, and jerky strips. "Could I ask for a roll of toilet paper?"

Whit chuckled. "Absolutely." She walked down the hall and grabbed two rolls. "Can you pack two?"

"I'll make it work," Timeless said as he packed the items in his backpack. "Thank you for the hospitality and the food. It was good seeing Whit and the boys and meeting you and Mark."

Eli asked, "Would you use a walking stick?"

"You made the ones these guys had? Heck yeah," he said.

"Come pick out one that fits you." Eli led him to the workshop, and he picked out a beautiful stick.

"This will travel many miles with me," he promised.

Eli smiled. "I hope you will stop by next time you hike the trail. You are more than welcome."

"Thanks. I will remember that."

"Are you ready to check out the forge before you go?" Mitch asked.

"Please," Timeless answered.

"We'll see you two for lunch," Eli said.

"Thanks again," he said, following Mitch and Mark up the trail.

✝

"He was an interesting character," Eli said after they left. "Do you need help inside?"

"Nope, I'm good. Are you going to unload and start some handles?"

"Yes, if you don't mind."

"Not at all. Do you need something to drink?"

"I'm okay, but I may come for one once I've unloaded."

"Love you," Whit said.

Eli watched her walk across the yard and slipped her gloves on. She took the saw back inside, then began to stack the wood beside her workbench." They had harvested more than she thought after looking at the stack. *That will keep me busy for a few days.*

†

Mitch gave Timeless the tour of the forge. "That was a brilliant idea to use this cave," he said.

"Whit and Eli's idea," Mark said.

Timeless looked over the blades and axes they were working on. "I'd love to have one of these trail knives."

"These are sold already, but here's my card. Let me know when you're home, and we'll set one aside for you from our next batch. If you lose the card, just look up Cast Iron Forge. That's the name of our business."

"I should be home in a couple of weeks. I'll drop you an email and set up payment."

"Sounds great. It was a pleasure to meet you. Both of my knuckleheads talk about you."

"Nice to meet you, too. You're raising two good young men." He shook Mark's hand and turned to Mitch. "Get back on the trail when you can."

"I will," Mitch replied. "Safe journeys."

Timeless nodded and started up the trail at a quick pace.

"He was a nice guy," Mark said.

"Yeah, I'm glad Whit and Eli ran into him. It was good to see him."

"Are you ready to get back to work?" Mark asked.

"I'm waiting on you." Mitch chuckled.

†

After supper, they sat around the fire pit and chatted with Julia and Carol. Mark and Mitch had left to shower and prepare for the next day. Eli worked on a walking stick as they relaxed. Carol noticed the glove.

"I'm glad Whit got you some protection." Carol chuckled.

"Me, too. I'm surprised at how comfortable it is." Eli lifted her left hand.

"Your doctor's appointment is Friday, correct?" Julia asked Whit.

Whit nodded. "We should be back by mid-afternoon."

"Carol and I would like to celebrate with you at the diner," Julia said. "The glow you have about you is something only an expecting mother has."

"Do you know already?" Carol asked.

Whit reached for Eli's hand. "We did a test last night, and it came back positive. We know it could be a false positive, but feel confident Friday's appointment will confirm the test."

"Dinner is on us then," Carol said.

"You have a deal," Eli replied.

"We'd better head home before it gets much later. You've got another few weeks of school," Julia reminded Carol.

"I know. I can hardly wait until school is out to help with the gardens."

"We'll start planting next week," Eli said. "Whit thinks the ground is warm enough."

"There will be plenty you can help with once we start harvesting," Whit said. "Will you plan to can some of the vegetables for yourselves for next winter? There will be plenty between three garden plots."

Carol chuckled. "If you teach us how to do it."

"That's no problem."

"We'll see you Friday night then," Julia said. "Do you want to meet us or ride together?"

"Let's be chauffeured," Whit teased.

"We will pick you up around five then," Julia said.

CHAPTER FIFTEEN

Whit saw the soft glow at the top of the mountain and felt her amulet warm against her skin. She felt something unusual. Whit imagined she was being called to the crystal cave. The more she glanced at the glow, the more determined she felt. Eli was concentrating on her project. "Would you mind if I visited the crystal cave?"

"Tonight?" Eli asked.

"Yes. It's weird, but I'm being called by the mountain."

Eli cocked her head at Whit's comment. "Only if I get to go with you," Eli said.

"I hoped you would. This feels important."

Eli set her project aside. "Go get our headlamps, and I'll bring a Gator around."

"Thank you." Whit stood and kissed Eli.

Eli could see the gemstone flare beneath Whit's shirt. She pulled hers out, too, and it was glowing. "That's odd."

"Grab my pistol, too, in case we run into a critter that wants to eat us," Eli said. "Okay for Cruz to come?"

"Yes, she will keep us safe."

"That she will. Come on, baby girl," Eli said as she walked to the barn. Eli felt odd about going to the cave at night, but Whit was determined, and she trusted Whit's instincts.

When they reached the head of the trail, Eli clipped the pistol to her hip, and they turned their headlamps on to light their path. The soft glow from the cave made it easy for them to find. Eli looked at Whit as they reached the trail in front of the cave. "You feel okay?"

"Yeah, I do," Whit said.

Cruz walked bravely in front of them as they walked toward the crystal cave. It felt warm when they entered and walked toward the large chamber. Cruz's hackles rose, but she did not growl, which seemed odd. Eli was surprised when Cruz rushed forward, and she lost sight of her. "What the hell?"

Eli was startled when they reached the chamber and found someone inside. He was petting Cruz, who seemed familiar to him. When he looked up, Eli saw amazing blue eyes. The eyes and blond hair made her think of Whit's story of her father.

He smiled and spoke. "Hello, Daughter."

Eli held onto Whit to support her, afraid she might faint, but Whit held strong.

"Hello, Father."

"Join me, please," he asked, pointing to the ground. "We have much to discuss. Eli, my second daughter, welcome. I have many names. The one you may be most familiar with is Zeus."

"The God of the sky and thunder," Whit stated.

"The Cherokee called us the Sky People and a name I can no longer remember," he said.

Eli helped Whit to ease down to the floor and sat beside her. "Us? There are others like you?" Eli asked.

"Thousands who have visited earth for hundreds of your earth years. We come from the sky, so that is the name we use most often."

"The blue light we see in the night sky. Is that you?" Whit asked.

He nodded. "I have come here for years to watch over you and your mother. I was saddened to learn she had a tragic end, but she created someone beautiful and special in you."

Eli had a difficult time understanding what was going on. "You travel here? From where?"

"I have lived all over this world for a hundred years. This is the place I claim as home." He spread his arms wide, and the gemstones flared.

"What is this place?" Eli asked.

"Other than my home, it's a place of power. The crystals around your necks are a power source for my capsule."

"So, the bright lights we see streaking across the sky sometimes, are you?"

"Yes, when I come to check on you." His hand softly stroked down Cruz's body.

"Why are you calling me now? After all these years when you could have revealed yourself to me."

His smile faded. "I did not wish to repeat the experience your mother suffered. She was not mature enough to understand the importance of our discretion. She was the most beautiful human I ever met, but she suffered great ridicule when she tried to convince others of my existence."

Eli saw the tears in Whit's eyes and reached for her hand.

"You have grown into a beautiful woman just as she would have and found great love in Eli. And now you are going to be a mother."

"How could you possibly know that?" Whit asked.

"Because you are a part of me. The whispering you've heard all your life on this mountain was me as I watched you grow."

"You've been here all this time?" Eli asked.

"No, only for short periods before I recycle and recharge, but I come as often as possible."

"I've never seen you, but I've sensed your presence and felt your memories here."

"I am only visible to you here, in this chamber. Outside I fade into the sky."

"That is why our crystals glow brighter when you're around?" Eli asked.

He nodded. "Yes, and to give you extra energy when needed. The brightness of the crystals you wear will always reveal my presence."

"Good to know," Eli replied.

He reached for Whit's hand.

Whit was surprised by the softness and warmth of his touch. She felt his gentle squeeze and looked into his eyes.

"I need to tell you something important. That's why I reached out to you tonight." He paused and looked at both of them. "The man you selected for your donor is a Star Child like you. Not mine, but another's."

"Is that why he felt so familiar?" Whit asked.

"I imagine you were both drawn to him," he answered. "Like you, he is brilliant and doing great work in the medical field. Your children will follow in your footsteps."

"Children?" Eli asked.

"Yes." He nodded. "Whit is carrying twins, one boy, and one girl. They will both be blessed with high intellect and become brilliant researchers that will advance medical care by many years. Whit will teach them from home, and they will move on to higher education when they are ready."

"Twins?" Eli let out a gasp.

Whit's hand went to her head. "How can you know all this?"

"Because you are a part of me, and this has been a hope for many years, that you would create the next generation of Star Children." He chuckled. "Your love for Eli gave me pause for a short time, but the love you share will help them grow into even more special people."

"This is a tad overwhelming," Whit said.

"There was no simple way to share this information with you. I'm sorry if it has upset you."

Whit shook her head rapidly. "No, not at all. It's just weird. You know all of this before the children are even born. This is just so much to process, and I'm sure I will have a thousand questions once all of this sinks in."

"I will be here for a short time. You, Eli, and this beautiful creature are the only ones that can see me," he said as he stroked Cruz.

"I can come back tomorrow?" Whit asked.

He smiled warmly. "Yes, I would like that. There's so much we can share."

Eli stood and helped Whit to her feet.

He looked at Eli. "Thank you for sharing your life with my daughter."

Eli felt speechless and nodded to him. "Are you ready? We will return tomorrow."

Whit smiled, stepped toward her father, and embraced him. "I'm glad to finally meet you."

"I've been here all along, just not an active part of your life for obvious reasons. I will look forward to seeing you again."

Eli nodded and led Whit from the cave. The cool air outside felt good against her skin. "Are you okay?" she asked Whit.

"Yes. I'm excited to meet my father, even under these circumstances. Are you sure we aren't dreaming?"

Eli leaned down and kissed Whit. "Did you feel that?"

"Yes, I did."

"We are not dreaming, then." Eli grinned. "Let's go home."

Whit nodded. "I need a cinnamon roll to talk this over with you."

"Coffee?"

"No, I think I need some milk," Whit answered. She looped her hand under Eli's elbow, and they returned to the Gator to drive home.

Eli closed the barn door and looked at Whit. "Twins?"

"I'm as surprised as you, but I'm pleased to know we will have them."

Whit took Eli's hand. "We have names to pick out and a nursery to prepare."

"We can't say anything until the doctor confirms this, but we can start planning," Eli said.

"People would think we are nuts." Whit grinned. "Mark and Mitch might understand, but this needs to be our secret. We are the only ones who can see him, so it would be hard to explain."

Eli smiled as they stepped onto the porch. "I'm glad he involved me in this."

"You are a critical part of me and will be crucial in raising the kids."

"Kids. Oh, my goodness. That is still hard to believe," Eli said. She walked to the refrigerator. "Grab a cinnamon roll, and I'll bring you some milk."

"Thanks," Whit said as she opened the box at the table.

†

They talked for over an hour at the kitchen table. "I think we need to lay down," Eli finally admitted.

After they were snuggled under the covers, Whit turned to Eli. "I wonder if the doctor can confirm twins on Friday?"

"Don't ask me. I don't know nothing about birthing babies," she teased.

"Me either, but it looks like we will be getting a crash course soon," Whit whispered.

"Yeah. Twins," Eli said.

Whit could hear the excitement in Eli's voice. "Are you pleased we will have a boy and a girl?"

"We could have more, and I would still be excited," Eli admitted.

"Whoa, two is plenty." Whit chuckled.

"For starters. We may change our minds later."

"Maybe," Whit agreed. "Let's survive these two first."

†

Eli woke and went downstairs to start breakfast. She looked up when she saw Whit start down the stairs. There was a glow around her and a beautiful smile on her face. "Good morning, my love."

"Good morning. Did you sleep well?" Whit asked.

"I dreamed of babies all night." Eli laughed. "Can you eat some bacon and scrambled eggs?"

"Yes. I'm hungry this morning. Will you add some cheese to the eggs?"

"I'll add anything you want," Eli replied.

"Pepper rings and black olives, then." Whit laughed.

"Sounds good. Coffee or juice?"

"Both," Whit answered. "I'll pour a cup. Do you need help with anything?"

"I've got this," Eli said as she whipped the eggs.

A knock on the door revealed Mitch had arrived.

"Good morning," he said when he walked in. "Dad sent me down to raid the henhouse. I went ahead and fed the animals for you. Do you need anything?" His hand sneaked a slice of bacon.

"No, we're good. Thanks for feeding the animals for me. We will spend the morning scouting more wood for handles, but we should return by lunch."

"Dad and I were talking about pizza or livers and wings," Mitch reported. He looked at Whit. "Does either sound good to you?"

"Both, actually." Whit chuckled. "Why don't you and I go to town and get the chicken for lunch and pick up pizzas to keep warm for supper?"

Mitch hugged her gently. "I think you should be pregnant more often," he teased. "Stop by when you come back from exploring, and we can call in orders and go."

"We will," Whit promised.

"See ya," Mitch said and left.

"You made his day." Eli grinned.

"That was pretty clever of you to tell him we were exploring this morning. Can we also go star gazing after dinner? There is so much I want to learn from my father."

Eli nodded as she added ingredients to the eggs. "We can go whenever you wish. If you want to visit alone, I'm okay with that, but only during daylight hours, please."

"That's reasonable," Whit answered. "I appreciate you going with me."

"My pleasure." Eli pulled two plates down and added toast and bacon to them while the eggs cooked. "Do you want some jelly?"

"Apple cinnamon?"

"Absolutely. We need to get you and Brad making some as soon as he gets here," Eli said as she pulled a jar from the fridge. "We are dangerously low."

"I will add supplies and more jars to a shopping list. Brad and Laura will be here next weekend, right?"

"Yes, either Friday night or Saturday morning. I'd bet Friday night." Eli smiled. "We can confirm with Mark today.

"Too bad they can't be here for the fish fry this weekend."

"We will have plenty more. Did Mr. Henry confirm?"

Whit nodded. "They will be here as soon as he gets off around lunchtime. He's excited to fish."

"The boys will return from the junkyard before then, and I will help them unload faster."

"Just stay out of their way. The three of them can handle things. You can help me get the fryer set up and other preps."

"Got it," Eli said as she plated the eggs and delivered breakfast to the table. "Breakfast is served," she said as she placed a plate in front of Whit.

"That's a lot of eggs. Do we need to buy more hens?" Whit teased.

"I think Mark is planning to start raising some. I think we can count Mitch out for a couple of days. His tiny home and furniture are being delivered on Tuesday."

"Would you shop with me on Monday to set him up?" Whit asked.

Eli shook her head. "I think Mitch needs to accompany you. He needs to understand all the steps of buying groceries and supplies for a home right off the bat. I will play gopher for Mark."

"That's a good point," Whit agreed. "We can load his truck up with dry goods, and he can store refrigerator or freezer foods at Marks until he's set up. This tastes great." She smiled as she bit into the eggs.

"Thanks. Eat up, and I'll cook more if you're still hungry."

"This should be plenty."

†

Eli loaded three camp chairs into the Gator, and they spent the morning chatting with Zeus. Whit had many questions that he patiently answered. When she asked where he was from, Eli was as shocked as Whit appeared.

"I'm not from another planet, as you must be wondering. I'm from this one, just in another dimension and time."

"You're right. I wasn't expecting that," Whit said.

They talked until Whit's stomach began growling.

"Will it be okay to return tonight to talk more?"

"I would like that," he answered.

"We will see you tonight then," Whit said as she and Eli stood to leave. "Thank you for all of these answers. It helps me to understand so much."

"I owe you that much." He smiled. "Eat and rest, and I will see you tonight."

They left the cave, and Whit pulled out her phone. "I'm calling Mitch as soon as we get service. I'm starved."

Mitch answered on the first ring. "I was about to go to town without you."

"Place our orders, and we are on our way," Whit replied.

†

Whit's mind was whirling as she fired question after question at her father. "How different will their DNA be? I was shocked to find mine wasn't exactly normal in college."

"The children's DNA, if ever tested, will appear normal, but it will be enhanced from what is considered normal. Not enough to throw up any red flags, though." He smiled. "They will advance even more quickly than you, and their IQs will be off the charts. You will teach them from home until you feel they are socially and academically ready for advanced studies. I'm sure you remember how socially awkward it was for you to be in university so young. You can prepare them for that. You both must understand that the children will be linked to you telepathically. They will communicate with you before they begin to speak. Don't be alarmed. This is normal."

"Thanks for the heads up on that. I can feel Whit sometimes, but the babies might have freaked me out," Eli admitted.

"You will be just as important to their physical and social development as Whit. I've seen how you interact with your nephews and brother, and it's precisely how the children need to grow up, with a sense of family and responsibility."

"I can guarantee they will be welcomed. Mitch and Mark are both excited about us having a child. When they learn they are twins, Mark will be over the moon excited." Eli smiled.

"It is important for both twins to experience similar events. They will be even more connected than normal human twins," he stated.

Whit frowned. "Will they be able to see you and learn from you?"

"For a while. But my life cycle will be completed before they are adults. I will teach them everything I can.

You have all the tools to teach them, and I will support and provide the background they need to develop."

Whit frowned. "Your life cycle?"

He nodded. "We live much longer than humans from this plane, but we are not immortal."

"Do you know in advance?" Eli asked.

"Yes, our cycle runs for two hundred years. That leaves me about twelve years. That will be plenty of time for as fast as the children will learn."

"But, that's not enough time for me. I'm just getting to know you," Whit stated.

Zeus reached out to stroke Whit's face. "We will spend as much time together as possible. I have enjoyed watching you grow, but I know you weren't given that same opportunity. Talking to you now, I think you may have understood earlier, but I couldn't risk damaging you."

Whit leaned into his touch, and it pulled on Eli's heart. It made her realize how much Whit missed out by not having a relationship with her father.

"Your grandparents did an excellent job raising you; I will forever be grateful for them."

"They gave me every advantage they could." Whit was silent for a minute.

Eli looked at Zeus. "You said there are thousands of your kind on earth. Are they procreating, and will we be able to recognize them if our paths cross?"

"Yes, they are procreating to build a solid second generation. I'm unsure if you can sense another Star Child, but Whit certainly will. The children will, too."

Eli nodded.

"There are hundreds of Star Children being born each year, and some have grown into prominent scholars at a young age."

"So, if a young person shows exceptional intellect, there is a good chance they are a Star Child?"

"A high probability, but the human race is also evolving into a more intellectual race. Most humans, anyhow," Zeus said. "Every race has its bad apples, even ours."

"What happens to the defective ones in your race?" Eli asked.

"If they show tendencies for violence or unethical behaviors, their life spans are escalated, and their souls are recycled."

"Will our children have a long life cycle?" Whit asked.

"They will live longer than an average human, but not as long as me," he replied.

Eli shook her head. "This is all so incredible."

Zeus nodded. "It's a lot of information to digest, and some must seem unbelievable. I can fully understand your confusion."

"I know human twins aren't usually carried a full term of nine months. Will ours?" Whit asked.

"You will give birth in the middle of your seventh month." He smiled. "Your babies will decide when it's time to be born."

"That is almost crazy to think about," Eli said. She smiled at Whit. "Knock, knock, Mommy, it's time for us to arrive."

Zeus chuckled. "It will happen just like that. They will let Whit know when it is time."

"Is there anything we need to be prepared for that is unusual from average babies?" Eli asked.

"They may wake you up during the night to be changed or fed, and you may pick up on their communication between themselves. They will grow faster, physically, emotionally, and intellectually." He looked at Eli. "They won't be perfect children. They will have tantrums and behaviors, and it will take a firm hand and patience to teach them the correct behavior."

"I think we can handle that," Whit replied.

"They will be extremely curious, so be prepared for a million 'why' questions and for them to experience things other children might not attempt at a much older age. They will have bumps and bruises, but hopefully will have Whit's gracefulness and not yours," Zeus teased Eli.

"Hey, now," Eli said and laughed. "It only took me one lesson to realize I can't fly."

Whit's eyes flew open. "Will they have superpowers we need to be concerned about?"

Zeus nodded. "The telepathic ability is the most common. They won't be able to fly, go invisible, or be exceptionally strong."

Eli sighed.

"They will learn at an incredible rate to toilet and feed themselves. Their physical growth will be above average, but not so much it draws unwanted attention. They will be healthy with a unique immune system. Do you ever remember being sick as a child?"

"No. Not even the typical childhood diseases."

"I've never seen you ever have the sniffles," Eli stated. "The only thing close was the one morning of morning sickness you had at the beach."

"That was because I wasn't wearing my amulet, right?" Whit asked him.

He nodded. "You haven't had a problem with nausea since you put it back on, have you?"

Whit shook her head. "I actually have a great appetite and an increased energy level."

Zeus laughed. "You will both need that to keep up with the twins."

The night had grown long, but Eli had one more question. "How do you know the children will be researchers or scientists?"

"It's included in their enhanced DNA. We have a different makeup, but Whit and the father are brilliant scientists, so the children will follow in their footsteps."

"So, they will be mini versions of you?" Eli asked as she looked at Whit.

Zeus answered. "Intellectually, yes, but your imprint on them will also be significant. They will learn social skills, love for others and animals, and nature from you."

"That should be easy for me to teach."

"Expect to learn from them as well," he said. "Sometimes they will seem like adults in a juvenile's body. Just remember to teach them to have fun." He looked at Whit. "I think those were some of the things you missed by not having a sibling. Your grandparents did their best, but I wish you could have experienced more fun growing up."

Whit smiled and took Eli's hand. "I didn't realize I was missing fun until you came into my life. We have done so much together in such a short time."

"Will I see you tomorrow?" Whit asked.

"Yes, I have another cycle of the sun before I need to leave for a short time."

"When will I know you're back?"

"I will contact you now that you know of my presence."

"I will see you tomorrow then." Whit stood and hugged him.

†

Whit was quiet during the ride home. When they entered the house, Eli looked at her.

"Are you craving a cinnamon roll?"

"I wasn't until you mentioned it, but yes. With some milk."

Eli poured a large glass of milk and placed a pastry on the plate for Whit. "You have been very quiet since we left the cave. Are you all right?"

Whit nodded. "I'm just trying to process everything."

"Do you feel safe visiting him alone tomorrow?"

"Yes, I do. Why?"

"I think you have many questions that only need to be answered for you," Eli explained. "I can work on some handles and tell the guys you are busy on a project."

"Yes, you're right. I have many more questions."

"I can drop you off and then come get you for lunch. You can always call me earlier, and I'll come to get you if you tire and need to rest."

"Thank you. I only have one more day with him until we see him again," Whit answered.

"Do ask him one question for me, though," Eli said. "If we and the children are the only ones who can see him, can he come into our home when the children are born and begin to teach them?"

"That's a good question I hadn't thought of," Whit replied. "That would be good to know, especially when the weather turns cold."

"It would cause much less suspicion if people wonder why you constantly take them to the cave. We can clear the back bedroom, use it for a classroom, and create a small chamber for him. If we need more crystals to do that, we can easily collect them."

"I will find that out and bring more crystals home with each trip. Is it too late for Mitch to cancel his furniture order?"

"We can see if it has shipped. If it has, I will find a place to store the furniture."

"I like that idea," Whit replied.

CHAPTER SIXTEEN

Whit was excited to go for her doctor's visit on Friday. She was expecting clarification that she was carrying twins, even though it was probably too early to tell. She had no reason to doubt her father's revelation. Eli sat next to her when the doctor came in.

He studied her blood results. "You are most definitely pregnant." He smiled. "How are you feeling?"

"I feel great. Good energy. Good appetite and sleeping well," Whit answered.

"No morning sickness?"

"Just once."

"That's amazing. Let's take a listen to your heart. Sorry if this is cold," the doctor teased.

"No problem," Whit replied when he placed the stethoscope on her chest.

They watched as a confused look came over his face. He rechecked Whit's heart and then moved down to her stomach. He looked at her and went to a computer to review her chart. "This is incredible," he said.

"Is everything okay?" Eli asked.

"Yes. Whit is healthy and pregnant, but there's something else. Hers isn't the only heartbeat I hear, which should be almost impossible since we just performed her procedure not even five weeks ago." He looked up at Whit. "You must have immediately conceived." He shook his head and rechecked the heartbeats in her stomach. "I've got to see this," he said.

He called the nurse to bring an ultrasound machine into the room. Once it arrived, he inserted the instrument and performed the test. "I have never seen this," he stammered. He turned the machine toward Whit and Eli. He pointed out two areas and turned up the volume.

Eli could see movement in two distinct areas and heard a sound that reminded her of a horse running. "It sounds like a stampede," she said.

"Not only are you pregnant, but you have twins," he told them. "I'm amazed they are so developed since it's only been a short time after your procedure. I'm afraid to even guess a due date," he said. "I want to see you again in two weeks, and we will repeat the tests. That will allow me to determine a date based on their growth rate."

He removed the instrument from Whit's body, still shaking his head. "Whatever you've been doing, continue. The heartbeats are strong, and you look fantastic."

"Thank you, Doc," Whit said. She looked at Eli. "We have lots of work to do." She grinned.

"Yeah," Eli replied. "Two of everything."

"Congratulations," he said. "I'll see you in two weeks."

†

Eli kissed Whit when they got back to the truck. "Not that I doubted, but this is so exciting."

"Yes, it is. We need to start some shopping. Car seats, bassinets, cribs. A ton of diapers." Whit chuckled.

Eli reached for Whit's hand. "I need your help with something."

"Anything." Whit smiled.

"I would like to ask Mark to help me make baby cribs. Will you help me pick out a pattern?"

"I would love to," Whit answered. "That's a great idea. Once we no longer need them, we can store them for Mitch and Brad."

"Family heirlooms. Yeah, I like that." Eli grinned. "Let's go home. We've got lots to do."

"Can we stop for some great cinnamon rolls in town?" Whit asked.

Eli chuckled. "I will buy as many as you want. You're eating for three."

"I think a dozen will last for a while," Whit answered.

"I will drive to town as often as you'd like if this will be your craved item," Eli said. "I've heard stories about pickles, ice cream, and other strange cravings. I'd rather watch you devour cinnamon rolls."

"They seem to be the only thing I crave so far."

"Do you want one with juice for the road?" Eli asked as she parked in front of the bakery?

"Yes, please," Whit said.

"I'll be right back." Eli smiled and left the truck.

†

Mark looked at Mitch, then at Eli. "Did I hear you correctly? You're having twins?"

"Yes, that's correct," Whit said.

Mark sat at the workbench. "Congratulations."

"Thank you. We've got something to ask both of you," Whit said.

"What do you need?" Mitch asked.

"First, would you mind if we canceled your bedroom furniture order?"

"Um, no, that won't be a problem. But why?"

"Eli and I have decided I will home-school the babies, and we want to set the back bedroom up as a classroom. We can always store the furniture if you stick with what you've ordered."

"Heck no, I'd love to have that set." Mitch smiled brightly.

"Good. We can move it when your house gets here Tuesday. I'll cancel the order today."

"What else?" Mitch said.

Eli looked at Mark. "I need your help and craftsmanship. I want to build cribs for the babies that we can pass on to Mitch and Brad one day."

"I'd love to help with that, and we have all the tools we need in the workshop." Mark was beaming from Eli's request. "When do we start?"

"Whit and I will research some patterns, but I want wood from our property, so we need to mill some boards."

"I can help with that," Mitch said. "Just point out the trees, and I can get them to the mill for Dad and me to cut."

"Good deal," Eli said. "Julia and Carol are treating us to the diner to celebrate tonight. Do you want my help in the morning with the junkyard trip?"

"No, Evan is coming out at six, so we can finish early and come back to fish," Mitch replied.

"Mr. Henry will be out to fish as soon as he finishes his route tomorrow, and Whit and I will get everything set up for a fish fry."

"Is it okay to tell Laura and Brad the good news?" Mark said.

"Absolutely," Whit replied. "I imagine Carol will call her to help set up a baby shower later this summer."

Mark nodded. "Two of everything. I think I'll buy stock in the diaper brand you choose."

Mitch looked at Whit. "When will you know the sex of my little cousins?"

Whit smiled at his excitement. "Not for a while yet, but I think it will be one of each."

Mark cocked his head at her. "That would be perfect."

"One other thing," Eli told Mitch.

"What?"

"I'm playing gopher for your dad Monday while you and Whit go grocery shopping for your home. She's already got a mile-long list, so be warned, it won't be a quick trip."

Whit shrugged. "Well, he is starting from scratch. He needs everything from linens to spices and cleaning supplies."

"That's true," Mitch said. "I'll need to go by the bank before we shop."

Eli shook her head. "We've decided the casino winnings will get you started in your new home. You will have plenty of opportunities to buy groceries and supplies once we get your basics."

"You can store any dry goods in your truck and put your refrigerated or frozen foods in your dad's freezer or ours," Whit said. "That way, you only unload once."

"That's smart," Mitch said.

†

Eli stood. "We'll see you tomorrow."

"Have fun tonight," Mark said.

"Be safe tomorrow," Eli said, then they walked to the truck.

"What do we do first?" Whit said.

"I'd like to look for a crib pattern to determine what kind of wood and how much we need," Eli suggested.

Whit nodded. "We have plenty of beech trees on the property. We would need to take the boards to a mill to be kiln dried, so the sooner, the better."

"I'll go get a Gator and a can of paint if you feel like looking for a couple of trees," Eli said. "Mitch and Evan can harvest them for us on Sunday."

"I'll grab some water and meet you outside after I hit the bathroom."

"Let's go, Cruz," Eli called, and they walked to the workshop for a can of paint. "Go get Molly," she told Cruz.

Cruz rushed ahead to enter the barn and open Molly's stall door. As Eli entered, they dashed out of the barn, and she walked to a Gator. She pulled in front of the house and smiled at Whit. "All aboard."

"Are you letting those two run for a bit?" she asked Eli.

Eli nodded. "Molly has been cooped up, and I think it would be good for both of them to run and play for a while."

"We all need that from time to time." Whit chuckled.

As they started up the trail, Molly and Cruz rushed past them. "They are having fun."

"Yeah, they are. What do you think of these three?" Eli asked as she rolled to a stop.

"Straight and tall," Whit agreed. "Do you think it will take three?"

"If leftovers exist, we can use the wood for other projects. We never seem to run out of ideas around here."

"That's true. Do you want me to mark those three, then?"

Eli handed her the can of spray paint. "I'll get us turned around while you do."

Whit marked the trees and climbed into the Gator. "Let's drop back by the forge and tell Mitch we've got the trees marked."

"Fine with me. Then we need to rest before Julia and Carol pick us up."

Whit nodded. "This day has flown by."

Mitch looked up when Eli pulled up in the Gator. "Everything okay?" Mitch asked.

"Yeah, we wanted to let you know we've marked three beech trees," Whit replied. "Will you see if Evan will help you harvest them Sunday? We need to get the boards milled and to a kiln in town for drying."

"Why don't we take a break from the forge? I can supervise you while you drop, limb, and section the trees?" Mark suggested. "We've gotten a lot done today." He looked at Eli. "I can start milling tomorrow if you help me while the others fish."

"You have a deal," Eli agreed.

"Ride with them, get the saws, and hook the trailer to the Gator. We can drop the sections at the mill and return the trailer for tomorrow's junkyard trip. I'll shut down here and be ready to go."

"Sounds like a plan to me," Mitch said, and climbed into the Gator.

†

Eli helped Mitch hitch the trailer to the Gator and then sat beside Whit on the steps to watch Molly and Cruz play once he left. "They are so funny to watch," Whit said.

"Just think. It won't be all that long before our kids are out here playing."

Whit leaned into Eli. "I know the years will pass all too quickly."

They sat together until the sound of a chainsaw broke the silence. "Well, there goes the neighborhood," Eli teased. "I'll get everyone fed for the night if you want to freshen up before supper."

"Are you sure you don't need my help?"

"I've got this," Eli said and stood to help Whit to her feet. "I'll be in shortly." She looked at the yard. "Let's go, Cruz and Molly," she called as she walked toward the barn.

"Love you," Whit called to her.

Eli turned back toward her and smiled. "Most," she answered.

"No way, man," Whit said and walked inside.

†

Mark was impressed with the precision Mitch employed to drop the three trees. They limbed them together, and Mitch looked at his dad. "What length do we need to cut these logs?"

"I think eight-foot sections will be fine. Smaller sections will be near the top, but it will be very usable wood."

"If you measure and mark, I will cut," Mitch replied.

Mark nodded and began measuring while Mitch took a drink. He carried a bottle to his dad and started cutting sections. Mark began moving the smaller sections to the trailer while Mitch finished cutting. When Mitch turned off the saw, he called him over. "Take a water break, and we'll finish loading together."

Mitch drained a bottle of water. "I can handle these longer sections if you aren't feeling well."

"I feel good," Mark said. "I don't think I'll tackle an eight-footer alone, but we can move them safely together."

Mitch grinned. He was really enjoying working beside his dad.

The sun started fading when they finished delivering the logs to the sawmill and pulled the trailer back to their place. Mark looked at Mitch when they hooked the trailer to his truck. "Are you okay with leftover pizza and a few cold beers?"

"That sounds perfect to me," Mitch said, wiping the sweat from his brow. "Evan will be here early, so we need a good night's sleep. If you warm up the pizza, I'll load the tools in your truck."

"Deal," Mark replied.

Mitch watched his father climb onto the deck and enter the house. He was surprised at how easily he accomplished the task. A few months ago, he would have needed the handrail or Mitch's help for the short climb. Even after the long work day, his dad moved much better. *Life is good.*

†

"Twins?" Carol asked a little louder than she had planned.

"Yes, twins." Eli smiled at her friend.

Carol looked at Julia. "We'd better get busy planning a baby shower."

"I believe we have plenty of time to plan, so relax," Julia told her.

"But, but two of everything." Carol sounded exasperated.

"It's all good," Whit promised Carol. She chuckled. "We've got at least six months to prepare."

"Six?" Carol asked.

"Twins often come early," Eli said. "We won't have an estimated due date until our next visit in two weeks."

Carol released a deep sigh. "Okay. It's not every day that two of my best friends have a baby, much less twins."

Eli nudged Whit. "Maybe we should have waited a few weeks to tell her about the twins."

"Are you kidding? School is out next week. It is perfect timing for me to start planning," Carol said.

†

"We'll see you tomorrow," Whit said when Julia stopped in front of their house.

"Come over any time you want. I'm going to help Mark mill some lumber while the others fish," Eli said.

"What's the lumber for?" Julia asked.

"Mark and I will build the cribs for the babies using some of our lumber. We will mill it tomorrow and maybe Sunday to take it to a drying kiln next week. That may take up to three weeks to process."

"Do you mind an extra set of hands? I can help stack the boards and stay clear of the kitchen," Julia stated.

"I think that's a great idea. I'll whip up the hushpuppy mix, get it chilling in the fridge, then turn the kitchen over to Whit and Carol. Miss Flora will be out when Mr. Henry finishes his mail route. She's bringing some of her goodies."

"Her baked beans?" Julia asked.

Eli nodded. "Potato salad and banana pudding, too."

"Oh hell yeah," Julia said.

"Evan is coming out early to go to the junkyard with Mark and Mitch to pick up more metal, but they should be back by mid-morning. Mark and I will start milling when they return."

"We'll come over after breakfast. I can help you set up the tables and fish cooker," Julia offered.

"Perfect," Eli said.

They watched their friends drive off, and Eli reached for Whit's hand. They walked over to the stack of logs Mark and Mitch had delivered. Eli breathed in deeply. "I love the smell of fresh-cut logs."

"The beech will have some beautiful grains and should be easy to work with," Whit said. "Do you want to go look up some crib patterns?"

"That sounds like the perfect way to end the evening," Eli replied. "I'm going to make a cup of coffee. Do you want some?"

"No, I have to get rid of that water I drank at the diner. Go ahead, and I'll get the computer turned on."

Eli opened the door to let Cruz out to potty. She left it open and walked to the kitchen to start the coffee. She was waiting on the coffee to brew when Whit passed by on her way to the computer. "Will you close the door behind our daughter?"

"Sure." Whit grinned, closed, and locked the door.

When Eli pulled a chair beside her, she saw Cruz with her head in Whit's lap. "Do you think she knows?"

Whit nodded. "I do. She follows me around more than normal. She's right beside me when I sit, often just like this."

Eli shrugged. "Cruz sees your father, so maybe she senses the babies."

"That would be my guess."

Two hours and two cups of coffee later, they had selected their two favorite crib patterns. "Do you think they need to match?" Eli said. "It would be easy to make one of each."

"I think they will have plenty of identical items throughout their childhoods. I think having a little difference in the patterns would be fine," Eli said.

"Yeah, there isn't a huge difference," Whit agreed. "I'll print out the patterns, cut sizes, and hardware we need. You and Mark can review the plans, but I'm positive we have more wood than we need."

"We can probably build a changing table and other items," Eli said. "I think we'll mill and dry two trees and use the third for outdoor projects around here."

"Like his chicken coop." Whit chuckled.

"Don't forget he wants a barn, too. I'll contact the park service to see if we can use some of the blow-down trees they had from the recent storm. What we don't use for the barn, we can split for firewood."

"We've got an extra pair of hands starting next weekend. Maybe you, Brad, and I can work on the smaller projects to let Mark and Mitch continue working in the forge."

Eli nodded. "You can supervise and play gopher."

"I promise to be careful. There's a lot I can help with, though."

"I know. Just no heavy lifting, please."

"Cross my heart," Whit teased. "I'll order the supplies for the chicken coop tomorrow, and we can pick them up next week."

"I'm going to take Cruz out. Will you be ready to go to bed when I get back?"

"I'm sure I will. This has been a long day."

"Let's go, Cruz."

Eli sat on the steps to wait on Cruz. She was lost in thought when Cruz nuzzled her hand and put a tennis ball in it. "Okay, I can take a hint." Eli tossed the ball for Cruz.

†

When Eli hadn't returned, Whit walked to the door. Eli sat on the steps with Cruz curled up beside her. She could tell Eli was deep in her thoughts as her hand instinctively stroked Cruz's coat. "A penny for your thoughts," she said and sat beside her.

Eli looked at Whit, her eyes full of emotion. "I was thinking of the future. Two of everything from cribs to clothing. I've decided they will only get one truck when it's time because they will be so close they will do everything together."

"Right. I'll believe that when I see it. I can see two new trucks sitting in the yard the day they turn sixteen."

Eli laughed softly. "You're probably right. I don't know what I was thinking. Hell, they may not even like trucks."

Whit smiled and laid her head on Eli's shoulder. Eli wrapped an arm around her as they stared into the darkness.

"We'll take it one glorious day at a time," Whit said.

CHAPTER SEVENTEEN

"Do you want something besides a cinnamon roll and a glass of milk?" Eli asked.

"No, I think that will be good this morning. I'll plan on making some sandwiches for lunch. I'm sure the boys will have worked up an appetite before they start fishing."

"That sounds good." Eli poured a cup of coffee and grabbed toast from the toaster. "I think I'll set up the small table for the fish fryer while I wait on Julia to help with the picnic tables."

"There's a jug of oil in the pantry ready to go," Whit said. "Fresh fish sounds good."

273

"Hopefully, the fish will be biting today. I know Mr. Henry is as excited as the boys to fish. I think I'll set him up in Brad's spot on the bridge, so he'll have a bench to sit on."

"I didn't think to ask if the girls are joining us," Whit stated.

Eli nodded. "They work until noon, then Erin and Jessie will join us."

"Maybe we can convince Mark to cook a butt next weekend, and we'll get Doc Loren and Macy to join us, too."

"That would be fun. It could be a welcome home for Brad and Laura. Evan can bring Hayden with him." Whit smiled.

"Brad would enjoy that. The crew could fish, so everyone will have filets to take home."

"Come in," Eli called out when she heard a knock.

Carol and Julia walked in. "I hope we're not too early," Julia said. "Carol's been ready for an hour," she teased.

"We're just finishing breakfast. Want some coffee?" Eli asked.

"No, we've already drunk a pot," Carol said.

"I guess we'd better get started then," Eli said. "I'll feed the crew, and we'll start setting the tables up for supper."

"I can feed the animals for you and check for eggs," Carol offered.

"Okay, that works for me. Let's go, Julia." Eli placed her coffee mug in the sink and grabbed the jug of oil from the pantry. "Was that coffee jet fuel?" Eli asked Julia. "Carol is a bit wired this morning."

"She's been up since five making lists of things she needs to do to set up a baby shower for y'all." Julia chuckled. "She's a wee bit excited to be an aunt."

"I can tell. I love it, though."

"She needed a project for the summer, so this is perfect timing. The gardens will help but won't keep her that busy."

"We plan on building a barn at Mark's place, so she can help with that. I'm positive we can find plenty to keep her occupied. Whit will make jelly, and once the gardens start producing, she can help with the harvest and canning."

"Do you think Whit would mind if we had some hens of our own?"

"I'm sure she would agree and help Carol build a mobile coop like ours," Eli said. She handed Julia the oil and picked up the small table they used for the fryer.

"I'll go back for the fryer while you set up the table," Julia said.

Julia frowned when she brought the fryer out. "The gas canister feels like it's almost empty."

"Crap, I didn't think to check it yesterday." She smiled at Julia. "A good project for Carol and Whit?"

"Yeah. I'll carry it to your truck," Julia said. "You can go give them instructions."

Eli walked into the house. "We have a minor issue. Our gas is low. Will you and Carol take my truck to exchange canisters?"

"Sure," Whit answered.

"Julia's got it loaded. We'll finish setting up the tables, and I'll work on the hushpuppy mix while you're gone."

†

"What can I help with?" Julia asked when they went into the kitchen.

Eli was pulling a large mixing bowl from the cabinet. "Go to the pantry and bring me the three bags of cornmeal. You can open three cans of Ro-Tel and corn for me also. I've already chopped the onion."

Eli poured the bags of cornmeal into the bowl and dumped the onion into the mix while Julia opened the cans. She returned to the pantry for a six-pack of Budweiser beer and a roll of plastic wrap.

Julia handed her the Ro-Tel and started opening the corn. "It smells good already."

"Dad's recipe," Eli said as she popped the top on the first beer can. "He cooked thousands of these for customers and family."

"He would be pleased you continue to use his recipe then, I'm sure," Julia said.

Eli nodded. "He was a great cook and taught Mark and me how to be creative in the kitchen."

"Drain the corn?" Julia asked.

"Yes, please," Eli said and began stirring the mixture. She added a second can of beer as Julia emptied the corn into the bowl.

When the mix was ready, Eli covered it with plastic wrap and placed it in the refrigerator. "We need to pull some buckets out of the barn for our fishermen." Eli chuckled.

"Do you not fish?" Julia asked.

"I sometimes do, but I have more fun watching the kids with the competitions to see who catches the most. I swear Mr. Henry looks younger when he's got a fishing rod in his hands."

"You really love it here, don't you?"

"I've never been this happy," Eli said as they walked to the barn.

They emerged from the barn when Whit pulled the truck into the yard. "Set out your buckets, and I'll get the gas set up."

Eli carried the buckets onto the porch. "Welcome back." She kissed Whit.

"We got two tanks, so we have a backup if needed."

"That was smart. The hushpuppy mix is in the refrigerator. I expect the guys to show up soon."

Whit nodded. "I saw them turning into the drive when I stopped for the mail."

"Julia and I will take a drink break while we wait for them. We've decided Carol needs a chicken coop." She smiled. "So double that supply order."

"No problem." Whit chuckled. "That's a great idea. What do you want to drink?"

"A glass of tea would be great," Eli answered. "I'll pull down Mitch's fishing gear."

"I'll bring two glasses to the porch for y'all."

†

Evan hugged Whit when the guys arrived. "Congratulations."

"Thank you. We're excited," Whit answered.

"Mark and Mitch are, too. That's all we've talked about this morning."

"I hope it wasn't too boring for you."

"Not at all. They've got me excited, too." Evan grinned. "I know you and Mark are building the cribs, but would you mind if Mitch and I tackle a changing table and diaper storage cabinet?"

"I'd love that," Whit told him. "Thank you, Evan."

"Wait until you see it first," he joked.

"I know you will do a great job on it," Whit replied. "Have fun fishing, but leave some for the girls and Mr. Henry."

"I'm sure there will be plenty to go around."

"Go ahead and plan for next Saturday, too. We'll talk Mark into a butt, and you youngins can load up everyone's coolers with fish filets."

"Perfect. What can I bring?" Evan asked.

"Nothing, we've got the food covered."

"Maybe an extra dessert?" Evan smiled.

"Well, we can never have too many desserts," Whit said. "Go, fish." She swatted him on the shoulder. "You're making me hungry."

†

"We've got an extra project," Eli told Mark while she pulled her gloves on. "Carol needs a chicken coop."

"That makes two, then." Mark chuckled. "Evan and Mitch are making you a changing table and diaper station."

"We need to start on your barn, too. When Brad arrives, I thought I'd check with the forestry service to see if we can harvest some blow-down logs from the last storm."

"That's a great idea. I like the sixteen-by-sixteen plan Whit created."

"The three of us can work on the wood for the barn while you and Mitch keep the forge fires glowing," Eli said.

"Are you comfortable running the mill?" he asked.

"I want to watch you a bit and then maybe try my hand at it," Eli said. "Julia and I will carry the boards to the trailer while you cut."

Mark started the mill and began trimming the boards. When he shut it down for a break, he took a bottle of water from Eli. "We're making good progress. I want to use the boards with the live edges for the chicken coops. They won't be suitable for furniture."

"That makes sense."

"Are you ready to run the mill?" Mark asked.

"I think so. We have plans for you to cook a butt next Saturday to welcome Brad and Laura home."

"That sounds good to me. We can pick out a couple and prepare to cook this weekend."

Eli nodded and finished her water. "Okay, I'm ready."

"The depth is already set. Just take it slow and be careful. Whit will kill me if you get hurt," Mark teased.

†

Eli cut six sections before Mark signaled her to break. "You did great."

"Thanks," Eli said and wiped the sweat from her brow. "I think I've got this."

"I think so, too. Let's check on our fishermen and stretch for a bit," Mark suggested. "We've got a good sized stack on the trailer already, and we haven't finished the second tree yet."

"Do you think we'll have room for all three?" Eli asked.

"We will even if we need to make two trips."

"That should give us enough live edge for two coops, won't it?"

"If not, we'll be damn close."

†

Eli grabbed a bucket when she saw Mr. Henry pull up with Miss Flora. "I've got the bridge reserved for you today."

"Go ahead. We'll help Miss Flora inside," Mark said.

Eli nodded. "Don't let him talk you into sampling the banana pudding, Miss Flora."

"Damn, Sis. You're no fun."

"Congratulations," Mr. Henry said as he pulled his fishing rod. "We are so excited for the two of you."

"Thanks, Mr. Henry. We're excited, too."

"I hope you know you'll have plenty baby sitters when you need a night off. Flora hasn't had a baby for years."

"That's good to know. I'm sure we'll have our hands full with two."

Eli placed the bucket beside the bench. "What can I bring you to drink?"

"Nothing yet. Are you going back to the mill?"

"Yes, we aren't done yet. How did you know?"

Mr. Henry smiled and pointed to her hair. "The trailer of boards also tipped me off."

Eli ran her hand through her hair, and the air filled with sawdust. She laughed and hugged Mr. Henry. "Smoked butt, next Saturday, so mark it on your social calendar. Brad and Laura will be here."

"Is Laura staying yet?"

"Not yet, she's got another year to get Brad through high school, and she can work remotely or retire. Brad will be here for the summer."

"Good. I miss Brad. He's such a clown."

"That he is. Good luck, and I'll check on you later."

"Thanks," Mr. Henry said.

†

Mark handed her a glass of tea. "The boys have got a few in their buckets. The girls should be out soon."

"Are you good to cut for a few more hours, then get cleaned up to start cooking?"

Mark smiled. "I've got clean clothes. I thought I'd shower in your laundry room to save time."

"That works. The boys can start cleaning the fish while we start cooking. They should have enough by the time I finish the hush puppies."

"If they don't, I'll clean and send them back to fish."

They heard Mitch holler as he hooked another fish. "I don't think we have to worry about having enough fish."

Mark nodded. "Let's get back to work. You good to cut a few more?"

"Sure," Eli said.

†

Mark watched Eli cut six more logs and signaled to turn off the mill. "I think that's good for today. We can finish the last few logs tomorrow."

Eli looked at the trailer. "I think we'll get the rest of them on the trailer, don't you?"

"I think so," Julia said.

Mark nodded. "I agree. Let's get cleaned up."

"I'll be back in a bit," Julia said.

"Check on Mr. Henry as you cross the bridge, please," Eli said.

"Will do," Julia said.

"I'll check on the ladies and hit the shower," Eli told Mark. "I'll start on the hushpuppies while the fish are cleaned."

Mark grabbed his clothes out of the truck. "If I finish before you, I'll get the oil heating."

†

Eli entered the house to find Whit, Carol, and Miss Flora sitting around the table. She smiled at Whit. "I'm going to shower quickly, and then we'll start cooking. Mr. Henry and the boys have been reeling in the fish."

"How are the boards coming?" Whit asked.

283

"Good, and I still have all my fingers." Eli laughed. She looked at Carol. "Julia ran home to shower, too."

Whit nodded. "We've got everything under control in here. We are discussing a baby shower."

"Have fun," Eli said and darted up the stairs.

†

When she returned, Eli gathered all her tools and supplies for the hushpuppies. Julia arrived just in time to help her carry them to the cooking table. Eli leaned down and kissed Whit. "Will you bring out three glasses of tea?"

"I'll come back if you have them ready," Julia said.

"Y'all go. I've got this," Carol said and stood. "I'll be right back."

Julia opened the door, and they started across the yard. Eli saw Mark at the cooker and the blue flames licking under the pot. "Damn, I forgot a roll of paper towels," Eli said when they set the mix and supplies on the table.

"Don't worry, we can get Carol to bring some out after she delivers our tea," Julia said.

Mark looked up and chuckled. "She must have been reading your mind."

They turned to find Carol carrying a tray of glasses filled with tea, a full pitcher, and a roll of paper towels. "Whit said you might need these," Carol replied, handing Eli the roll.

"Thanks," Eli answered.

"I'm going to check on Mr. Henry and the boys," Mark said. "There's no need for all three of us to watch the oil heat."

"That's fine. The girls just pulled up. Will you give them a bucket for their fish? They normally fish the west creek."

"I'm on it, boss." Mark grinned.

Eli hollered when Erin and Jessie walked past them a few minutes later. "Good luck, you've got catching up to do."

"We're feeling lucky today." Erin grinned back at them.

Eli lined the pans with paper towels and began cooking hushpuppies when the oil was heated.

†

Mark and the boys started fileting the fish and brought a pan to Eli for cooking. "What do you want us to do with all the fish scraps?" Mitch asked.

"Dump them in the garden, and I will till them into the soil next week before I plant."

"That's a great idea," Julia said. "Carol is so excited about planting her first garden."

"Whit plans to supervise her next week. She and Mitch will shop Monday to buy his supplies, but she's free the rest of the week."

"I bet Mitch is about to burst with excitement," Julia replied.

"He is. The tiny home will be delivered and set up Tuesday. He and Whit already have his solar panels installed and charging, and his water lines run."

"That will be an exciting day."

"I can't tell if he's more nervous or excited. I know he'll still be close to Mark, but this is his first solo venture."

"It's a good thing he got Tink. She will keep him company."

"That's true," Eli said as she dipped hushpuppies from the oil. "Let these cool, and we'll give them a taste."

†

It didn't take long for Erin and Jessie to fill their bucket, and Mark decided there was plenty of fish for supper. Jessie groaned when he pulled them off the creek. "You can come back tomorrow and fish to fill some coolers," Mark promised.

The boys carried the cold dishes from the house and helped Carol and Whit set the table while Eli and Mark finished cooking the fish.

"This all looks terrific," Mr. Henry said as he sat beside his wife. "I had so much fun, too."

"The kids plan on more fishing tomorrow, so bring a cooler and join them. You can add some fish to your freezer." Mark smiled at him. "Will you bless this meal for us?"

†

Mark and Eli loaded the last of the milled lumber onto the trailer. "That is some impressive lumber if I say so." Mark grinned at Eli.

"We can deliver it to the kiln tomorrow while Whit and Mitch shop," Eli answered.

"What about the four of us having a nice steak after everyone finishes fishing today?"

Eli smiled at her brother. "I love that idea. Right now, I will see if any of Miss Flora's banana pudding is left. I think she and Whit are making sandwiches for everyone."

"I do like the way you think, Sis."

†

"Evan said he will come out Tuesday to help me move the furniture into my tiny home," Mitch informed Mark during lunch.

"I'm glad you two youngins will carry that to your loft. There's no way I could make it." Mark chuckled.

"We will all pitch in and set up your kitchen," Whit told him. "It shouldn't take us long."

"We can unload your truck, and you can arrange everything as you like after we leave," Eli added. "Make it your home."

"I'm looking forward to it," Mitch replied. "I'll have everything I need except a laundry set up."

"You can use ours or your dad's," Whit replied. "That's the only drawback to a tiny home. Maybe one day we can add onto it."

"Will you and Evan load the cooler for Mr. Henry after we finish cleaning the fish?"

"Of course, Dad. That should keep you in filets for a few months." Mitch grinned at Mr. Henry. "If you run out, you know where to come."

"I've enjoyed fishing with you young folks. I haven't had this much fun in years." Mr. Henry looked at his wife. "We've been eating well since you all arrived."

Eli shot Mark a wink. "Our dad taught us that sharing food with friends and family is about as good as it gets. Growing up, we had a crowd every weekend if the weather was nice."

"Great hurricane parties, too, when it wasn't so nice." Mark chuckled.

"That's true." Eli remembered.

"Everyone is coming back for pulled pork on Saturday, right?" Mark asked.

"We've already got the menu set," Whit replied. "Anyone who wants can fish; the rest of us will relax."

"That sounds great to me." Eli draped an arm over Whit's shoulder.

CHAPTER EIGHTEEN

"I guess we will have an exciting new year," Eli said as she fastened her seat belt.

"Are you disappointed we don't have more of a definite range for the baby's arrival?" Whit asked.

Eli shook her head. "No, we have plenty of time to get everything in order. Mark and I will start working on the cribs as soon as the wood is ready."

"Carol and I have been working on a registry for the baby shower. It may be a good thing we cleared out that bedroom early. We need room for storage," Whit reported.

"I'd like to start researching names," Eli said.

"We can start that tonight." Whit smiled at Eli. "I think it's a chicken wing and liver day."

Eli chuckled. "Call the boys and tell them we're bringing lunch."

†

"I never would have dreamed it would be so hard to pick out names," Eli said as they sat in front of the computer.

"So many options to consider," Whit replied. "Names with the same first letter, biblical names, mythological names, etc."

"It's probably a good thing we have time to decide. This is an important decision." Eli sighed. "Are there any names you are drawn to?"

"I like Zackary, but I'm not positive yet."

"Like I said, we have time." Eli smiled.

†

They were so busy the summer passed quickly. Mitch was living well independently, and Mark's business was thriving. Whit and Eli spent long days harvesting and canning vegetables. One morning when they had stepped out of the shower, Eli knelt before Whit. "You have finally started showing," she teased, kissing Whit's stomach. "Good morning, our babies," she whispered.

"Remember the doctor said once I start showing, I'll blow up like a balloon," Whit reminded her.

"I couldn't love you more," Eli said, kissing her sweetly.

Whit grinned at her. "I hope you have French toast planned for breakfast. I ate my last cinnamon roll last night, and I'm craving a cinnamon fix."

"French toast it is, then. Why don't we ride to town for some rolls later? We can take a break from canning to enjoy the day."

"We have been working hard. Why don't you see what the guys would like for lunch, and we'll bring something back?"

"We haven't had pizza in a while. Would you be good if Mitch recommends that?"

Whit rubbed her stomach. "Yes, pizza would do just fine."

†

Whit smiled at Eli and touched her stomach. "I think the babies are enjoying the smell of the pizza. They are wiggling around." She reached for Eli's hand to feel the movement.

Eli's eyes grew wide when she felt the movement inside Whit. "It's probably a good thing we are on an open road," she teased as she pulled her truck back into her lane. "We should probably do that when we are sitting still."

"They are starting to become more active," Whit replied. "What do you think of Zackary and Mackenzie?"

Eli thought about the names for a few seconds. "We could shorten them to Mack and Zack." She grinned.

"Or Zack and Kenzie," Whit added. "Ooh, I think they like those. One of them just gave me a good kick."

"I could live with those names," Eli said. "I won't even kick ya," she teased.

†

When Eli pulled up to the forge, Mitch jogged out to greet them and opened the door for Whit. He offered her his hand and helped her from the truck.

"Good morning, my little cousins," he said as he touched her stomach and smiled at Whit.

Eli grabbed the pizza from the back seat, but she could still see Mitch's face and read his joy as he interacted with Whit. She walked around to meet them at the front of the truck. "What do you think about Zackary and Mackenzie?" she asked.

"Zack and Mack. I like that," Mitch stated.

"I swear you two are just alike." Whit smiled at Eli. "Or Zack and Kenzie," she added.

"You can call her whatever, but she'll be my Mack," Mitch teased.

"What's this?" Mark asked as he joined them at the picnic table and overheard Mitch's comment.

"I think we've decided on names," Eli told him. "Mackenzie and Zackary."

293

"Mack and Zack. I like that," Mark replied.

Eli placed her hand over her face. "It must be a Fortner thing," she teased, and they all laughed. She put her hand on her stomach. "Sorry, Kenzie, you'll probably be called Mack."

Eli smiled at Whit. "It could have been worse. We could have picked Matilda and called her Tilly."

"No freaking way." Whit smiled. "I still may call you Kenzie."

"As much love as those two will get, you can call them anything," Mark said. "How are you feeling?"

"Starved," Whit teased and reached for pizza.

†

When they returned home, Whit dozed in the hammock, and Eli did some carving down by the creek. The sound of the water was relaxing, and Whit drifted off quickly. Eli watched her sleeping for several minutes and began working on a new walking stick. Mark had invited everyone for supper on the grill.

"Zack and Mack," she whispered. "I really do like those names." Eli carved until the gentle sound of the water made her eyes grow heavy. She placed her knife beside her and sat back in the chair for a short nap.

Hours later, Whit woke her, needing help to get out of the hammock. "I really need to pee," she said after calling Eli's name.

Eli helped her to the ground and walked inside with her. "That's probably my last visit to the hammock for a while," Whit said when she emerged from the bathroom.

"I can get a chaise lounge like Mark's if you'd be comfortable. It's so beautiful by the creek. I'd hate for you to miss it."

"That might not be a bad idea," Whit replied. "I'll still probably need help getting up and down, but it will be much easier than the hammock."

"Are you up to going today?"

"Sure, just let me grab a snack for the trip."

"Let me guess. A cinnamon roll and apple juice."

"Absolutely." Whit smiled. "Do you want anything?"

"I'm good. Thanks."

†

Eli called Mitch to meet them to help her unload the new furniture. They bought two, so they could stretch out together by the creek.

"Those are nice," he said as they lifted the first from the truck. "I may have to get one for myself."

"Better hurry then. The store is running low on clearance."

"Call Evan to bring one out for you," Whit suggested.

"Yeah, That's a great idea. Are there any that aren't all flowery?"

Eli chuckled. "I'm sure Evan can find you one that's manly."

"I'm on it. See you for supper?"

"We'll be up in a little while. We want to test out these chairs first."

"You want me to feed the animals while I'm here?" he offered.

"That would be great," Eli replied.

"See ya." Mitch grinned and jogged away.

†

Mark and Eli entered the workshop after dinner. "Are you ready to start cutting some of the crib patterns?"

"I'll sand while you cut," Eli said. "Much safer that way."

"You have a valid point." He grinned. "How do you feel about tongue and groove joints? I would like to reduce the risk of injury from metal hardware."

"I like that idea. Can you teach me how to use the router for that?"

Mark nodded. "Let's work on cutting and sanding tonight, and I can teach you the router this weekend. Everyone else will be busy with projects, so we can sneak in some time."

"Perfect," Eli agreed. "I can work on sanding until then."

The Sky People

†

It was close to eleven before Eli showered and climbed in next to Whit. "Did you and Mark have a good night?"

"Yes, we did. I think we've got some good plans for the cribs. I'll continue to sand the wood this week, and we'll get together again this weekend."

"I promised Julia and Carol I would help them harvest and do some canning."

"I know. That's when Mark and I will work together, so I'll stay out of your way." Eli chuckled.

"Thanks for a relaxing day," Whit said.

"We will have as many as you need," Eli promised. "We are in great shape here and can afford some days off to rest and relax."

"That sounds good to me."

†

Eli caressed Whit's baby bump with her fingertips. "That tickles."

"What tickles?" she asked Whit.

"What do you mean?" Whit looked confused.

"Did you not just say, 'That tickles?'" Eli looked at Whit.

"No, it wasn't me," Whit replied.

Eli's eyes grew wide as her hand caressed Whit's stomach. She heard giggling in her head. "What tickles?"

"You running your fingers across us," a tiny voice answered.

"What the heck?" Eli looked up at Whit, shocked.

Eli laid her head on Whit's stomach. "Zack and Mackenzie. Is that you?"

"Yes, Da," a voice answered. "But we prefer Zack and Mack."

"Are you hearing this?" Eli asked Whit.

Whit nodded her head. "Zack and Mack, it is then."

"Thanks, Mommy a tiny female voice answered."

"You're welcome, Mack."

"How long have you two been listening to us?" Eli asked.

"Since yesterday, Da," Zack answered. "When we heard our names being called, it woke us."

Eli shook her head to clear the cobwebs from her brain. "Seriously?"

"Yes," Zack repeated.

Eli lowered her head and kissed Whit's stomach. "Good morning, my babies."

"Good morning, Da," Zack answered.

"Why, Da?" Whit asked.

"Does it offend you?" Mack answered.

"No, not at all," Eli said. She smiled at Whit in disbelief.

"We have a Mommy who carries us and a Da to protect us. Would you rather we call you something else?"

"Absolutely not. Da is perfect," Eli told them.

"Da, will you feed Mommy then? We're hungry," Zack said.

"What are we eating today?" Eli asked.

"I think she calls it French toast," Mack replied.

"I am on my way to the kitchen," Eli said, climbing from bed. "I'll get breakfast started, Mommy."

"I've got to empty my bladder from where these two have been using it for a punching bag, and I'll be right down," Whit answered.

"Sorry, Mommy. It's starting to get a little cramped in here," Zack answered.

"If you keep growing, you won't fit much longer," Whit said as she waddled toward the bathroom.

"You will be meeting us soon," Mack replied. "We are ready to see you, Da, and our cousin Mitch."

"He is already crazy about you, and you haven't been born yet," Whit answered.

"We can feel the love you share," Mack said.

"He would be jealous if he knew we could talk to you," Whit said. "He is so excited to have cousins."

"We could talk to him through you," Zack said.

"I don't think we are ready for that just yet. Mitch and Mark know much about my background but don't know you are second-generation Star Children. I think it's best to keep that secret for now."

"Yes, Mommy," Zack answered. "We'll sleep now so you can enjoy your meal."

Whit slipped on her robe and joined Eli in the kitchen.

Eli turned to her with a massive smile on her face. "Can you believe what just happened?"

"No, but I think it's pretty awesome. The twins are napping while we eat," she told Eli.

"I'm glad you can hear them. I thought I was losing my mind for a minute. I know your father said this would possibly happen, but wow. Just wow."

"I have a feeling their 'awakening' will trigger a visit from him soon. I'm sure he has much to say to them."

"I wouldn't be surprised either." Eli plated two slices of French toast and handed them to Whit. "Apple juice?"

"Please," Whit answered. "Are you not eating with me?"

"I'm too excited to eat. I'll have some coffee, though."

"Do you have a busy day planned?"

"I do now. I will buckle down and finish sanding the wood for the cribs. I have a feeling the twins will arrive ahead of schedule. Mark and I can assemble them this weekend, and I can stain them next week."

"I guess I need to order the mattresses and a mat for the changing table," Whit said. "Can you think of anything else we haven't planned for?"

"I don't know if we will need them, but what about rocking chairs in case they get colic?"

"I don't think they will, but rocking chairs would be nice to have in the living room. I don't think they will fit anywhere else."

"What about the landing at the top of the stairs? It's big enough and will be a quiet area," Eli suggested.

"I'll see what we can get. If Evan brings out a chaise for Mitch, maybe he can add a few rockers. I'll call him this morning."

"Call the guys and see if they want to join us for supper. I can think of something to whip up."

"Too late. Mark is cooking baby backs, sweet potatoes, and street corn. I'm tossing a salad."

"Delicious," Eli said. "Did you have enough to eat?"

Eli nodded. "I have cinnamon rolls to snack on if I get hungry. How do tomato sandwiches sound for lunch?"

"Great. I think this year's crop is better than last year."

"They will continue to improve each year as the soil develops," Whit told her.

"I'll be in the workshop and have my phone if you need me." Eli leaned over to kiss Whit. "I love you."

"I love you, too. Do you want me to bring you a thermos of coffee in a little while?"

"Yes, please, if you would."

"I'll see you in a bit then."

†

Eli fed the animals and let Molly out to play with Cruz. She left the door to the workshop open so she could smell the clean scent in the air. Eli was halfway through one stack when Whit arrived with coffee.

"You have been busy," Whit said as she refilled Eli's cup.

"It's not hard to do, just time-consuming to smooth each section. Well worth the effort for our little ones." Eli leaned forward and kissed Whit's stomach. "Are they still asleep?"

"Not anymore," Whit replied.

"We wanted to hear what you're doing, Da," Zack said.

"Your Uncle Mark and I are building cribs for you and your sister to sleep in," Eli explained. "We didn't want you in just any old store-bought crib, so we're building them from wood we harvested from the mountain."

"That sounds good. I can hear the love in your voice when you speak of them, so I know they will be well done."

"Only the best for our children," Eli said.

"I've got the rocking chairs ordered. Evan will bring them out tonight and join us for dinner. Mattresses and changing table mats have been ordered, too."

"I'm not the only one that's been busy." Eli smiled. "Do you need me to pick some tomatoes for you?"

"No, I need some time in the sun," Whit replied.

Eli nodded. "Call me when it's time for sandwiches. Thanks for the coffee."

"You're very welcome."

"Bye, Zack and Mack."

"Bye, Da," they answered.

Eli's cheeks were starting to ache from smiling so hard. She returned to the sanding and didn't notice when Mark entered the workshop. She turned off the sander when she finally saw him. Mark let out a whistle.

"You have been busy. These look great," he said, inspecting a wooden slat.

"I think the twins will be arriving sooner than expected," Eli said.

"Is everything okay?" Mark asked.

"Perfect. I think the twins are getting restless and ready to be born."

"When is the next doctor's visit?"

"Friday. After that, it may be weekly until they are born."

"Exciting news. I know you can't wait. Holding your firstborn is like nothing I have ever experienced. Your heart will feel like it will beat out of your chest."

"I'm looking forward to meeting our children. Can we assemble the cribs this weekend so I can start staining them next week?"

"We will make it happen. Whit asked me to come to get you for lunch, so take a break, and let's go eat some homegrown tomatoes."

†

Evan pulled up in the yard just as Eli finished feeding the animals. "I hear two rocking chairs will be needed soon." He grinned.

Whit stepped onto the porch. "Those look beautiful, Evan. Ask your dad to bill me, and I'll pay for them."

"No can do. These are my gifts to y'all for everything you have done for me," Evan said. "Just tell me where you want them, and don't argue with me." He smiled. "Please."

"The top of the stairs in the alcove," Eli said. "Do you need help?"

"No, ma'am, I've got this. I'm headed up to drop Mitch's chair off and have supper. Do you want a ride?"

"Thanks, but I've already got a Gator warming up. We may come home before you're ready to leave." Eli grinned. "I heard Mitch talking to his dad about shooting some pool tonight."

"Okay, then, I guess I'll see you there," Evan said after setting up the second chair.

"We won't be far behind you." Eli followed him out and walked to the barn for the Gator. When she pulled to the porch, Whit tucked her amulet inside her shirt. "No flare yet?"

"Not yet, but soon."

"Let's go introduce our babies to Mark's BBQ."

CHAPTER NINETEEN

Mark and Eli were up early on Saturday and had one of the cribs assembled by mid-afternoon.

"You did such a remarkable job on these joints that we could get away without gluing them, but we're doing it anyway."

"They need to last for many years." Eli grinned. "I'm impressed by how well this turned out."

"Wait until you see it stained, and I'm sure you will have a tear or two in your eyes."

"You're probably right about that."

The door to the workshop was open, and Eli could hear Mitch and Evan as they built the changing table. "Dude, this is awesome," she heard Mitch tell Evan.

"It sounds like the guys are finishing their project," she told Mark. "Let's check on them and see what we want to plan for supper."

"I'm ready for wings and livers," Mark said. "Maybe the boys will make a run into town."

"I'm sure that can be arranged."

"That is gorgeous." Eli smiled when she saw the table. She ran her hands across the fine grain wood.

"We want to blow off any remaining dust and get a coat of stain on it today," Evan replied.

"Maybe a second coat if it dries quickly, and we can clear coat it tomorrow," Mitch added.

"That sounds great. Can we talk you into another project?" Eli asked.

"Anything. What do you need?"

Eli smiled at Mitch. "We need two young men to run into town for wings and livers if Whit is fine with that for supper."

"A chicken run, bro," Evan teased.

"We'd love that," Mitch replied. "Check with the boss and have her call in an order and let us know when to pick it up."

"I will," Eli said. "Be right back. Do y'all need anything to drink? I think Whit has some lemonade in the fridge."

"That sounds great. I'll walk with you and bring it back," Mark said.

†

Mark and Eli entered the kitchen, and she walked over for a kiss. "We thought we would raid the fridge for the lemonade. The boys are ready to start staining, and we have one crib assembled."

"You need to come out and take a look. I think you'll be impressed with both projects," Mark said.

"We also thought we'd send the boys to town for livers and wings if that sounds good to you."

"That sounds good, Da. We're getting hungry. Love you."

Without thinking, Eli bent down and kissed Whit's stomach. "Love you, too, Zack."

"That's perfect. I'll place an order and come out to tell them when to pick them up. I'm starting to get hungry, so the sooner, the better. Okay with y'all?"

"We can always eat," Mark teased as he pulled the pitcher from the fridge and filled four glasses with ice. "I'll take these out and get started on crib number two."

"I'll be there in a few," Eli replied.

When Mark left, Whit looked at Eli. "Did you see Mark's face when you were talking with Zack?"

"No, what did I miss?"

"He was a bit surprised, I think. Maybe I'm just overthinking what I observed."

"I've gotten so used to talking with the twins I didn't think about Mark being here." Eli shrugged.

"He'll probably just think you're a crazy expectant parent." Whit chuckled.

"Well, I can't say he's wrong about that. I can hardly wait until these two arrive."

"Soon, Da," Zack said.

"I'll see you in a few. Order big. We're all hungry," Eli said and touched Whit's stomach.

†

When Mark and Eli started building the second crib, he looked at Eli. "I may just be imagining things, but earlier, were you talking to the twins?"

Eli hesitated and looked at Mark. "Just an overexcited expectant parent," she answered.

"Okay," Mark replied. "That makes sense."

Eli touched his shoulder. "Actually, Mark, that's not the truth. We might want to sit down for this conversation, though."

Mark shook his head after Eli explained. "So, you can talk to them like baby adults? That's incredible."

"It totally freaked me out when I heard them the first time. I thought I was losing my mind, but Whit heard them, too." She chuckled. "I think it's cute they call me Da and Whit Mommy."

"I know I can't share this news with anyone, but thank you for telling me."

"I slipped up and was so comfortable with you around, I answered Zack without thinking. Thankfully it was you and not someone else."

"They would have thought you were a crazy expectant parent, but I saw much more than that."

"You know me too well. I couldn't keep it from you after that slip."

"I know, and I'm excited to meet my niece and nephew. We better get back to work, so these babies will have cribs to sleep in," he said and picked up the next piece. He looked at Eli. "You know you could make this into a business with the quality of this crib."

Eli shook her head. "These were made with love. I have plenty of projects to do here without adding to the list. Thank you for the compliment."

"You know, Dad and Grandpa would be proud of your workmanship. They, too, were perfectionists when it came to building things."

"I guess it's a good thing we got their genes." Eli smiled at Mark.

†

Eli placed an arm around Whit when the cribs and table were arranged in the nursery.

"They came out well, didn't they?" Eli asked.

"Beautiful, now you just need to add the babies," Mark teased.

Eli and Whit laughed with them. "I don't think it will be too much longer," Whit said.

"Do you have your ready bag in the truck?" Mark asked.

Eli nodded. "It's been ready for weeks."

"Is there anything we haven't thought of they will need?" Mitch asked.

"Not that we can think of," Eli replied. "That will probably change once we bring them home."

"You'll call and let us know when you go to the hospital, right?"

"You will be my first call, so keep your phone on," Eli teased.

"And charged," Mark added.

"I will." Mitch nodded.

†

Two weeks later, Eli and Whit were relaxed on the couch and preparing to go upstairs for the evening. Whit felt a twinge of muscles in her lower belly. "Da, Mommy, it's time," Zack said.

"What?" Eli said, jumping off the couch.

"It's time," Zack repeated. "There is time to drive slow," he reminded Eli. "We will arrive in the morning."

"Okay, you relax here while I pull the truck to the steps," Eli said.

"Eli?"

"Yes?"

Whit reached for her and pulled her in for a kiss. "Relax. We've got this."

Eli took a deep breath. "Yes, we do. Will you call Mitch and tell them we are heading to the hospital?"

"I'm on it," Whit said and picked up the phone.

†

"Hello," Mitch answered with a groggy voice.

"Are you in bed already?" Whit teased.

"Wait. What? Is everything okay?" He immediately sprang to life.

"I wanted to let you and your dad know we are heading to the hospital. I will probably be in labor most of the night, so there's no rush to sit and wait. Will you feed the animals in the morning and come then?"

"Yes, no problem. I'll call Dad. Is Eli okay to drive? I can drive you."

"Eli will be fine, Mitch, but thanks for offering. I'll see you tomorrow. Love you."

"I love you, too."

Mitch hung up and called his dad. "They are going to the hospital. Whit said to feed up and come in the morning.

She sounded pretty calm for someone about to give birth," Mitch said.

"How was Eli?"

"Whit says she is good and can drive them safely."

"The hell with waiting until the morning. Shower and get dressed. I'll call Carol and Julia and ask them to feed the animals in the morning. We can drop Cruz at their house when we leave."

"Sounds good."

"Oh, and Son, dress comfortably. It could be a long night."

"On it, Dad," Mitch said. "I'll see you soon."

†

Eli's hands trembled as she placed the key in the ignition. "Get a grip," she growled at herself and let out a slow, deep breath. She pulled the truck up near the steps and jogged inside for Whit. Cruz was lying on the couch beside her with her head in Whit's lap.

"When you see us next, the babies will be with us," Whit said, stroking her head. "Mitch will come in the morning to feed you."

Cruz climbed down from the couch when Whit stood, and Eli escorted her from the house. "We'll be back soon," she promised Cruz and closed the door. After buckling Whit into her seat, she asked. "Is there anything else you need?"

Whit nodded with a smile. "A kiss."

Eli leaned in and kissed her sweetly. "Let's roll."

†

"Breathe, Da. Mommy's the one having babies," Zack teased to lighten the mood in the truck.

Eli reached over and covered Whit's hand on her stomach. "I am breathing." She chuckled. "Have you given thought to who arrives first? Whoever it is will be the firstborn and will always be the older sibling."

"Zack will be first and always be my protector," Mack replied.

"I like that answer," Eli said. "I'm so excited to finally get to see you."

"As we are," Zack replied. "We can't wait to be in your arms."

"Hey. What am I, chopped liver? I've carried you all these months," Whit teased.

"Yours will be the first face we see, Mommy," Zack answered.

Eli returned her hand to the steering wheel and carefully drove to the hospital.

When the nurse wheeled Whit into the birthing room, Eli turned to Whit. "I'll be right back once I park the truck."

"Don't worry. We'll get Whit set up and comfortable. Your doctor has been notified and is on his way in," the nurse told them.

†

When the doctor arrived, he completed an examination. "You are in labor, but your body is not ready to give birth yet. It's going to be several hours yet, I'm afraid. Are you in much pain?"

Whit shook her head. "Nothing I can't handle. Are the babies ready?"

He looked at her and smiled. "I've never seen twins more ready to be born. Everything looks good. My only concern is that you haven't developed enough breast milk to feed them both, but there are many good formulas we will start them on." He grinned up at Eli. "You must help at every feeding so one twin doesn't feel slighted."

"That is not a problem." Eli smiled. "They will both be well fed."

"I'll check back on you in a little while. Ring for the nurse if you need anything, and try to relax and let your body do what it was born to do."

Whit nodded and laid back against the pillow. She reached for Eli's hand. "Tomorrow, we'll be parents."

"Yes, we will. Are you disappointed in having to bottle feed?"

"A little, but I want our babies to get everything they need. We will need to buy a bunch of bottles, though. The hospital will send us home with some as a start, but we will need more."

"Oh, crap. I knew I forgot something," Eli said and smacked her head.

"What?"

"The car seats," Eli groaned.

"We have plenty of time. I will probably be here for a day or so until it's determined the formulas satisfy the babies. You can go home and get them then, or we can have Mark and Mitch bring them. I want you to go home, shower, and rest, not camp out here."

"Once everyone is settled, I'll go home for a while."

"Promise?"

"I promise." Eli leaned in and kissed her. She placed her other hand on Whit's stomach. "How are you two feeling?"

"Ready to be born," Zack answered. "We are sorry for the pain it is causing you, Mommy."

"Don't worry about that," Whit said. "It's all a part of the process. It will be over soon."

"Relax, and we will let you know when it's time," Zack whispered to both of them. Mack's getting a nap, and I'll do the same."

†

"Holy shit, hang on a second, Dad," Mitch cried out, jumping out of the truck to run inside. When he returned moments later carrying a bag, Mark smiled at him. "I almost forgot the welcoming presents for the babies."

316

"What did you get them?" Mark asked.

"For me to know and you to find out." Mitch chuckled. "I've kept it a secret for two weeks, so a few more hours won't hurt."

"I'm very proud of you, Son. Jealous, too, that I didn't think of getting a welcome present," Mark said.

"I'm sure we will have ample opportunities to spoil them for years," Mitch replied.

"Don't you know it," Mark said, putting the truck in gear. "Let's go get Cruz and be on our way. We probably need to hit a coffee shop close to the hospital. Hospital coffee is sometimes not the greatest."

"Relax, Dad, hospitals have improved since we were born. The hospital has a twenty-four-hour coffee shop with every coffee you could want."

"That's good to know. It will be our first stop when we arrive."

†

Several hours had passed since they arrived, and the doctor frequently visited throughout the night. "It won't be much longer now," he promised.

Eli was finishing her third cup of coffee. "This is excellent stuff," she told Mitch and Mark. "Thank you."

"We all needed a boost," Mark said.

"We didn't intend for you to come in last night. You could have waited until later," Whit said.

"And miss the birth of my cousins?" Mitch declared. "Hell, no."

"Enough said then." Eli chuckled.

"There was no way I would keep him away after that call."

"We are glad you are here with us," Whit said.

†

Zack stretched when waking from his nap. "Are you ready, Mommy?"

Whit looked at Eli. "It's time. Will you get the nurse to get you gowned and gloved up?"

"That's our cue to leave, Son," Mark said. "We'll be in the waiting room. Good luck."

"Ready," Whit said and took Eli's gloved hand.

The doctor did a final examination and looked up. "It's time we meet your twins. Try to relax and let your body do the work. Eli, are you okay?"

"Yeah, I'm fine, Doc."

"Good, we don't need two patients to tend to here. If you start feeling funny, please sit down."

"I will," Eli promised.

†

Whit clamped her teeth together as Zack began to arrive. She squeezed Eli's hand and listened for the babies.

318

"Almost here, Mommy," she heard Zack say. "Mack is following right behind, so I won't be much older."

"Just get here soon," Eli told him.

The doctor looked up at her. "The first is almost here."

Zack arrived, and the doctor smacked him on the butt to hear him cry, then Eli cut his cord.

Eli could barely contain her laughter when she heard Zack warn Mack. "You better come out crying, or you'll get your first spanking."

"Nothing wrong with those lungs." The doctor chuckled and handed Zack to the nurse for bathing. "Sister seems to be hurrying to follow," he told Whit.

"That's fine with me," Whit said. Her hair was plastered to her head with sweat. "I'm ready."

"Give her one final push, then."

Whit grunted with all her might, and Mack was born, crying at the moment she took in air.

"Perfect," the doctor stated when Eli cut the second cord. "If you give us some time, we will care for Whit and the babies. A nurse will tell you the room number when Whit has arrived, and then you can properly greet your new family. Congratulations."

"Thank you. I'll be with the boys in the waiting room. I love you," she told Whit.

"I love you, too, Da," Whit answered with a smile.

Eli looked at the twins. "I will see you soon."

†

"They will get Whit, and the babies settled into a room and come get us," Eli said.

"Congratulations," Mark said and pulled her into a hug.

"Thank you." She looked at a grinning Mitch, who was clutching onto a bag. "I can't wait to see what's inside that bag."

"You will see soon. Hopefully, you and Whit will approve."

"I'm sure we will," Eli said. "Man, what a night. I appreciate you both being here. I didn't expect you to sit with us all night."

"I don't think either of us would have slept a wink. Carol has Cruz, and they will feed for us in the morning and come up. Is there anything we need to do?"

"We will have to feed the babies formula. Once we determine which type and what bottles we need, I may send you shopping. We hadn't planned for that, but Whit doesn't have the milk to support them."

"That's not uncommon for twins, from what I've heard. That means you'll both be feeding simultaneously," Mark said.

"I'm good with that." Eli nodded.

"If you teach me, I can help, too," Mitch offered.

"You will be a great cousin and can help raise the twins. I'll take all the help we can get."

Mitch beamed with joy. "Thanks, Aunt Eli. I can't wait to teach them to fish." He grinned. "We are going to kick everybody's ass."

"I think you have a few years to practice for that," Mark teased.

"Doesn't hurt to plan. Can I get one of those backpacks to carry the babies around on the mountain until they start walking?"

Eli laughed. "Knock yourself out."

†

"Are you ready to meet your babies?" the nurse asked Eli.

"Yes, I am." She jumped to her feet.

"Come with me, and I'll take you to her room."

"Is there a waiting room for us?" Mark asked.

"No way. You're coming in with me," Eli said. "That's okay, right?"

"Three people max, though, for now." The nurse smiled. "Follow me."

†

Eli felt like her heart would explode with joy when she walked into the room, Whit was propped up in bed with a baby on each arm. She looked tired, but the smile on her face showed the love she felt for the babies.

"Hey, beautiful. How are you feeling?"

"Tired but relieved these guys are finally here. Da, meet Zack and Mack." Whit smiled.

Eli couldn't hold back the tears when she looked at their babies. They were beautiful, tiny versions of Whit. Zack fixed his eyes on her. "I love you, Da." Eli bent down to take him from Whit's arms.

"You'd better sit down," Whit teased.

"He's so handsome, and they are both perfect little versions of you," Eli said as tears began to roll down her cheeks.

"Mitch, would you like to hold Mack?" Whit asked.

Mitch dropped the bag and stared at Whit. "How do I hold her? She's so tiny."

"Mark, will you show him how?" Whit asked.

"Take a seat, Son," Mark said, then bent down to pick up Mack. "She's a Fortner, so she's tough and won't break, but treat her gently."

Mitch cradled Mack in his arms, and when she reached out to wrap her tiny little hand around his finger, Mitch looked up at Whit and lost it. "She's so perfect," he said between sniffles. "Hello, Mack," he spoke.

"Is cousin Mitch okay?" Mack asked her mommy.

"Yes, we are all happy to finally meet you," Whit answered her. "Everything is good."

Mark stepped back and pulled out his camera. "I have got to take some pictures, or I will be shot." He snapped pictures of Eli and Zack, Mitch and Mack, and all four next to Whit.

"My hair probably looks hideous," Whit said.

"More beautiful than tears running down my manly cheeks," Mitch said as he wiped his face.

Mark looked at the photos. "They are all beautiful. Is it okay to start sending them out?"

Eli looked at Whit, who nodded. "Go ahead," Whit said.

†

The nurse gave them several minutes to visit before returning to the room. "I'm going to ask you two to leave now, so we can start trying these two on formulas."

"We'll wait for you in the family room," Mark said.

"Wait. I want to see what's in that bag," Whit told Mitch.

Mitch smiled and pulled a box to hand to Whit. "I wanted to buy the twins something."

Whit opened the box and smiled up at Mitch. "These are perfect going-home outfits," she replied and held up two matching denim onesies and caps with their names embroidered. "Thank you, Mitch, these are priceless."

"No, the smile on your face is priceless. Love y'all," Mitch said, leaning down to kiss Whit's cheek.

"Love you most," Whit replied.

"No way, Love Muffin." He grinned.

"Get him out of here." Eli laughed. "I'll get you when you can visit again."

†

They were lucky that both twins tolerated the first formula they tried without hesitancy. "It's not Da's French Toast, but it's not bad," Zack said.

"That's an advantage for us to hear you. Please tell us when there are things you don't like," Whit said.

"Like that big needle she's carrying?" Zack replied.

"We don't have control over some things. You need vitamins and some vaccines right off the bat. They won't hurt long," Eli promised.

"That's a good girl," the nurse cooed when Mack took the injections without whimpering.

"Are you going to let your sister show you up?" Eli asked.

"No, Da. I won't make a sound," Zack said, but she felt him flinch when the nurse inserted the needle."

Once the babies were fed and given their shots, Mark and Mitch were allowed to return to the room. Mitch went immediately for Mack while Mark took Zack from Eli.

"Brad and Laura send their congratulations, as do Carol and Julia. Everyone is fed, and they will visit later today after you've had an opportunity to rest."

"I don't suppose I can convince you to go home and rest," Whit asked Eli.

"No, not yet. I may go for a while when Carol and Julia come up. I can nap right here with you and the babies."

"Do you think they will make it into their bassinets anytime soon?" Whit asked.

"It doesn't look like it," Eli said. "They both look perfectly content."

"Are we talking babies or men?"

"Both." Eli smiled.

"Let us know when you need to nap," Eli told the twins.

"We're good, Da," Mack replied, smiling at Mitch.

"I love the outfits you picked for them," Eli told Mitch. "When were you able to do that?"

"I researched and found a shop here in town that made them. Jessie and I came over one afternoon instead of going to the movies and bought them. The lady even gift-wrapped them for me."

"The hats, too?" Whit asked.

"She whipped them out in a matter of minutes," Mitch said.

"Do you know how long you will be in here?" Mark asked.

"If today goes well, we'll be home tomorrow night. They want to ensure both twins tolerate the formula and elimination is normal."

"That's peeing and pooping for us country folk," Mark teased Mitch.

"I've got to remember to put the car seats in the truck tonight, then," Eli said.

"We can help. I think I can do those in my sleep."

"Even after all these years?" Mitch teased.

"Excellent muscle memory. Seat belts haven't changed much, but I'll read the directions," Mark assured Eli.

"We bought the ones that the carriers pop out, so you don't have to lug those heavy seats everywhere you go." Eli grinned.

"What about strollers?" Mitch asked.

"We have a double one for when we come to town."

"I wonder if John Deere makes baby booster seats to fit the Gator?"

Eli looked at Mitch. "If not, I think we should invent some. That's a great idea."

Mark saw the weariness on Whit's face. "I think it's time for us to head home and let these two rest. Is there anything you need before we go?"

"No, I think we're good. Thanks for being here," Eli said and hugged them both after they placed the babies in the bassinets beside the bed.

When Mark opened the door, a nurse delivered a recliner for Eli. "It's not as comfy as your bed, but I feel we won't have much luck getting you out of here."

"She's promised to go home later today," Whit said.

"I'll be back for tonight, though," Eli clarified.

"I'm here until seven, and I'll check on you frequently, but if you need anything, just call me."

"Can you provide me with the name of the formula and the bottles we'll need?" Mark asked. "We can pick them up on our way home."

"Sure, but don't go crazy and buy much until we confirm the babies will tolerate the formula."

"Got it," Mark said.

"Follow me, and I'll write everything down for you."

Mark turned back to them. "I love you all and I'm happy for the additions to the family."

"Thank you. I'll let you know when I'm home."

"See you soon, Whit," Mark said. "Y'all get some rest."

CHAPTER TWENTY

When they arrived home, Mitch was eager to learn how to care for the twins. He quickly became an expert on bottle feeding and did well with changing diapers. Eli had to suppress a laugh when she walked in to find Mitch changing Zack.

"Don't even think about hosing me down," he told Zack.

"Be good to your cousin," Eli told him.

"But it's cold, Da," Zack answered. Eli could hear his soft laughter, and he started peeing as soon as Mitch opened the diaper.

"Damn, Zack," Mitch said, then laughed.

"I think I've figured him out," Eli said. "If you'll take one of the warmed wipes to immediately cover him, it helps. If he still goes, at least it's into the wipe."

"I will try that next time. Not cool, little man." Mitch chuckled.

†

Mitch and Mark were doing so well in the forge that Mitch decided to take a year off from school. Every morning, he arrived to feed the animals, and fed a twin while Eli or Whit showered. Mitch often visited at lunch and again at supper to help. He quickly became a great help to Whit and Eli.

"You know, Dad and I could babysit for you one night if you need a break to go adulting," Mitch offered. "Dinner and a movie or something."

"Are you sure you're ready for that?" Eli asked.

"I'm positive I am. It's you and Whit that will worry about leaving the twins."

"I know they will be in good hands, and I will discuss it with Whit. Thanks, Mitch. That's very thoughtful of you."

"I love these guys," Mitch said, lifting Mack over his head.

"They love you, too," Eli replied. Zack and Mack told her often how much they loved being with Mitch, but she couldn't explain that to him.

†

He surprised her one day when they were returning from the grocery store. He had pulled over at the mailbox and turned to Eli. "I know the twins are unique because they are a part of Whit, but can they put thoughts in my head? Sometimes I feel like they are trying to communicate with me."

"Turn off the truck," Eli answered. "Zack and Mack are very unique. We didn't know until after the procedure, but the biological father is also a Star Child, like Whit."

"Holy shit," Mitch cried out. "So, are they going to be super babies?"

"They will be brilliant at a young age, even more so than Whit was, and they both have destinies to fulfill. They will grow and learn faster than normal human babies, and yes, they can communicate telepathically. It was just with Whit and me and between the twins. They must feel bonded with you as well."

"I knew it," Mitch said.

"You can't share that with anyone. Not even your dad. The twin's identities must be protected at all costs. Even your dad doesn't know. He knows we can communicate with them telepathically, but doesn't know the rest."

"So, how do I communicate with them?"

"Through your thoughts, or if you're alone with them, talk to them as usual. Doing it in front of others would throw up a red flag."

"I promise I will keep their secret and guard them with my life if it ever came to that."

"I know you would. There is much more to the story, but that's a conversation for a later time."

"Did it kind of freak you out at the beginning?"

"Very much so, but it's nice to know how they feel when hungry and precisely what they need. Naming them woke them up, and we've talked ever since. They want you to know how much they love you, so now they can tell you themselves."

"Cool," Mitch said and started the truck. "I'm cooking steaks tonight at Dad's, and Whit said y'all would come."

"It's decided then." Eli chuckled. "Do we need to bring something?"

"That's why I got four extra boxes of brownie mix." Mitch grinned.

"Perfect," Eli said as they pulled up to the house.

Epilogue

Zeus returned when the babies were six months old to begin their training. Both were taking a few steps and babbling away. His prediction of a flood of "why" questions came through, but Eli, Whit, and Mitch answered them with love and patience. He was surprised at the bond the children had created with Mitch, but he was pleased that he would become an essential part of their lives.

He was able to spend several hours teaching the children in the nursery, but they were the only ones that could see or communicate with him. "You have brought two beautiful and brilliant children into the world," he told Whit one day after a challenging session. "They are already asking questions way beyond what I had anticipated."

"They have begun reading, and Eli has bought them both iPads. They have learned to scour the internet and research articles beyond what we can sometimes comprehend."

He nodded. "They will be challenging to teach, but they are progressing well. They tell me of the adventures with Eli on the mountain and Mitch's explanation of fly fishing. He will make an excellent father one day."

"He will, and he adores both kids. They have been good for him, too," Whit replied. "They make him think long and hard before answering some of their questions."

†

The intellectual and physical growth of the twins amazed Eli. She was happy that even though they were walking and eating baby food, they still enjoyed being cuddled on the couch or in a rocker. They loved listening to stories and had two favorites: how she and Whit met and the Sky People.

One evening after dinner, they were cuddling on the couch before a roaring fire. The winter had been mild, but they expected a late snowstorm to arrive. Zack looked into Eli's eyes. "Will you tell us about the Sky People, Da?"

Eli chuckled. "You have heard that one a hundred times," she teased. Eli thought she would change the story a bit. "Tonight, will be a little different."

Three sets of eyes were glued to Eli as she began her story. "You already know that the Cherokee Indians were native to this area and created the term Sky People. Your grandfather and others from his time have visited our world for hundreds if not thousands of years. Since they came from the sky, the name fits them well. As relationships grew, there were special children born."

"Like Mommy?" Mack asked.

"Yes, like Mommy. She is a Star Child." Eli smiled at Whit. "Star children are born to help our society advance in many areas and to bring beautiful gifts of learning, love, and kindness to our world in much-needed times." Eli looked at Mack. "Mommy is a brilliant scientist who has contributed much knowledge to other students and scientists. She's always had a love for the stars. One day soon, we will take you to her lab so she can begin teaching you about the stars and different universes. We have spent hours looking toward the heavens at the beautiful stars and waiting for your grandfather to return."

"How do you know if you don't always see him arrive?" Zack asked.

Whit pulled the amulet from underneath her shirt. "This crystal is a power source that flares when your grandfather is near."

"Only for him, or others as well?" Zack asked.

Whit's eyebrows knitted together. "I don't know the answer to that. That will be a good question for him. To my knowledge, he is the only Sky Person I've met."

Eli nodded. "I'm not exactly sure, but it appears brightest for Mommy, but mine glows as well, so maybe it's a family thing."

"The man who helped you create us is also a Star Child, right?" Mack asked.

"Yes, but we didn't know until after you were conceived. Your da and I both felt an attraction to him when we reviewed his profile, but it was your grandfather who confirmed the fact."

"So, we're Sky People and Star Children?" Zack asked Eli.

"Yes. A next generation that will help our society move forward on a positive path. You will study and learn here with Mommy and Grandfather and then go to a university to further your education. You are destined to become brilliant researchers at a young age."

Zack's face turned into a frown. "I don't ever want to leave you, Da."

Eli smiled at him sweetly. "You will never truly leave Mommy or me. We will always carry you in our hearts, but there will be a time we can no longer teach you. It will be a short time, and then if you choose, you can return here to continue your work."

Zack snuggled next to Eli. "I will definitely choose to return."

Whit smiled at him. "You may feel differently once you experience the world outside our mountain, but this will always be your home."

"We love you, Mommy and Da," Mack said.

"We love you, too. Our lives changed forever the day you came into our lives," Eli answered Mack and looked to find tears in Whit's eyes.

ABOUT THE AUTHOR

Ali Spooner lives in beautiful northwest Florida with several fur babies. Ali's writing began as a hobby, and with the assistance of the Affinity Rainbow Publishing team has advanced her love of storytelling to a new level.

Ali's characters are primarily everyday people, from cowgirls to psychics. Ali also has created a few supernatural characters in her paranormal series. Several of her thirty-plus books have been Amazon-rated number one choices and always include a happily ever after. Ali's hobbies include photography, reading, travel, college sports, and spending time with family and friends.

OTHER AFFINITY BOOKS

<u>Love Bonds by Annette Mori</u>

When Mila Thompson, a rookie police officer, discovers her mother is missing, she engages the assistance of San Diego's number one detective, who is more than a little reluctant to enter the fray, noting she works in homicide, not missing persons.

Bernie doesn't play well with others, which is why she doesn't have a partner at work or in her personal life. When Mila approaches her, she tries hard to refuse the request, but Mila will not accept no for an answer. For reasons she does not understand, Bernie doesn't want to say no to Mila, who can charm her way into anything, including smoothing the rough edges of Bernie's crusty heart.

Things get complicated when the women in The Organization have an unusual tie to Mila's mother. This sets up an action-packed adventure with twists and turns and a healthy dose of love. Find out the future of The Organization and whether an unlikely pair can find their way to love.

Holy Water and Whiskey Scars by Ali Spooner
Faith Wilson and Logan Bronson have family secrets to protect and a legacy to uphold to support their small rural Appalachian community. Their commitment to each other is strong, and their desire to aid the struggling families however they can, lead them both down an exciting but dangerous path. Will their love continue to grow and be the glue that binds the community together, or will they flee the withering community?

Politics of Love by Annette Mori
Governor Sandra Murphy is rethinking the sanity of allowing her mother to talk her into considering becoming the democratic party's choice for the presidential nominee. Sandra has enough to contend with after surviving a bomb attack, thanks to the brave border control agent working alongside the clever undercover FBI agent. Now she has to worry about a pesky reporter who seems to be everywhere scoping stories Sandra would prefer Wynter Holmes steer far away from.

Wynter admires the charismatic governor. After all, she voted for the woman. But that doesn't give Governor Murphy a free pass. A breaking story is what Wynter lives for, and she isn't about to stop digging just because the engaging governor is attractive, single, and an out lesbian. Reporting for the famously biased, right-wing media conglomerate is not exactly making Wynter a friend of the enigmatic leader.

Will repeated attempts on Governor Murphy's life where Wynter might be collateral damage bring them closer together or tear them apart from what might be a perfect match?

Out and Loud by Ali Spooner

The Bentleys have begun celebrating their success by performing live in small venues and outdoor concerts. Their music and love for one another continue to grow as their number drops to four. Stone is needed at home to run the business during his father's rehabilitation, but the Bentleys drive forward. Cedra's challenge to her bandmates to create original songs for their next album turns into brilliant love songs, rockabilly, and a Pride Festival anthem. Ride along with the Bentleys as they capture the hearts of country music lovers across the nation.

Undercover Love by Annette Mori

When the domestic terrorist cell Emma Schmidt has infiltrated summons her to an abandoned warehouse for a loyalty test, Emma immediately recognizes the battered woman. Emma must act fast to protect her cover and save the woman, Jimena Aguilar, she's never forgotten.

Emma and Jimena team up on a dangerous mission to take down the terrorist cell and save the life of the popular California governor.

Will this lead them back to the closeness they once shared or have the years in between hardened their hearts to love.

Changing Times by Jen Silver

Thirty years on from when we first met Dani Barker and Camila Callaghan in *Changing Perspectives*, they're enjoying marriage and semi-retirement in a luxury flat near London.

Dani's niece, Holly, runs their mixed media business, now gaining a foothold in the highly competitive online games market. Holly's older sibling, Luc, influences people to take action on climate issues with their website, Gaia One: One Earth, One Chance.

Romance has been in short supply for both Holly and Luc. Immersed in her work, Holly's dating life is non-existent. For Luc, family prejudices stand in the way of a relationship with the love of their life.

Can Holly and Luc succeed in making the changes

necessary to achieve their own happy ever afters?

Midnight in Nashville by Ali Spooner
  The Bentleys have successfully finished cutting their first album, *Six Strings, and a Dream*. When the Covid-19 epidemic hits, tours and live performances are cancelled as the world goes into lockdown. With the closing of the restaurant, employment for the band members has been severely impacted. The group comes together to make life work at Ma Bentley's Boarding House. They take advantage of their down time and use of the studio to record more songs. Cedra has challenged each of her bandmates to create a song for their next album. Juliet's song, "Midnight in Nashville," is chosen as the title track. Join the group as they venture into new marketing avenues and create their first music video for the title track.

Compound Interest by Annette Mori
  The kick-ass women in The Organization are back and they have their sights set on a few new recruits. Not everyone is jumping for joy at the choices, considering subterfuge is front and center in the games the new recruits have been playing.
  Dani is supposed to get her happily ever after, but she's not sure what's real anymore including Candy's feelings for her. When a new enemy takes Candy captive, Dani vows to uncover the truth by insisting on going on the mission to save

her. Candy is not what she seems, and that presents a new set of complications for Dani and her feelings.

The Organization continues to have challenges when those damn book magicians and book witches keep popping back in to warn them of new catastrophes on the horizon. She doesn't have time for their warnings, until their enemies intersect once again to keep them working together.

From award-winning author, Annette Mori, find out what happens in this final chapter of the combined Asset Management/Book Addict series.

Six Strings and a Dream by Ali Spooner

Cedra Tyler's dream of becoming a songwriter in Nashville was put on hold due to her mother's failing health. When the time came for Cedra to start her journey, she left her home in south Alabama with a heavy heart.

Arriving at Ma Bentley's boarding house, meeting her housemates, also fledgling musicians, she feels the warmth she was missing since leaving home.

Her housemates realize Cedra's talent as a song writer and begin to gel as a group. The pain and loss she had experienced added a layer of emotion and longing in her lyrics unusual for someone of her age.

They form a band, The Bentley's, named after Ma who is much more than a landlord to them all. Cedra falls for bandmate Juliet, and that inspires her creativity even more.

Will The Bentley's achieve their dream of making it big in Music City? Has Cedra found her forever in the arms of Juliet?

Trouble in Paradise-Trophy Wives Club book 4 – Ali Spooner & Annette Mori
The gang from the Trophy Wives Club is back. This time they're taking their fun to a new and exciting location. The club's future is looking bright, and as a thank you, Lindy rewards the crew with an all-expenses paid trip to paradise over the holidays. Soon after arriving on the island, an attractive stranger catches the eye of more than one person in their tight-knit group, but Lindy is especially intrigued. Could Angel Dubois, the owner of an all-woman financial planning company be the answer to Lindy's crushing feelings of loneliness? Along with fun in the sun, the gang navigates treacherous waters to ring in the New Year.

Affinity
Rainbow Publications

eBooks, Print, Free eBooks

Visit our website for more publications available online.

www.affinityebooks.com

Published by Affinity Rainbow Publications
A Division of Affinity eBook Press NZ LTD
Canterbury, New Zealand

Registered Company 2517228